Quickies 2

QUICKIES 2

Short Short Fiction on Gay Male Desire

Edited by
JAMES C. JOHNSTONE

ARSENAL PULP PRESS

Vancouver

QUICKIES 2
Stories copyright © 1999 by the authors
Introduction copyright © 1999 by James C. Johnstone

ARSENAL PULP PRESS
103-1014 Homer Street
Vancouver, BC Canada V6B 2W9
www.arsenalpulp.com

The publisher gratefully acknowledges the support of the
Canada Council for the Arts and the B.C. Arts Council for its
publishing program.

Canadä The publisher gratefully acknowledges the support of the
Government of Canada through the Book Publishing Industry
Development Program for its publishing activities.

Typeset for the press by Robert Ballantyne
Author photo by Judson Young
Printed and bound in Canada

CANADIAN CATALOGUING IN PUBLICATION DATA
Main entry under title:
Quickies 2

ISBN 1-55152-069-9

1. Gay men's writings. 2. Gay men-Fiction. I. Johnstone, James C.
(James Compton)
PN 6120.92.G39Q52 1999   808.83'108353   C99-910951-0

Acknowledgements

A heartfelt thanks to Brian Lam, Blaine Kyllo, and Robert Ballantyne at Arsenal Pulp Press for their ongoing enthusiasm and support for my various projects. You guys are the best!

For ongoing encouragement (not to mention understanding and patience), friendship, and for keeping me sane and on track on a day to day basis, I would like to thank my partner Richard Rooney, and my housemate Keith Stuart. As well, I would like to thank my friends and fellow writer/anthologists Karen X. Tulchinsky and Robert Thomson, Daniel Collins and all the members of the Sunday Gay Writer's Group, Alfredo Ferreira, Jeff Fisher and Alex Verdecchia of the fabulous Gang of Four, Jules Sievert, Laura Mayne, and my daughter Jayka.

For their friendship, generosity and hospitality while I was on the road with the first volume of *Quickies*, I would like to thank: Steven Simms, Tony Speakman, Alan Workman, Antony Audain, Patrick Duggan, Mohammed Khaki, Bob Tivey, and Paul Yee. Thanks to all of you, everywhere I go feels like home.

I would also like to acknowledge Don MacLean, Shawn Syms, and the staff of Canadian Male, Dean Odorico and the staff of Woody's and Sailors in Toronto, Ron Van Streun and the staff of the Odyssey in Vancouver, as well as Richard Labonté and Tommi Avicolli Mecca of A Different Light Bookstore in San Francisco, for their efforts in making the launches in these three cities both successful, fun, and unforgettable experiences.

Thanks again to Val Speidel for a masterful rendering of Daniel Collins' imaginative and eye-catching photo of models Robert Dean and Edmund Wong. You make the best book covers!

Lastly, I would like to express my deep gratitude to the hundreds of writers from all over the globe that continue to share their gifts with me. I am honoured.

For my partner, Richard Rooney

Contents

Introduction

Back for another *Quickie*? This second international collection of short short fiction on gay male desire features 69-plus stories by well-known and emerging gay writers from seven different countries. Each of them, in one thousand words or less, explores the wild and wonderful world of gay men's sexuality from a rich diversity of perspectives, backgrounds, experience, and well—*positions*.

As I read through the stories sent for this collection, I was amazed at how many strongly resonated for me, how many of them triggered vivid memories. Many included in this book remind me of events from my childhood. I was six or seven when I first became aware of my fascination for the male body—that I was interested in boys, not girls. I can't remember what came first. It might have been seeing Robert Conrad shirtless in a *Wild, Wild West* episode or one from *Route 66*, or that picture of ancient Greek athletes wrestling naked in *National Geographic*'s *Everyday Life in Ancient Times*. Maybe it was those body-building ads in the back of comic books I read. Or perhaps it was the muscular, older neighbour boy who liked to box and always mowed his lawn bare-chested and in cut-offs, whom I found so fascinating that I almost took up boxing just to get closer to him. Whatever it was, these stimuli evoked a definite, intense, and often scary response in me, and though I didn't know where they would take me, I was painfully aware of the power of my desire.

Throughout my later childhood and adolescence, right up to my last year in university, I struggled with my attraction. The entire period, until my eventual coming out, was spent peeking, maybe not from under a bed or through keyholes like in some of the stories included in this volume, but I was peeking all the same. I became quite skilled at sneaking looks at the vital, mature, muscled male bodies I saw blooming naked in the school change room, or sporting boxer trunks at the beach. How I longed to reach out and touch. . . .

In spite of all these clear hormonal urgings, religion intervened in the form of a hands-on-the-television born-again conversion experience. It wasn't until I was twenty-four that I actually had sex with another man. I was denied the boyhood circle jerks and summer camp gropings I heard about later from other gay men. I also missed out on the teenage sexual initiations and school and university experiences featured in some of these stories. I was—*sigh*—a late bloomer, but I've done and am doing my best to catch up.

When I began to work on the order of stories for this book, I knew immediately which story I wanted to begin with and which story I wanted at the end. Stringing the remaining stories between was an adventure. Some are arranged in what I perceived as a chronological progression, an arc of diverse and often starkly contrasting gay male experience: from youthful imaginings to first sexual experiences and coming out, through cruising, dating, falling in love and making love, to betrayal, break-up and attempts at revenge. Other stories are grouped by topic and theme, while some stories are so unique I had to let them shine by themselves.

Several times I got to wondering how the characters in these stories would turn out in later years; how their early experiences would influence their later gay sexual lives, determine their fetishes, shape their fantasies and life choices. Does the little boy in David Garnes' "Under The Mexicali Moon" ever find his one true cowboy? Does the student in Jim Eigo's "Here At St. Peter's Prep" end up so strongly imprinted by his experience with the custodian that he'll only go for working class tops? I also wondered what sort of family interactions and early experiences shaped the characters in some of the other stories. And what magical combination of circumstances must happen in your early life in order to get a circus trapeze artist to land in your lap later on as in Billy Cowan's "Flying"?

Desire keeps gay men busy, both mentally and physically. It motivates us; makes us write poetry, climb mountains, ford rivers, cross oceans, speak and spend foolishly. It moves us to shape, shave, tattoo and pierce our bodies. It makes us defy convention, tradition, common sense, and speed limits. It brings us to tears, drives us to distraction, and makes us mental. It is a compelling and pervasive force, sometimes insidious, frightening and even destructive, and can inspire and liberate as well as betray and enslave. And no—despite all the rumours and the press among the religious right—it doesn't always lead us to bed and a good boffing. It doesn't always translate into an orgy or even an orgasm. As gay men, and more broadly, as

11

homosexual men, our experience of desire, the role sex plays in our lives—how we are as sexual and sex-needing beings—is bigger and more complex than that. Sometimes our desire is validated, our fantasies fulfilled. Sometimes it is frustrated and voided. We can be charged up with all the desire we could possibly want and still live in a hit and miss world.

The stories in this collection reflect both the diversity of our community and the broad spectrum of our experience, from youth and innocence, through maturity, the onset of jadedness and the mellowing of aging—our courage, passion, tenderness, humour, tenacity, and love. They are snapshots from the great male homosexual odyssey. And, in spite of their brevity, speak volumes to the power that our desire and sexual imagination have over our lives.

As I mentioned in the acknowledgements for the first volume of *Quickies*, the idea for this book came from New York writer and anthologist extraordinaire Lawrence Schimel. That was an incredible and very generous gift. Working on *Quickies* and *Quickies 2* introduced me to a whole new world of gay male writers and their writing. I am gratified by the attention and respect received by the first volume. It is my sincere hope that *Quickies 2* follows in that tradition of compelling, thought-provoking, and entertaining writing on gay male desire—that this second book satisfies as well, if not better than, the first. It has been great fun putting this book together. I hope you enjoy the read.

—James C. Johnstone
Vancouver
August 1999

DAVID GARNES

Under the Mexicali Moon

No football pennants or little league plaques adorned Gary's bedroom walls. Instead, hung in neatly ordered rows, were twenty-two photos of Cisco Colt, the famous singing cowboy. Gary much preferred Cisco to Roy Rogers or Gene Autry. Gene could sing okay and Roy was handsome and had a pretty voice, but Cisco was taller and more muscular. Cisco also tended to have more hair—*jet black*—not to mention those slanty ice-blue eyes that crinkled up when he smiled.

One summer day the local paper reported that Cisco Colt was coming to town on a personal appearance tour. Escorted by the mayor, Cisco and his horse El Noche would ride down Main Street to the Rivoli, where his new movie *High Sierra Serenade* was opening.

Gary had received many signed photos from Cisco, but this was a once-in-a-lifetime opportunity to see Cisco and El Noche up close and in person. In one of the few full-colour photos on Gary's bedroom wall, Cisco and his big stallion were outlined against a sky streaked orange and pink, in gorgeous contrast to El Noche's glossy black coat. Cisco was wearing a beautiful scarlet shirt with a thick white fringe, tight white pants, and black boots studded with fancy silver flowers.

On the day of Cisco's appearance, Gary left his house early, informing his mother that he wouldn't be back until evening. She wasn't surprised. Gary often sat through Cisco's movies more than once. Earlier that summer he had watched four showings of *Melody of Old Monterey* and had missed dinner altogether.

Gary debated whether to wait at the train station or stake out a spot at the Rivoli. He finally decided on this second course of action, since he wanted to have a bird's eye view of Cisco on-stage. He stopped by early at the theatre and bought a child's ticket. Gary sometimes had to lie about his age, but he looked young for fourteen and this time the lady at the box-office didn't bat an eye.

As he had hoped, Gary had a great view as Cisco and El Noche arrived amidst cheers from the crowd. For a while, they pranced around in the hot sun in front of the theatre, but soon Cisco swung his leg over the saddle and dismounted.

Cisco was resplendent in a costume of royal blue and white. Swirls of black chest hair were visible above the loosened top buttons of his satin shirt. Gary also noticed that the leather chaps over Cisco's tight pants made them bunch up in the front, just under his studded silver belt.

As he strolled past Gary, Cisco said, "Howdy, amigo."

Gary blushed. "Hi, Cisco," he shyly replied.

Gary was at the head of the line entering the theatre and managed to get a seat right in the front row. Local radio disc jockey Randy Clark introduced Cisco to whistles and wild applause. Cisco played his guitar and sang one of his most famous songs, "Take Me Back to San Luis Obispo."

Then he said, "Amigos, I need one of you to help me out."

Gary didn't raise his hand, although he had been staring at Cisco during his entire song. Cisco looked down at Gary and said, "Hey, how about you, young fella?"

Gary awkwardly made his way up the darkened steps and into the bright stage spotlight.

"What's your name, pardner?" Cisco asked.

"Gary, Cisco. I mean, just Gary." Cisco smiled and everyone laughed.

"Okay, Gary, you stand there as nice and still as can be," Cisco said. He moved away from Gary and picked up a thick lariat from the stage floor. Cisco carefully spun the heavy rope and let fly.

Now, Gary knew for a fact that Cisco was an expert at lassoing. The lariat whirled through the air, scattering particles of dust in the glare of the spotlight. Sure enough, the lasso dropped right over Gary's head. Cisco gently tugged the rope around Gary's waist. Gary had seen enough movies to know what to do next. He dropped to his knees and hung his head.

The theatre was suddenly quiet as Cisco ran up to Gary and said, "Gary, are you okay?"

"Yes," Gary whispered. "I'm your prisoner now."

Cisco chuckled. "Say, amigo, you really get into it, don't you?" He turned to the audience. "Let's hear it for my outlaw Gary!" he said. Then Cisco helped Gary up, dusted off the front of Gary's trousers, and patted the seat of his pants. Cisco shook Gary's hand and tousled his hair. Then Cisco untied his neckerchief, wiped his forehead, and handed the scarf to Gary.

Gary stumbled down the steps and back to his seat, where he watched in a daze as the mayor gave Cisco a fat gold key to the city. Cisco smiled and waved as he left the stage.

After the second showing of *High Sierra Serenade*, Gary waited until everyone in the audience had left. Then he slowly made his way through the deserted lobby.

On the sidewalk outside the theatre stood a big cardboard cutout of Cisco: eyes narrowed, body tensed, six-shooter in hand. Gary had admired this cutout the previous week when he had come to see another of his favourites, Lash LaRue, in *This Whip for Hire*.

Without a second thought, Gary scooped Cisco up in his arms and continued walking straight on down the street. Nobody stopped him.

When he got home, Gary's father said, "What in hell is this?"

Gary replied, "It's a life-size cutout of Cisco Colt."

Up in his room Gary carefully arranged Cisco in a corner where he could see him from his bed. Later that night, Gary lay looking at Cisco. His bedroom light was off, but the yellow August moon cast a pale glow on Cisco's face and the big silver revolver in his gloved hand.

Gary kicked the sheet back and slowly wriggled out of his BVDS. He took Cisco's white neckerchief from under his pillow and stepped down from the bed. Slowly, he walked over to Cisco, stood on his tip-toes, and kissed him. He stroked the smooth surface of Cisco's silk shirt and pressed his legs against Cisco's leather chaps.

Gary closed his eyes and whispered, "Cisco, Cisco."

Then he kissed him again.

MATTHEW R. K. HAYNES

Peeking

You can never see well enough from under the bed. Their feet hang over the foot board. You smile, bite your bottom lip, buck teeth digging deep into chapped, chewy flesh, centre tender, over-baked, flaky, yum-yum lip. You roll onto your back, grabbing your heart, attempting to silence its heavy hurried pound, thinking they might hear it. Your knees ache and you arch them as much as you can, careful not to nudge the springs that sag. You just listen. Muffled mouth-to-mouth laughter. Hushed moans. You giggle inside. Delicate. Almost bored. You play with your hair, laden with two days' dirt and sweat, hardened with sun and air. Time.

This reminds you of the moment that you sat with painful posture outside of the bathroom door as your brother lay in water, sequential steam rising, seeping through window pane age cracks. You peeked through an old house keyhole where a small wad of toilet paper would normally be. You viewed through your scope tilting and tacking, looking for the perfect angle—trying to see what he looked like. How his body was. What he did in the bathroom.

And now as you listen to the slops of tongues, you again wonder about his body. Probably warm and tenuous. Slighted with muscle that screams through his skin like a cat in a blanket, curved and loping like a million dollar coaster ride. Surely hairy, now that he's older. Definitely excited, his dick erect. You roll to your stomach and wonder if you too will ever be in a bed, kissing, touching, moving, and moving on. But for now you just listen. You hear a girly giggle and her say, "What is this?" Your body jumps and tingles when you hear a solid thud against the wall, but regains composure when a tanned, exhausted, left-handed baseball mitt strikes the carpet, bouncing once.

And this reminds you of the time when you stood in his closet for hours, looking through his clothes and trying on his shoes. Pretending they were your trophies. Wondering if you'd grow up, too. And then he came in. You hid behind boxes of clothes he never used, and dried flowers in cheap vases. And he went to his closet and took off his shirt, threw it to the floor, rustled through hanging garments, posed for a moment, his thighs hard and molded. And then he left the closet. Door slightly open. His music coursing loud and thick, bass waves and drum booms. Carefully, you moved from your spot and peeked through the crack and saw him dancing with himself. Perhaps practicing. Perhaps dreaming. And then he removed his soccer shorts and from the left side of his surely damp jock-strap he extracted his dick, half hard and thick. And you watched as a mouse, trying to remain unnoticed while he roamed around the room rubbing himself on pep rally posters, kissing new trophies. And when he came, shooting short spasms of clear liquid, he did so in his baseball mitt. The one he never used because he couldn't throw anymore because his arm abandoned him at his pubescent prime.

And now, here you are face to face with that urn, that reliquary. And you are sure that you can smell the salt from times past. You breathe deeply only to inhale the scent of old pizza from Super Bowl Sunday. The sound of a zipper pricks up your ears. You move to your elbows and stretch your neck, prodding the air with your head as far as it will go. The giggle again and then a moan. Brother moan. Then girl moan. And then her "No" and then "Stop, Nathan." And your temples tingle and a swell squeals in your nose, a burn, a sneeze without a release. You hear a slap and then a harder one, a whimper and muffled cries. And you wish it was the scent of the rotting, manhandled pizza that is cramping your stomach, pulling at your intestines. But it is the sound of nothing coherent and the deep smell of salt and sweat that pours off the sheets and moving first into your nasal passage and your throat, a taste on your tongue, and then into your bowels. You bite your lip. The bed moves hard and the springs bite your back. In rhythms. In pulses. And you hear the tear. Pubic splitting. And you want to scream and you wished you'd never seen him in the bathroom or his glove.

And then it stops.

She cries softly. Injured. Feeling guilty. And his feet fall in front of your face. Faded blue denim greets you with soiled tube socks. He stands. Moves two steps. Says, "I'm gonna shower." Pauses. Then kicks his mitt.

MICHAEL THOMAS FORD

The Memories of Boys

Gym class. Eighth grade. Forget the horror of facing thrice-weekly rounds of bombardment. Forget picking the ball up on the soccer field thinking it's out-of-bounds and hearing the jeers of teammates. Forget even the anxiety produced while waiting to be chosen last for basketball teams. Or for any teams.

No, the real horror came after the final merciful bell rang and those things were already-fading memories. It came in the locker room, while rushing to get dressed and safely away before an army of naked boys could appear, their skins a rosy pink as they emerged from the scrim of steam produced by the communal showers, their hair wet and glistening like the fur of seals.

That was the dangerous time, the time when the placement of eyes was of utmost importance. The time when one too-long look at an exposed crotch or a passing pale ass could mean the difference between just another horrible adolescent memory and something much worse. And it was gotten through by holding the breath and praying until the suffocating heat of hot water and adolescent need was replaced by the cool safety of the hallway and the comforting sound of footsteps echoing along the corridor as I hurried away, willing my eyes to forget.

These are the moments I remember most from those years—the times spent in escape, in running not from others so much as from myself. The stings of "queer," spat like acid as it was so often, have faded to dull throbs. The days of not belonging have faded into one vague stretch of grey. But even now I remember the running.

The one who carried the most danger for me was Ray Donnelly, wearing it like a second skin that fit him more comfortably than his own. Tall, with the muscles of the farmboy he was, he was closer to manhood than the rest of us, as though at birth he'd been dealt a right to take up more space and had ignored even that generous offering. Adopted—I don't know how I knew this—he was a mystery, his dark hair and blue eyes so dissimilar from those of the red-haired, fair-skinned family that chose him, like the most rambunctious puppy, from the rest of the litter.

What I remember now, in addition to the blueness of his eyes, are his teeth, crooked and sharp in his mouth. And, of course, the cock, for that is what made Ray famous in the locker room of Poland Central School. The cock was huge, hanging thickly between Ray's legs like a full-grown man's before he'd even reached the age of thirteen. Besides its size, Ray's dick was, for some reason, uncut. Ostensibly, this is why the other boys felt they could remark upon it without fear of crossing the line into queerdom. Difference was a safe topic of conversation; size was certainly not, although that didn't stop some imaginative redneck from nicknaming Ray "Horse."

It was Ray's cock that I feared, and not so much Ray himself, although he and I had a history of animosity since once, in fifth grade, he had threatened to kill me for calling him an asshole on the playground. It says something about the both of us that I waited for the next six years for him to carry out this promise, and that he never did.

But in fifth grade I had not yet seen Ray's cock. When I did, it changed something between us, even though I'm sure he could never recall the exact moment it happened, as I still can even twenty years later. I have only to think back and see vividly the grey skins of the lockers, reserved for the high school boys and seemingly sacred, and feel the smoothness of the tile floor as though I'd just walked through the door of that room. I remember, too, the wooden bench, and Ray bent over it, his balls hanging down between his legs. He turns, and

I see his cock, the wrinkled skin folded over the head, the black hair around it still wet from the shower.

The actual event was hardly momentous, a fleeting glimpse of his prick as he turned to say something to a friend and I darted out the door to the safety of English class, where I could move words around the page as skillfully as Ray moved the ball around the basketball court, not that it saved me from the curse of being the school fag. Afterwards, though, there was a subtle shift in the way Ray made his way through my world. Where before I avoided him in the halls out of general fear, now I did so for far different reasons. I feared what he made me feel, despite my hatred of him and him of me. I hated that sometimes at night, my cock hard from thoughts that came seemingly out of nowhere, I recalled the sight of his dick as I stroked myself into a wadded-up tissue. When one day I was kneeling on the gym floor tying my shoe and Ray, passing by, said, "Hey, faggot, while you're down there why don't you give me a blow job?" The words hung before me, ripe with hatred. But despite their bitterness, I wanted nothing more than to swallow them down.

I never saw Ray's cock again. And after a hurried departure from high school three years later, I never saw Ray himself again. Yet sometimes I see a similar face, or perhaps a similar hatred reflected in the eyes of a man on the street or on the subway, and I am reminded of him. And still sometimes I close my eyes and imagine sucking a cock, long and thick. Its owner's hands hold my head, not in love but in hate, as he fucks my mouth. It is an act of need, pure and simple. And inevitably, when I open my eyes and look up, I am in a junior high locker room, and it is Ray's cold blue eyes looking down as he releases his load into my throat and, happily, I swallow.

DAVID LYNDON BROWN

Elysian Fields

James Leslie and Donald Smith were champion gymnasts. I used to watch them practicing in the auditorium which doubled as a gymnasium at our school. I was in love with James. Donald was his best friend. They were rivals, constantly striving to eclipse each other on the high bar, the pommel horse, the mat, and the rings, while I glumly observed them from the periphery, a jealous exile.

Donald was compact and swarthy, with prematurely hairy legs and black swatches in his armpits. His ripe nipples protruded through the thin nylon of his gym singlet. James was a whip of muscles woven from ginger leather. He had red hair and mismatched eyes. One was the sea and one was the sky.

After the exams at the end of the year, Donald and James were allowed extra time in the auditorium to practice for the National Secondary Schools Gymnastics Competition. I was committed to *A Streetcar Named Desire*. I had designed the set for the Drama Club's production and I was busy painting the backdrop. I would look down from the tropical shadows of New Orleans and pause, brush in hand, on the ladder, to watch James Leslie arcing through the air, perfecting his Yamashita, his Valdez, his Suicide Tuck Back. Donald

Smith's speciality was the rings. He would hang there swaying, cru-cified for minutes on end, the veins in his arms engorged, his eyes turned up to heaven. Then he would drop, hang, swing, and then somersault back to earth. He was having a few problems with his landing.

One day, after school, I was working late on the set. The play was due to open in a few days. It was the beginning of summer and the afternoon sunlight slanted down through the high windows of the auditorium, casting the stage into an eerie dusk. It was the kind of moody, wistful twilight which Miss DuBois would have appreci-ated. I was creating a bower for Blanche, tacking up draperies of pink satin and organdie, hanging paper lanterns, secretly revelling in the tawdry glamour.

I heard voices, footsteps echoing, then the sound of something heavy being dragged across the wooden floor of the auditorium, the thunk of a dropped mat, the clank of metal. I peered out from Blanche's boudoir. Donald and James were assembling the parallel bars, positioning the vaulting horse. They were wearing just their white gym shorts. From behind the satin curtain I watched the yel-low light come down on them, gilding their foreheads with diadems of sweat. I watched the orchestration of their muscles as they lim-bered up. I was too dazzled by their architecture to utter a word. Cowering on Blanche DuBois' makeshift divan I felt as though I was suffocating in a miasma of dust, spilt perfume, and longing.

I listened to the thuds and gasps as they practiced their routines, straining their wings. Through the diaphanous curtain, I glimpsed a shoulder, a hairy leg, the trajectory of a torso, drenched in gold, hurtling through the air. I heard James say, "One of us has to win and if it's not me it's gotta be you. So you better fucking nail that dismount." I waited for ages in the claustrophobic gloom, listening. I had an aching hard-on. The hammer was still in my hand.

Finally I heard a grunt and an exhalation and then the sounds of physical expenditure ceased. It was quiet in the auditorium and I hoped that maybe I could sneak away while James and Donald were in the shower. I edged out of the Kowalskis' apartment, past the fake magnolia, and crouched behind the baroque papier mâché fountain I was so proud of.

Donald Smith and James Leslie were locked together on the

canvas mat. James had Donald pinned. Donald's legs were wrapped around his buttocks, he had James's arm twisted up his back. They were face to face, eye to eye, immobilized in some kind of stalemate. They were panting. The air was green with the smell of their sweat. Suddenly James thrust himself up with his free arm, I could almost hear the wrench of his sinews, and Donald relented. Then James lunged down and bit into the tendons of Donald's neck. An electrical shudder rang through Donald's body and echoed into James. I felt my bones soften. I had to grip onto the rough wooden struts that supported the phoney fountain.

The dark corners of the auditorium were encroaching. The sunlight had just about finished. James and Donald lay collapsed in a glittering tangle. Their shadows seeped into the mat like blood. It looked as though there had been some dreadful accident; a slaughter. I shut my eyes. I wondered how I was going to account for the stain on my trousers when I got home. I'd have to say it was spilt paint. Or paste. Then I heard the suck of skin separating. They got up. James stretched and smiled. Donald adjusted his shorts. In a distant classroom, someone was practicing scales on a piano. Somewhere a phone was ringing, then it stopped.

J . E I G O

Here at St. Peter's Prep

A boy steps out of the sun into the shade of a favourite group of trees for one last time. An indistinct motion like that of an animal draws his eyes across an expanse of grass. On the other side of the lawn that runs behind the school's main building: a man is rising from a bed of earth. The sight takes hold of the boy like a hairy hand over either ear.

When the man has risen to his full height, the sun hits the top of his head. Of apparent Mediterranean descent and indeterminate accent, he's roamed among the boys of the school for months, its Custodian. The attentive student will have gathered few hard statistics about the man in charge of the campus physical plant, shards, a narrative archipelago. Almost blond though his surname's Raimondo, behind his back the freshmen call him Sunray.

But any thread between bare facts that the student discerns he'll have stitched for himself. Biography's significant accidents remain in the care of Custodian alone. Into the gap of fact about him, the onlooker's full attention pitches headlong. By today, the boy's graduation day, Custodian has grown to contain all that school will ever mean for the boy, the quiet centre of St. Peter's Prep and its full span, ranging daily over demanding gardens and lawns.

Not so much older than the boy himself, Custodian bears unmistakable marks of a guy who has grown up. Swell of muscle, shadowy jaw, absence of any softness: to the boy they body forth a man. Collar of Custodian's sweat-drenched t-shirt dips to disclose a rolling upper chest and its lustrous spray of hair. Enough underbrush to get lost in: dare the boy allow himself such luxury now? In contrast to the uniformly burnished hair on the standing man's head, strands of his nest of chest hair range from light to jet.

The subject's sudden motion interrupts the boy's inspection. Along the sides of his trouser legs, the man brushes the moist earth from his hands. What, the boy asks, might this action forecast? He ceases for a moment to breathe, the better to see.

The man is moving in the general direction of the boy. The soft material of loose summer trousers flows like a stream of water or air over the core of the boy's imaginings. The waves of heat rising from the lawn render the man and his parts intermittent mirage. A monumental set of unseen genitals consistently rearranges itself, drawing from the boy a noiseless gasp. The pendulous swing keeps counterpoint to the rippling cloth. Confinement may diminish its arc, but hardly contains it.

The man stops at a mid-lawn strip of earth. The boy as he peers from behind a tree knows from experience: if Custodian hews to his usual pattern, he now will piss in the seedbed, shake his shapely tool, and split. And in fact he now unzips, but today he reaches with unaccustomed deliberateness into the opening he's made. Possibilities are not unlimited, yet somehow the potential is.

Chrysanthemum, peony, zinnia, penis. Everything looks like sex to the late adolescent. From the shadowed gap in his pants, Custodian pulls the long veiny tuber of his sex. With thrilling indifference he rolls the foreskin back from the tip. Like a single strain of steady rain, the arc of urine glistens, instantly its own rainbow.

But today, although Custodian has pumped from his cock the last few drops, still, to the spectator's shock, it lies across the palm of the hand of its owner who still stands there, appraising his extended member like a snake he's apprehended. As he turns his eye in the direction of his hidden witness, his prick flexes, an action that appears to hasten its rapid expansion and its lift-off.

Primeval fruits, the testicles dangle blindly; it's up to the man's sensible cock to sniff out its prey. It points to the boy who, now at the eye of a pocket of pressure, stands stock-still. There's a sound, as of someone running up behind him. He spins around, but it's only his own heart pounding in his head. Might a priest now, ghostly in black, be looking down from the bell tower? A steamed pane can only mirror. Let these men of death dress the part; the boy rather unbuttons his collar, loosens his tie.

By the time the boy turns back, Custodian has nearly closed the distance from centre to periphery. Above the horizon line, a great, inflated penis looms, like an alien form of life—or like a phantom. Until the boy can touch it, the cock of this man will be no more substantial to him than a plume of smoke or a god.

Custodian steps out of the sun, into the shade, up to the boy. Odour rolls off him like a fog. And like a fist at the door, the heart in the chest of the boy just pounds. Wind sends a spray of hair—so unlike Custodian's own—down over the boy's brow. Custodian reaches out to feel it, moves his hand till the tip of his index touches the back of the boy's head, centre of the whorl of hair.

Like the strings of a marionette might snap, the boy in his every joint collapses, drops to his knees. Although his eyes roll back, his lips part in approximate smile. Peter hovers at the pearls of heaven's gate. But a mouth strained to its limits can as well recall the jaws of hell.

There are baby birds that seem ancient. His fine-haired head craned back, this late adolescent appears as paradoxical, an aged baby. How can need this eternal be unnatural? The man standing above the supplicant approaches the paternal. Straddling the hungry head, he lowers his scrotum to the open hole. Heat and aroma all but overwhelm his recipient. But as they close over the vibrant trophy, the lips of the graduate hum something akin to contentment.

MICHAEL WYNNE

Jayo

I never could fathom why Jayo chose to move to Sligo from his native north Dublin. It still irks me, sometimes—the not knowing.

I sublet a small house for a London-based couple; it's on Harmony Hill, which overlooks the main street of Sligo town. When I first opened the door to the sight of Jayo's frame, which almost filled the doorway and blocked out the September sun, I felt both amused and a little sympathetic. Never, certainly not in this town, had I seen a man of such an apparently laboursome size. As he lumbered by me with a laconic remark about having seen the ad for the room in a nearby window, I openly took in the parodoxically outsize shoulders, the ponderous semi-spheres of the chest, the huge cylindrical arms. Alongside the obvious lust, tainted as it was in this case with faint contempt, I instantly saw him, maybe unfairly, as essentially laughable, and achingly pathetic in his boyishly self-obsessive quest to become his idea of what was the ultimate, unquestionable man. But the lust over-rode all the rest, and fifteen minutes later, without mention of a reference or the sniff of a deposit, it was settled: he got the room.

I admit I've always been a great one for misjudging character.

My last boyfriend, whom I'd just sloughed off when Jayo came on the scene, while starting out to me to seem composed, prudent, attractively aloof, had turned out to be indiscreet, erratic, a dead weight with no solid values or good sense to speak of. So in a way, mindful of my record, it really wasn't a shock to learn that Jayo had shades of homophobia, all the more sinister because they were just that: tentative half-hints of a strange, facetious hate that came with a dimpled one-sided smile, and a searching look as if he were testing me for a reaction. Besides this, it turned out, unexpectedly, that he had aspirations of a certain cerebral kind, though to what end would be anyone's guess. He was well-read on things metaphysical, and had a penchant for the dark side of Celtic learning. He also spoke Gaelic like a Connemara man, which, delivered in the strained gutteral accent of the north side of the capital, was one of the most bizarre things I've ever heard.

I began to discover something of all this one evening shortly after he moved in, when he joined me and the other tenant, Eric, a young Mayonian in his first year at the regional college, as we sat in the TV room. Settling his bulk onto the couch next to Eric, he asked of no one in particular about the rates the local gyms had to offer. While Eric, who clearly knew about such things, timidly volunteered the information, I quietly studied this outlandish new addition to the house, took in the inverted pentacle tattooed at the slope of the overhanging tumulus that was the left pectoral muscle, made visible by the low neck of the black cotton top—just tight enough, typically, to show each over-bloated contour. On his lap sat a book on Druidic rituals. When Jayo interrupted his talk with Eric to make some mock-lewd comment on the homosexual characters of the soap that was on, which he followed with a stealthy, searching look at us both, I wondered, if put to it, what ancient black rites would our Jayo resurrect to blast such deviancy as the screen depicted. After this, I made sure to finish what in fact I'd already started: the absolute de-queering of all communal areas of the house.

Over the next couple of months I came to dislike and fear Jayo more and more. But these feelings were complicated by the contemptuous hunger for him that persisted; and as they grew, so also did he, the muscles of his trunk continuing to swell, to fill out, ridiculously, into giant cannonballs. At my circumspection in domestic matters he would scoff nastily in Irish, always, I thought, with undertones directed clearly at my sexuality. He had no job, and stayed in the house most of the day, reading a good bit, but mainly sweating and cursing raucously over his own weights: he supplemented his gym-work with a solitary evening routine in his room. Once, to get the rent, I walked in on him and caught him gazing absractedly into his bulging eyes as, dripping, he lifted a barbell to his chest before the wardrobe mirror. More than anything, it seemed a blatant exhibition of shameless self-love. Distractedly he dropped the bar and spat out, "*Go dtachtfaidh an diabhal thu.*" This means, "May the devil choke you." I know because it's something my mother said to me as a child. Clearly we had mutual scorn for each other, mine based on the obvious, his on what I was convinced were classic heterosexist suspicions.

So it was all the more jarring to me when I discovered them both, Jayo and Eric, with their faces buried in the cracks of each other's arse that day when I nipped into the latter's room to borrow a pair of tweezers. The curtains were drawn, and a couple of candles that smelled like beeswax were burning by the bed on which, facing me, Eric's face was pressed into the dark crevice between the great shining convexities of Jayo's buttocks. Disregarding me, his head moved on Jayo like an automaton, while at the other end, beyond the striated ridge of his upper back, Jayo's head pumped likewise.

I left the room, shaken, and, yes, riven with jealousy. For days there was no sign of Jayo, until I realized he was gone, perhaps back to Dublin, but certainly away from Sligo. As for Eric, he remained resolutely tight-lipped on the subject, as much as though Jayo had been a figment of a shared, shameful fantasy.

It took me a while to willingly face the fact that I had misconstrued Jayo's attempts to suss the sexual territory as subtle, glee-filled slights. But as I said, no one misreads character like I do.

STEVE NUGENT

Remnants

I'm Irish. Dublin actually, but you wouldn't know it by my accent. When I was twelve, me father sent me to one of those tony English boarding schools where everybody talked as if they had a stick up their ass. Actually it was more me dad's lover who sent me. He was getting to find that I was in the way of their nightly drunken fuck-fests. I'd hammer on their door after a few minutes of the heavy-duty bust-the-bed action, all ending usually with me dad at the top of his voice yelling "Fuck" when he came. I couldn't sleep until after the final act when Frank would jack himself off to me dad's snores and his own grunts and moans. A real romantic ritual. None of it got me in the least excited, in fact it was kind of boring when I got past the fact that I wasn't getting much sleep any night, and falling into a doze at school during the afternoon.

So Frank suggested one day that it might be interesting for me to go abroad to school and polish up my languages. I didn't want to go far from home so I settled for just outside London. In fact, I really didn't want to go too far from Dad, for what Frank didn't know was that when he wasn't around I was getting on like a house on fire, and I mean fire, with Dad.

I loved me dad, not so much in the usual son-father way, but by the fact that he was so seductive and hot as chili. He started out with me in such a way that I was hooked without a chance. He'd get himself into the bathroom and leave the door open while he was in the bath with it's soapy Palmolive smell, lying back, steam rising, the taps dripping into the silence. I'd leave off my homework, go to the door, and stand looking in. He'd slowly turn his gaze to me and smile while I watched him soap his cock to full size. Then I'd go in and he'd stand up in the bath and I'd soap him all over. He liked me to get between his legs and up into his hole with my fingers, "Yes, yes . . . there," while I let my tongue slick his balls and shaft, and he'd stand with his arms above his head as he watched me.

When I got to the school, I was a natural for all that kind of stuff. I was the Expert and sought after by the bigger boys who called me the Princess. The smaller boys liked me to pay a visit to their bedsides after lights out. I'd reach under their sheets and gently pull their moist hands away, then lick their bodies like a purring cat until they abruptly shuddered. I considered I was doing them a service, like giving them an education.

The older ones liked the shower room or locker scene, standing around looking slyly over their shoulders for me to approach, soaping up, throwing their heads back under the streaming water, blowing small spurts of water from their mouths and separating their buttocks, as if accidentally, for me to see their pink oysters pouting as they waited for me. Sometimes I'd fuck them, pushing them up against the tiled wall, all silent, as if nothing was happening at all. Sometimes three or four others might join in, or just watch in a detached way. I'd do whatever they wanted. I got to know what that was. Then they'd dry off quickly and comb their hair carefully back into place. I didn't exist for them anywhere else.

After I was there for about a year, I fell in love with James from the village and he, of course, didn't want me playing the field. I'd actually run into him in the village bookstore. After looking at each other for a while we went into the woods close by. We used to go to his house in the afternoons when his family was out. That was different. I'd smell his skin—he'd use his father's aftershave—kiss him, deep into his mouth, and play with his tongue while I felt his smooth, steely body. We'd tell each other how much we were in love, and how we'd be together forever. He was a jealous type though, which I found hard to deal with sometimes, but I liked feeling so special that he'd want to punch someone for just looking at me.

I went back to Dublin when I heard that me dad had died suddenly. His body seemed small and shrunken where he was laid out. I wanted to sneak a look at his cock, just for old times sake, a good-bye kind of, but there were too many nosy relatives around.

Frank damp-handed me at the graveside without looking at me. He still smelled of Old Spice.

My life has just kind of meandered on, with sex here and there, and a companion or two to pass the time away. I've never understood why the sex feelings all started out so intense, and then sort of faded.

I know one thing, though. Even if I wanted to, I couldn't stop thinking about how fierce good me dad used to look standing up in the bath, and what we did together, and how he'd say so softly. "That's good, boy, that's good, that's a good boy, it's good, that's it, that's what I like . . . ," and how the warm cum would splatter over my back and then melt away down my thighs.

BOB CONDRON

Fruit to Root

Turning his back, Dave "Duffo" Duffy gripped the waistband on his jogging pants and, bending over slightly, yanked them down to rest below the packed shelf of his solid buttocks. Bare-arsed, he glanced over his shoulder and grinned.

"Feast your eyes on that. Isn't it a beauty?"

He was being a tease. Was always teasing me these days. Ever since my tortured confession. . . . And it was beginning to fuck me right off.

The beer from the bar had quickly filtered through his bladder and had to be released. He pissed in the wash basin, letting out a groan of relief, swaying slightly. His six-foot frame, a powerhouse of muscle, visibly relaxed.

Bleary-eyed, I sat down on the single bed and looked around his campus room by the light of his bedside lamp. Halls of residence had sounded very grand in the university prospectus, but the reality was otherwise. His room, like mine, amounted to a cramped rectangle, sparsely furnished. Not much more than a cell. Still, at least it was warm. Too warm. I was beginning to sweat.

He'd stopped pissing and was leisurely shaking the last few drips from his foreskin as my eyes fixed once again on his sumptuous arse.

He peered into the mirror above the wash stand, casually rubbing a hand over the blond stubble on his shaven head.

The hard edge of his Yorkshire accent punctured the silence. "Put your tongue away," he sniggered. "Shouldn't let it hang out like a fuckin' dog!"

He was slurring his words. Drunk. We both were. He took his time pulling up his leggings. He enjoyed this, enjoyed the power he held over me whilst my stomach ached from wanting him. How could he be such a bastard?

It was at times like this that I wished I'd never told him the truth. Wished I'd never confessed to my "gay" feelings. The consequence of beer and intimacy. We were close. It felt safe to tell him. I'd assured him he wasn't the object of my desire. Who was I fooling? I'd kept myself in check for the longest time but once the games began, once the teasing began, I was lost. Aroused. Permanently aroused by him.

As he opened the picture window, a cold gust of wind blew a scattering of snowflakes inside. He quickly retrieved a couple of beer cans from the plastic bag that hung outside and tossed one over to me. I'd lost count of how many we'd gone through already that evening.

"Nicely chilled," he remarked, slamming the window shut. "Get that beer down your neck. . . ."

Outside the snow lay three feet deep. So much for a weekend away. All roads leading home were snowbound. Typical for the North of England. One heavy snowfall and the country ground to a standstill. We were marooned on campus, our only sustenance provided by the college bar.

Placing his can on the bedside table, he pulled off his rugby shirt and I knew the nightly ritual had begun. Soon he would be naked save for a pair of tiny briefs. Then he'd lay down on the bed with his goods proudly on display. And that look would be on his face, his want me look, his look-but-don't-touch smirk. Why did I stand for it?

And I thought: Would it wipe that all too familiar smirk off his face if he knew how often I'd had him? In my imagination only, of course. But if he knew the intimate details? For there was nothing we hadn't done together in my creative imagination. Nothing censored.

swallowed him whole. Had had him sit on my wriggling tongue. Had had him shaft me in every possible location including, most memorably, the communal showers while the whole Sunday I.C. Soccer team looked on and jerked off. On and on and . . .

I was dragged back from my fantasy world by an awareness of him on the bed beside me. Stripped and resting back on his elbows now, the muscles on his stomach taut and solid. Sturdy footballer's thighs spread wide and the silk coating of his boxers bunched up around his ball sac, creating the effect of a well-stuffed pillow. Was it just my imagination or was the pillow even more plumped up than usual? His eyes were fixed on me. Heavy-lidded. A weird look crossed his face. Something was different tonight. A charge in the air.

"What you lookin' at?"

"Nothin'." Taking a long, slow gulp from his can, Duffo ran a coarse palm over the flat of his hairy belly, letting the middle finger first find, and then toy with, his navel.

"Fuckin' typical," he complained, "Friday night and I should be home gettin' laid instead of which I'm stuck here with your ugly mug."

Here we go. . . .

"My nuts are killing me," he complained some more. "Full to the fuckin' brim and threatening to explode!"

I'd had enough. "What do you want me to do about it? . . . Suck you off?"

"You wouldn't dare!"

"Don't dare me, Duffo!"

He hooked a thumb under the elastic waistband and tugged it down to reveal his pride and joy. His free hand clasped the rapidly inflating shaft and slipped down from fruit to root, easing back the tight foreskin until it was fully retracted. He slapped his dick hard against his stomach. The veins popped out proudly as he held fast and squeezed; a long, thick tube sprouted up from the base and branched out into numerous offshoots leading up to the smooth, rose pink cockhead.

"You wouldn't dare. . . . "

My mouth watered. I gulped, "Yes, Duffo, I dare. I do fuckin' dare."

"Okay, prove it!" He lay back and closed his eyes as I bent my head towards his crotch. "Prove it. . . . "

D A V E   F O R D

My Dead Body

Today I make my move.

I could call Mark angelic, but our English teacher Miss Slams says, "Shun the obvious." So, okay: paper skin, spiky hair, spidery hands. He finishes homework on time, which sets him apart. Everyone drools over him. That's why I picture fucking him on a desk like a guy in a porno video. Corpses float around rumours about his dad, awash in wreaths. It lends Mark an edge he otherwise lacks.

The bell rings. Mark and I push out the door with the herd. "Hi," I say. He looks at the floor, then back at me. I think, I got him —I think. But he holds my gaze and my stomach contracts.

He says he works for his dad after school. I think, *At least you have one*, meaning a job. Now we're in the sun-blasted yard and I ask him what he does.

Mark says something, and I stare at the tiny pencil-dot mole on his neck. His hand lands on my arm. I barely manage not to jump.

"What?" I say.

"Do you. . . ."

I think: *How cool to sort of—stain him.* "What?" I say.

"I said, do you want to come over tonight or something?"

Errr. Friday's my night to lurk at the mall, but I picture Mark's bedroom and my jeans tent, so, "Sure," I say. The bell rings, and we wave goodbye.

Okay. My hair looks great. I roll a few joints but hold off on the Ecstasy I scored last week. Don't want to be too twisted too early. Still, I bring two hits.

His house is a ho-hum monstrosity: huge door, silent hinges. Mark stands smiling. Nice teeth: slightly crooked spots look, well, original. He asks what I want to drink.

"A beer?" I wish I'd said Coke. I picture being radiant like him. I resolve: no drugs this whole weekend, or maybe ever again. But he yanks two beers from a humungo steel fridge, so I decide I'll drink just one.

Upstairs, he turns and says, "Here's my room." Posters, computer, MTV. No babe pics; a good sign. I look at his bed (so neatly made) and feel guilty. It's like Mark can still be violated in a way I can't any more. I mean, I only feel like I've had sex. Yet I can't picture Mark watching porno, for example.

Mark plops on the bed next to me. We blab. Finally, I blurt, "You wanna smoke a joint?"

He says, "I wish we had some Ex." I nearly topple, then coolly produce the two hits. We chase them with beer, clinking our bottles in a matey silent toast. I light the joint, stick the lit end in my mouth, and blow. He purses his mountainous lips and sucks. The air gets soft and smoky. Nice.

Mark stands. Aha. I'm not the only one with a boner. He says, "I want to show you something."

I say, "What?" thinking maybe he'll strip.

But: "It's where my dad works."

Oh, well. I'm loaded, it's Friday night, we have the world to ourselves. I draw the obvious conclusion and relax.

We walk. Twenty minutes? Two hours? The Ex hits. I smell air, feel my ears, hear cars whoosh. Mark's teeth fit behind lips that roll like offshore breakers. I want to take his hand in mine, feel electricty vibrating between us like a TV set or a high wire act.

"Shun the obvious."

"What?" he says. He laughs. A thousand years crag on his face under the streetlight blare. Then he disappears and I feel him right next to me.

"Here," he says. A low-lying white building. Bushes squat like sentries. The door wheezes. Mark pulls me in. The door wheezes. A room without din. I melt along the liquid carpet.

Mark bares his lumberyard teeth; the smile hugs his eyes. He claws my palm. My hand trembles; his vibrates. Maybe I want to go where love is. Mark tugs another door, tugs my hand, and I think: love exists! The simple message clangs like a traffic light, and means something aside from words. Words! What a waste.

Now we're somewhere else and I can't see. Mark flicks a lighter. Jagged trails arc in the shadowy dark. The flame kisses a candle wick, another, another. It's a small room with a coffin on a riser and some chairs. I want to cling to Mark's hand, but it left to light candles. The emptiness in my palm shoots through my heart. I see, anyway, that Mark and I are rising above all that, lifting together in eternal oneness. . . .

Mark lifts the casket top. A face leaps out. I jump back, almost scream. Oops. I see he's kind of—hot. "Motorcycle accident," Mark mumbles. A picture forms: this stud rattles down the highway, like Dad, in a leather jacket. I'm riding shotgun, smelling his hair, clutching him, turned on or sobbing; I can't tell which.

Mark turns on me and mouths, "Don't say a word." He opens the suit, pulls off the tie, unbuttons the shirt. Whiteness sings. My stomach glurps. The belt buckle tinkles like our porch wind chimes; Dad and I used to sit and watch the sun burn the sky, our knees touching. Mark loops the belt around my neck. It sizzles. A scary crease sketches between Mark's eyes. He yanks the pants down the stiff body.

I see dead cock. Mark's blue jeans flop. He mounts the coffin. His perfect ass rises and falls like time-lapse mountain ranges forming. I—I am not seeing what I am seeing. I try to reconnect to my desire to elevate with him. I almost sob, or touch him, or join him, and then the corpse elevates with the face of my father and says, "Don't say a word."

The rest of the weekend I smoke a lot of cigarettes. In Monday's English class Mark smiles at me once, shyly or slyly. His homework's done. The next Friday I head for the mall, where everyone flirts, and life, however it's attached to love, vibrates under bright, bright, bright lights.

GEORGE ILSLEY

Random Acts of Hatred

You never know with men. Any man could glimpse flashes of ass and thigh in the ripped back jeans, glance up to Todd's large eyes, his loopy grin, shaved head, and gorgeous skull; hate feeling attracted, hate their impulse to fuck him, hate his knowing disdain, hate their second orgasm, and especially hate, when later, they're sucked in all over again.

A surly Newfie skinhead, Todd cruises and services construction workers, fake cops from the Tool Box, leather daddies from the Barn, any man who will let him. Except suits. "You gotta have standards," Todd would say. "Old enough to get an erection, and anyone but suits. Men are bad enough. But suits—can't stand the fuckers."

Todd likes men with hair on their chest and stomach who know what they want.

This man was like the rest of them. They were starting to blur for Todd, one burly aura blending into the next hairy torso. Wearing faded jeans, black leather chaps and a dirty t-shirt, the man had left the Barn, glared at Todd, hooked his thumbs into his belt, his meaty hands framing his crotch, and invited Todd up to his apartment with a jerk of his head. Closing the door behind them, he ordered Todd to his knees, unbuttoned his fly, and brought out a large handful of meat. "C'mere, punk. Come take care of this." The man's cock approached horizontal, the crooked knob glistening moistly.

"It's your fucking fault, punk. Your fucking mess. Clean it up. With your tongue."

The hairy balls stride his nose, Todd licked and licked and then sucked the sweet, salty shaft. Todd, on his knees, the cock of a man he hated, hated stretching his lips until cum drooled out the corners of his mouth.

Todd spat and wiped off his face. "You came so fucking fast, like it's a fucking race or something." Annoyed, Todd didn't even bother to finish jerking off. Idly stroking his chest, he wondered how long before that cock, a small sticky mess like a hairy dessert, would become hard and demanding again.

Growing up in Come By Chance, Newfoundland, too pretty for a boy, Todd feared those men, reeking of fish bait, who followed him into the night, caught him where it was dark, pulled him towards them and forced his face down into their crotch. More than one guy cuffed Todd upside the head for scraping his hard-on getting it out. *Kneeling on gravel in the dark, guiding boners out through flaps and zippers—Christ, it's easier getting dogfish out of a gillnet. Couldn't they just unbuckle and drop their drawers? Noooo. That would be too much of a commitment.*

Todd learned to cocksuck years ago, practicing first on his brother Steve, then on his brother's friend Matt, who was cute but brutal, and once with Steve and Matt together, back and forth between them, everyone pretending it was the first time anything like that had ever happened. *Looka the faggot,* Matt said, stroking his own drooling cock. *Looka the cocksucker. His own brother the cocksucker. Wants cock so bad. C'mere, you fucking faggot.*

Steve and Matt each shot a load in Todd's face, then spat on him in ejaculation replays. They sneered at the cocksucker, punched one another in the chest, and that was that. It never happened again.

Except—just before Steve's wedding. Christ, Todd hated weddings. There was something about getting married that makes guys keen for a blowjob. And they could be pretty pushy about it, especially if they'd been drinking, and who didn't just before tying the knot. Steve wasn't that rough when he was fifteen, sixteen, and only spit on Todd that once with Matt, which was okay—even if he did spit first. Matt was Matt and he had to show off. Matt's lingering need to despise Todd was volatile, insistent, feral, and kept secret. The best man at Steve's wedding, Matt pulled Todd into a bathroom, unzipped the fly of his rented tux and said, *You don't deserve this, you cocksucker. Not for one fucking minute.*

Steve too was suddenly rough. Just before Steve's wedding, Todd learned to deep throat—had to, or else choke to death and Steve wouldn't have noticed. Steve's calloused hands grasped his little brother's head and worked it on his cock, hips jerking, buttocks clenching, eyes closed, face a grimace. Todd hated that Steve went so far away while his cock was down his throat.

Soon after the wedding, Todd shaved his head and left for the big city. There he was fucked with abandon. Fucked by men who desired him for an hour, fucked by men who hated him from the start. Fucked by men who carried a torch, and fucked by men who carried self-replicating strings of genetic material.

Todd hated that the big city turned out to be so much like his family.

As a teenager, after practicing with Steve and Matt, Todd went to work for Uncle Fred. Fred lived down the way and used to be married, but she left. Now he needed help around the place.

Fred paid very little and actually expected yard work—mowing, raking, pruning. "It's hot," Fred said. "Take off your shirt, and I'll grab a couple beer." His uncle's eyes crawling up his back felt like bugs Todd couldn't brush off.

After enough beer, resenting working overtime for no more money, Todd returned his uncle's gaze. Fred, paunchy and moody, sauntered over. "There's work to be done in here," he said, directing the boy into the potting shed. Fred's moustache scratched and his kiss tasted foul—like ashtrays and old beer and something rotten. Todd flinched when his uncle grabbed his ass. To distract him, Todd felt up his uncle's crotch, then squatted down. His uncle's cock was loathsome; sharp piss and whatever it was, that smelly smegma paste like festering locker rooms and curdled cottage cheese. Beer and cigarettes, that's what Uncle Fred was like. Second-hand beer, cigarettes, smegma and piss.

One day Fred wouldn't let Todd fall to his knees. He held him up, pulled him into a slobbery embrace, and then bent him face down over a shelf for transplants. Pushing one joint of a blunt thumb into Todd's butt, Fred spit repeatedly into his other hand. Removing his thumb, he pressed the head of his prick against Todd's asshole, gripped the boy firmly, and pushed. Todd almost passed out from the pain. He cried while his uncle fucked him. He never hated anyone as much as he did his uncle at that moment. As the summer went by, Todd cried each time his uncle fucked him after yard work, until that scarlet yellow day—it was the fall—he didn't cry, he let go somehow and said *Yes, oh god, yes.*

That was the last time his uncle ever fucked him.

T O M   M c D O N A L D

A Date with Ray Ray

Ray Ray's already waiting by the time I get to the corner. I get into his car, my hair still wet from the shower.

"About fucking time!" he says. "Think I got all the fucking time in the world to wait for your mother fucking lazy ass?"

I apologize, want to tell him I'm five minutes early, but instead tell him it's nice to see him all dressed up.

"Well, this shit ain't for you," he says. "I got me some real plans when you and me done."

His voice is deep, sexy, turns me on.

"You got me covered, right, baby?" he says, pulling into a deli.

I hand him a twenty, watch as he struts his tall, broad self into the store, my mouth open at the sight of his high, tight butt. He returns with a six-pack of Rolling Rocks, two packs of Kools, pockets the change.

At the beach he lights a joint, throws back a few beers. I ask him how he's been but he shuts me up, turns up the radio. I sit back and think about how lucky I am that a guy like Ray Ray could dig a guy like me.

Ray Ray's song ends. He unzips. His meaty cock takes on a life of its own, growing to full erection. I kiss the head, lick the shaft up and down, run my tongue underneath his foreskin, slide his pants down and lick his balls, bite his thighs, think about the night I asked if I could kiss him. He said I had to eat out his ass first, which I did. And afterwards he laughed, said, "I ain't gonna have no faggot's butt-smelling tongue in my mouth." And I haven't pressed it since.

Now he's got me by the hair and is fucking my face, forcing me all the way down so my nose is buried in his pubes, the smell sickly intoxicating, my breathing seriously stunted, and he alternates between savage face-fucking and burying his cock full force down my throat until I can't decide if I'm going to vomit or suffocate and the whole time he's saying, "Oh yeah, baby, suck that dick," and then he pulls my head away and tells me to get outside.

I do like I did last time, dropping my pants and underwear to my ankles, leaning across his hood, my butt raised high. I pull a condom out of my coat pocket and hand it to him. He gave me an argument the first time, reluctantly agreed to drive to the 7-11 so I could buy some. I hand him a tiny package of lube which he throws to the ground with a "Fuck this shit" and he pushes the head of his cock around my crack until he finds my asshole and then he shoves it in, saying, "Yeah, you like that shit, don't ya, baby," as I grunt in pain. I grit my teeth as he goes in and out, taking long, violent jabs, slapping my thighs and ass, calling me a bitch and a whore and a cocksucker and a cheap motherfucking slut and I'm thinking how easy it would be for some other car to drive in here, the police even, and how much pain I'm in, and then I think about how much Ray Ray is enjoying it and eventually the burning pain turns to pure fucking ecstasy so even when he's pulling all the way out and shoving it all the way back in, it feels good, and I lose track of time until he pulls out, turns me around, gets me on my knees and shoots his cum all over my hair and face, globs of it dripping onto my shirt.

"Make sure you wipe that shit off before you get back in the car," he says.

I don't have any napkins so he throws me an old tissue. I wind up rubbing most of it in so at least it won't drip.

He is quiet on the ride back, smoking a Kool, sipping a Rolling Rock. I ask him if he'd like to get something to eat, my treat.

"Are you fucking deaf or just stupid? I told you I got me some plans."

He drops me off on the corner. I want to ask him why he doesn't call me more often or return my calls when I beep. But I just sit there thinking how handsome he is.

"You think you could get out sometime tonight?" he asks.

I get out, close the door, watch him drive off. It hurts to walk. I go up to the apartment, glad to find nobody's home. I go to the bathroom and look in the mirror for a long, long time, trying to figure out if I'm ugly or what, and I can see Ray Ray's cum in my hair, dried on my face, the stains it made on my shirt.

I go to bed, not bothering to brush my teeth or wash my face. I want to taste and feel Ray Ray as long as I can. I rub my cock against the mattress, hold my pillow tight in my arms, and say, "I'm glad you liked it, Ray Ray."

NOTHING KRISTOFER WOLFE

Everything

I'm sixteen years old. Youth is probably the only thing that I truly have going for me in this life. I sit here before you waiting for something to happen. You stare in my direction but I'm invisible to you. You don't realize I exist. I doubt you will ever understand.

If you'd look at me you'd see a child's face. Hair bleached white. Brown eyes, sunken like death. Body cloaked in a black short-sleeved T-shirt. NIN stretched across a protruding breastbone. Initials of a distorted attempt to face reality.

The jeans I wear are old and faded. As I wait for a ride—for someone to remove me from the dirt-stained highway's wall—I braid a few of the white strings which have frayed at my knee, the only way to relieve myself of the boredom and the expectancies of the house of incest.

I open the door. The darkness draws me inside. My lungs fill with the musky scent of decay. The familiar feeling sets in. The children are lined up against the walls like corpses. Some of them are alive but most are slowly dying since junk became their lives. Now they are just sleepers, waiting for their next fix.

I've promised myself never to get like them. The thought of fixing, of injecting a drug into my veins, sends as many chills now as the first time I ever watched Michael fix himself. The children are in constant need. I turn up the volume on my headphones to smother their sound, but still I can feel their cries tearing at my heart.

An unmade bed lays in the corner of the room, a filthy mattress with cum-stained sheets and half-stuffed pillows. Empty bottles litter the floor around the bed: Chartreuse and cheap vodka stolen from shoppers who would never have expected to be jumped by someone so young. I find a bottle that is still half-full and take a quick shot. The liquid burns my throat, and I cough loud enough to create a stir from the bed. My presence now revealed, I watch as Michael watches me, his dirty cock in his hand.

"Take off your clothes."

His words are laced with drunken venom. For a moment I contemplate running, leaving forever and never looking back. But this is me. Michael is the only one who will take care of me. I feel my body move closer to the bed. I watch as the blond-haired boy peels his shirt from his nakedness. The material sticks to his skin for a moment, revealing a thin layer of nervous sweat. I've watched this movie many times before. I know the roles better than any producer ever could.

Michael thinks that I am beautiful. My skin is soft as a baby's. Two tiny nipples jut out from a little boy's body, hairless and smooth. My bony ribcage sticks out. I wrap my arms around my nakedness for a moment. I try to hide myself, not wanting Michael's eyes on me. Black sheets cover the windows. Darkness dominates. It's how Michael likes it. I should know that by now.

He calls me, impatience in his voice. I kick a hole in the collection of needles and trash that surrounds the bed and pull open my belt. My jeans fall to the ground. I wear nothing underneath. I see no point. Michael always just tears them off.

"Come to me now."

I feel my cock begin to harden as I approach the bed. Two wraith-like hands reach out and grab at it. An arm wraps itself around my hipbones and pulls me down on top of him. I feel his lips against my face, my mouth, my cock. His fingers brush against the softness of my cheek as he leads my mouth to his aching cock. He forces it down my throat and I suck at it as demanded. His lips attack my chest, his mouth biting at my nipples until they start to bleed. I force back tears. His fingers play with my cock, stroking it roughly. Fingernails slice into the skin. I whimper silently and he does it again. He wants to make me cry. I won't surrender, though. I will not give him that pleasure.

Michael kisses my thighs. One peck softly on the left one, another on the right. His lips trace up the shaft of my cock, licking and tasting, kissing and sucking. I close my eyes tightly, forcing the tears back. His mouth slides over my cock, the sucking motions centred on the head. I begin to fall as Michael plays games of sadism and ecstasy with his tongue. Electricity shoots through my body. My orgasm floods Michael's throat. I open my eyes to the familiar darkness. A tear trails down from my eye and soaks into the pillow. I lay frozen, afraid that Michael will sense my fear, but he is too busy rummaging around for a cigarette.

"You want one?"

He throws the cigarette at me like money to a whore. It bounces off my naked chest and rolls down over my flat stomach. I place it against my lips and light it with a nearby candle. After the first drag, I find myself falling again. The tobacco is laced with some sort of shit, but it doesn't matter. This is all that I have. This is all that I really wanted. This night. The coke. Michael. Everything.

KEVIN KNOX

Love in the World

When he was a small child, he asked his mother where he came from. She said he fell down from the stars. Sometimes, when I watch him sleep, I think maybe he did; maybe he is one. He is that impossible to touch. I guard his restless limbs as if I am holding a vigil for the boy he was, and for the man he doesn't know how to be.

When he was four, his father left. Days later, his mother deposited him at his grandmother's house. They stood there on the front steps, this flower child with a child of her own, already growing like a weed. She left him there and told him not to cry, told him she'd be back. She left him there and walked out of his life for ten years. By the time she returned he was beyond control; hers, or anyone's. A distant boy infatuated with night, with things that happen in the dark. In love with the prick of the needle and the hum in the blood that says Rest, Rest, All is well.

Everything he knows he learned in those years, learned in alleys and abandoned cars, under bridges at the hands of strangers. Because he won't talk about it, because I've learned not to ask, there's so much I don't know. I don't know how old he is now, and he claims not to know either. He spent his sixteenth birthday in a locked ward, his eighteenth in rehab. He says he stopped counting after that.

I don't know when I'm going to see him next; he arrives unannounced and uninvited, disturbing my sleep like an ambulance siren. That is, if I *have* been sleeping; if I am not lying awake, lying in wait. The night belongs as much to him now as it does to the moon.

I don't know what to do, what to give him. I cooked for him once; after two bites he lit a cigarette, and the food sat untouched. He is beyond the reach of appetite now—every appetite but one.

I light candles. Not for an atmosphere of romance, but because he says light hurts his eyes. Often, I fill the tub with water and give him a bath. I bathe him because he forgets to do it himself. I bathe him because it allows me to touch him all over.

He eases into the tub and I kneel beside it, like a handmaiden, like a geisha. Leaning back with his eyes closed, he looks almost cadaverous. His ribs shine beneath his skin; his mottled arms float at his sides. I think of Charlotte Rampling and Dirk Bogarde in *The Night Porter*. I think of a *pietà*.

I used to ask myself: What do I get out of this? I wondered and pondered, worried it like a dog with a bone, enumerated words and events like rosary beads. One day, an answer materialized, clear as rain. What do I get out of this? Nothing.

Listen: When I was seven, my parents took me to the ocean for the first time. Though the breakers were taller than me, I ran headlong into them to be tumbled and tossed, the sound of the roar the size of the world. When it looked like I was in too deep, my father, never more than two steps behind, would drag me out. I couldn't wait to be engulfed—couldn't wait to be rescued.

I begin by scrubbing his chest, spreading a layer of bubbles like foam on a wave. I work the washcloth over his skin slowly, concentrating under his arms. He leans forward so that I can wash his back, which is as pale as a saint's, and as holy to me. His vertebrae are small hills in a field of ice, and I polish them with tender familiarity. When I have finished washing the top half of his body, he straightens up, somewhat revived, and I help him to his feet.

Having already taken off my shirt, which is wringing wet, I remove the last of my clothes and get into the tub with him. Crouched before him, I work up a lather in my hands and stroke it into his thighs, rubbing upward toward his groin. Briefly, I cup his balls in my hand, loose now from soaking in the water, and rub them together lightly. I comb froth through his pubic hair and spread it down the shaft of his cock, pausing to tug at the salmon-coloured head. Occasionally it swells slightly, more out of reflex than as an indication of desire.

I've tried that, though—that distraction, that bribe, that old bag of tricks. He stood impassive while I touched and probed, nuzzled with my nose and lips, cupped his ass, one soap-slick finger pushing into the furrow, teasing. His penis hung reproachfully, a clapper with no bell to ring, and I had to concede defeat. I want to take him out of himself; he wants to go further in. And where he goes, he goes alone.

After I dry him off, I take him into my room and turn down the bed. I pull him close, knowing that his nocturnal turnings will remove him from my tentative arms. I fold myself around him, imagining that I can dream heat into his cold bones, that my being here beside him matters at all.

Early in the morning, propped up on one elbow, I watch as he sucks his thumb, his face flushed and hot, and I remember something my mother told me, a long time ago. I picked you up, she said, every time you cried. I wanted you to know that there was love in the world.

D A R R I N   H A G E N

Remember

Remember.

Lazy days of sky and wind and brilliant sun and land stretching everywhere to nowhere and back, beckoning with their extraordinary emptiness, the loneliest place in the world. A sky that big could crush you, suffocate you. And hide you. Hide in the emptiness. It's just over that hill . . . no, the next one . . . no, the next one. . . .

Remember.

A wind so strong you could hear it coming for miles, with all the dust and leaves it sees fit to travel with. You could watch the dust cloud form past that first range, then race toward the plains. Remember sneaking into a dark bedroom like a frightened hunter, aching for that touch of young skin, but knowing that the uneasy sleep of a boy is too fragile for touching.

Knowing that, and touching anyway. The fear as you looked into his waking eyes in the dark, caught. He was hard in your hand. He didn't move or breathe and you didn't move your hand and then he stirred enough that you knew to continue. His eyes burned through the black room as your mouth filled with his smooth, clean, eager scent.

Remember waking in the dark with that same hardness forcing its way into your mouth.

Does he remember?

Of course. Who wouldn't be haunted by that? A servant to your desire, a warm wetness at your mercy. No strings, whenever the mood struck. More often as hormones surged, fueled by alcohol and porn and girlfriends at the drive-in who can fire a guy up so he's hard as a rock and then don't go all the way.

Something's gotta give.

Remember the night he tried to kill himself. You carried him around the yard in his underwear, trying to get him to walk off the pills. But there were too many pills, and he started to slip into unconsciousness. In the car, both in nothing but underwear, racing into town, through stop signs and intersections at top speed, him slumped against the car door, shivering. His smooth skin glowed from the sweat, the muscles under the skin vibrated.

Remember watching under his door as he masturbated to a magazine. Memorizing his caresses, in case it's ever my turn. Our climaxes were almost always simultaneous.

Remember the night he looked straight at the spot you were watching him from. Through the darkness, his eyes burned into yours. The way he didn't stop, even though he knew you were there. Even though he knew you were watching. He shifted so that you had a better view. Made it look like it was not what he was doing at all. It was all part of the game.

Remember the first time he reached for you, in your car. Remember your promise.

Remember the fantasies, the dreams, the sensuality, the excitement of watching him pleasure himself, the casual ease of his grace, the slender curve of his hardness, the arc of his success landing on his rippling muscles.

Remember when it all ended. The summer he moved out. Remember how he broke your heart, even though he never knew.

Remember the huge sky that hid us from view, hid our boys' games from the prying adult eyes.

Remember that freedom. That feeling of never getting caught. Remember dreaming about your future, and him always being in it. By your side.

BILLY COWAN

Flying

We met one night at the circus. He was the trapeze artist. I was his voyeur.

Entranced by his muscular torso, his shaven head, the bulge in his sparkling tights, I watched and worshipped as he spun and swirled a hundred feet above my head.

I'd never seen such a sight before. Dazzling, mesmerizing, dangerous. A light to which I was drawn uncontrollably.

After the show I went looking for him. Out back, with the horses, the lions, the clowns, the sequinned women. Out where the smells of hot, sweating animals consorted with the smells of hot, sweating humans. Smells that made my own body drip with excitement, anticipation, possibility.

I asked the ringmaster where I could find him. He pointed, and like a slave to desire, I followed his direction.

Passing the caged lions I came upon him, standing beside a wooden trough filled with water, washing down his body with a sponge. He was naked, except for a skin-coloured jock strap.

I stopped.

My heart raced as if I'd just been involved in an accident. I was suddenly nervous, unsure. What was I going to say? What would make sense? Should I tell him the truth? Tell him that I wanted to touch him, hold him, lick him, suck him, fuck him, love him? To feel him on top of me, inside me, all over me? Can a stranger tell these things to another?

Before I could make up my mind, he spoke.

"Hi, what can I do for you?" His voice was deep, but surprisingly sweet, like black treacle.

"Uhm. . . uhm . . . could I have your autograph?"

How ridiculous, pathetic.

"Sure. Have you got a pen and paper?"

I searched in my jacket as he dried himself with a towel. I held out the pen and paper with a shaking hand. He took them from me and then, raising his thigh to lean on, signed his name. I could see a thin curve of scrotum sticking out from beneath the elastic of his jock strap. I quickly raised my eyes as he handed back the pen and paper.

"Thanks," I said.

"No problem."

Not knowing what else to do, I turned to go.

"Would you like a beer?"

His voice stopped me and I turned to see the most devilish chipped-front-tooth smile.

Instantly, I knew he was to be mine.

We went to his trailer. We talked. We kissed. He removed my clothes. I removed his jock strap. He lay down and allowed me to rub oil over his smooth, firm flesh.

I told him that I wanted to slip inside him. He told me to wait. Then, taking my hand, he led me out of the trailer.

Running naked through the dark, I tried to cover my erection, but he told me not to worry, that I was among circus people.

We arrived at a small enclosed area to the side of the main tent, in the centre of which, suspended from a metal pole, was a low trapeze, about six feet from the ground.

"This is where I train," he explained, then jumped up and grabbed the trapeze. Wrapping his legs around the bar, he hung upside down.

"Come closer," he said.

I stepped forward. His face was level with my groin. He opened his mouth and swallowed my erection. I stretched forward and took him in as well. We sucked on each other like newly born pups. Hard and fast. As my legs started to tremble, he stopped and pulled himself up.

"Come up and join me. There's some steps over there to help you climb up."

I climbed onto the trapeze where he now stood, and sat down. He began to rock back and forth until we swung gently in the cool air. He smiled down at me, and then turned his back and took the weight of his body onto his arms, lifting his legs straight out in front of him at ninety degrees, parallel to the ground. He began to lower himself. My cock throbbed as I realized he was going to sit on me.

I positioned myself more accurately below his oiled hole as his round buttocks descended closer to my cock. With a groan he slid onto me, enclosing my full length inside his tight warmth. I kissed his back as we swung gently back and forth. The air tickled my skin, and though we were only six feet above the ground, I felt as if we were flying amongst the stars; free falling in space like two astronautical lovers.

Galactic sensations filled my body as he used the muscles of his strong arms to work himself up and down my shaft. Riding me faster and faster I soon felt the walls of his ass tighten with the onset of orgasm. Feeling the heat rise in my own groin, I held on tight to the trapeze. It only took a few more seconds for us both to explode. My body convulsed as my stardust shot into his black hole. His shot out into the black night like a super-nova.

The spasms caused us to fall onto the cushioned floor below, and there we lay for a time, side by side, just watching the trapeze above us swing back and forth until it came to a rest.

"It's time to go," he finally said. The blackness was giving way to morning grey. "Circus people are early risers."

We went back to the trailer where he dressed me, kissed me, and said goodbye.

That morning the circus left town—the horses, the lions, the clowns and the sequinned women, and one trapeze artist with a devilish chipped-front-tooth smile.

GARY PROBE

Just Wait

Greg looks at his watch. He has been sitting in the cubicle for an hour now waiting for a man to come into the Woolworth's bathroom to relieve himself. He is highly aroused. Occasionally he runs the fingers of his left hand along the underside of his penis to ensure that he will be ready for anything at a moment's notice.

Until a few days ago, Greg had never considered the possibility that sex could even be gotten in a public washroom. He had been posting a recipe for Gay Pride Neapolitan ice cream cake in his Members of the Same Sex newsgroup when one titled "Toilets Around Town" caught his attention. He studied the various locations thoroughly. He read and memorized several important bathroom sex etiquette tips. Then he decided to pay a visit to the downtown Woolworth's bathroom before retiring to his bedroom to masturbate about the plan.

The fluorescent tubes flicker overhead. Occasionally Greg catches the faint whiff of piss and man sweat beneath the overpowering smell of what must be a dozen crystalline deodorizing hockey pucks plunked into every urinal. He reads the jackknife and Bic pen scrawlings covering the cubical.

"HEY ASSHOLE, QUIT READING THIS—YER PISSING ON YOUR SHOES," says one.

He touches a finger to the most promising demand, "SUCK MY COCK, YOU HORNY BASTARD," and then scratches an exclamation point on the end of the sentence with his car key.

The sudden rush of water splashing automatically into the urinals startles him and he drops his keys. When he bends down to pick them up, he peeks underneath the stall door to scan the washroom floor. No one has slipped in during the commotion.

Greg leans down into the wall and studies the rudimentary glory hole fashioned by cocksuckers of yore. "Hmmm," he thinks. "Wonder what they used to make this? It's not very round." Greg would have used his portable rechargeable Black and Decker hand drill to cut the wood in a circular series of perforations before popping it through in a manly flourish using the butt of his drill. He imagines the dramatic emergence of his engorged penis on the other side of the wall and the chapped lips that utter, "Oh, yeah, baby," before swallowing him whole.

On closer inspection, though, it seems that the wood grain on the inside of the glory hole runs toward him. He squeezes his legs together involuntarily feeling the painful phantom splinter lodged firmly into his tender foreskin. "Maybe I should switch to the other side," Greg thinks. As he stands up and begins to push his hard-on back into his cotton boxers, he hears the washroom door swing open with a squeaky whine. He sits back down.

The footsteps squeak toward Greg's end of the washroom and then stop. Water begins to run into the sink and Greg peeks through the space in the door to see a sliver's worth of the back of a white t-shirt tucked into a sliver's worth of tight, faded blue jeans, and white running shoes. The water stops running in the sink and the bathroom becomes silent again save for the paper towel wiping of freshly cleaned man hands. The door to the next stall swings open and slams with a bang as the stranger sits himself down on the toilet. Greg races through the list of ways to make bathroom sex contact:

The stranger may slowly edge his running shoe-clad foot over and nudge Greg's foot, waiting for an encouraging nudge back. He may drop a wadded-up piece of paper and slide his hand slowly under the wall of the cubicle in a languorous invitation to be touched. Or, he may simply push his penis through the glory hole demanding Greg to feed until a gush of semen signals an end to the encounter.

"At least he's on the good side for avoiding splinters," Greg thinks.

The main door squeaks open and closed again and another man

walks in. He stops across from the cubicles. Greg sits motionless, squeezing his keys tightly in his right hand. He hasn't planned for the potential complications of bathroom sex at all. Could the newcomer be a store security guard or just someone wanting to have a bowel movement in one of the two occupied cubicle toilets?

He hears the man step up to the cubicles. Greg wonders if he can be arrested for having a ninety-minute crap. He notices a flake of paint sticking to the end of his car key. He flicks it off to conceal any connection to him and the new exclamation point on the cubicle wall.

The man taps lightly three times on the other stall door. Greg hears the stranger mutter, "Hey, man," to Greg's potential date. "Hey," says Greg's date as he opens the door and quietly welcomes in the stranger. They proceed without speaking. Only the clacking thud of two loose belt buckles thumping together announces what is taking place. Greg looks under the wall as their pants drop down around their ankles and a hand touches the floor for balance. He can hear the wet sounds of fellatio, the licking lips, the sliding, lubricated smack of saliva mixed with pre-cum. Greg does the only thing he can think of. He wads up a piece of paper and tosses it onto the floor of their cubicle. It is kicked back as the men reposition themselves with a thump against the other side of their adjoining wall. Greg nudges the white running shoe with his Hush Puppy two or three times. There is no reaction at all except for a breathy "Ohhh, fuck" that Greg is sure has little to do with him at all.

He wraps his hand around his throbbing dick and directs it toward the glory hole in a last ditch effort to enter the world of cubicle number two. It bumps into the hairy flesh of someone's buttock sealing off the hole from the other side. Greg drops his keys to the floor and begins jerking furiously. As the climaxing grunts of the two other men intensify, he turns and plucks a hair from the little mound of flesh pushing in through the glory hole. "Ow!" says one of the men. "I think I got a fucking splinter up my ass." Greg grinds the solitary ass hair into his own pubic hair and then comes into the palm of his hand. He slumps over, catching his breath as the other men shuffle and bump back into their clothes and leave the room.

Greg looks at his hand for a moment and then wipes his semen with a flourish across the wall. He takes his keys and scratches "GREG WAS HERE" around the circumference of the glory hole. Then he buckles his belt, zips up his fly, and strides confidently out of the Woolworth's men's washroom without washing his hands.

A N D Y   Q U A N

If It Sticks Out

If it sticks out: look at it. Is it as small as a pearl, glistening and taking in the world around it onto its lustrous surface? Or big as a roasted leg of lamb, the juices still sizzling and dripping, delicious and pink? Somewhere in between? Examine your own body. Can it fit somewhere? One, two, maybe three places. How does it lean? Does it point towards the sun or the moon, inland or the coast, the sky, or hidden places below?

Is it round? Circle it. Mirror it with your eyes, your pupils the same shape. Trace its aureole. Cup it with your hand. Put your ear against it. Bounce off of it. Rebound onto it. Kiss it, closed-mouth. Close your eyes. Draw it from memory.

If it sticks out, lick it. Orbit it with your tongue, clockwise, counter-clockwise. Ten times. Inhale, and let the breath dry the saliva on your tongue. Extend that tongue, curl it towards gravity, approach the object, roll your head into it like a cat, like a golfer's swing, slow motion. Withdraw your tongue into your mouth and taste it. Rub it against your upper palate, close your eyes and see the shelf where all the tastes in the world are stored. Is it there, this ruby you've gathered up between your lips? If it is, point it out. Nod, pay it respect. If it's new, place it in a glass case of your favourite colour.

Make space for it on the shelf.

If it sticks out, cover it. Form spit on your tongue, get the saliva flowing from your gums and cheeks. Part your lips gently, just the front, as if about to whistle. Position yourself over it and let fall one shining drop. Listen to the sound it makes. Continue until it's slick with spittle, until the dry roof has been covered in autumn rain. Is it shining? Blow on it. Steadily and then in sharp hot breaths. Give it a wolf-whistle.

If it sticks out, it's a monument, it's a tourist attraction. Look up, and see it above you. The lights at night falling over you like the start of rain. Now, climb its stairs. You can take the elevator but you'll have to pay. Enjoy the view.

If it sticks out, engulf it, seal up the borders. You're China; it's Hong Kong, pre-'97. You surround it but it belongs to someone else. Be glad you don't own it. Treasure it like a gift from a foreign land that you'd never seen or heard of before.

Is it beautiful? Does it know it's beautiful? Wrap it in leather straps. No, bind it. Tight so the skin pushes out from beneath, and the blood boils near the surface.

If it is the longest or the shortest day of the year, or any spirit day that you wish to celebrate, use the straps laced with shiny studs. Bind it twice. Adorn it with your finest jewelry, gold studs and silver bars. Pierce it. Show it no fear.

If it sticks out, suck it. Like your life depends on it. This is the soother you've been waiting for. Pull it in, feel it slide past your lips. Introduce it to the darkness inside your mouth. Compare the shape of it with your tongue's shape. Comfort it. The silk of your palate and the insides of your cheeks, soft and clean. Like submerging in a freshwater lake some black summer night, a lightning storm in the distance. Suck harder. Feel it at the back of your throat, like a premonition. Jostling with your uvula. This cavity that's been bothering you lately—it's filled and the pain is gone.

If it sticks out, paint it. You've got a palette with colours that have no names in this language. Oils and powders made from bumblebees' legs, seahorses' gullets, the wings of a hummingbird, distilled sapphires, the plume of a South China dragon. Here's your blank canvas, its cells and pores open up to you. Paint something from a part of your mind you haven't visited lately. Spell out the word, "desire." Sketch in an outline at first, or not at all. Go free-form, slather it on, you can always thin it out, or paint over it. Remember the hottest you've ever felt, and make a picture of it. Or the reddest. Or blue if you prefer. Or the loudest sound you've ever heard. The time you almost went blind. Go on. Use your imagination.

If it sticks out, sit on it. Have a seat and swing your legs like you're sitting on a tiny outcrop above the Grand Canyon. Half the world's wonder is there, and a whole mountain could fit in, or the Black Forest, or the lake which you grew up beside. Feel it beneath you, on your backside, the object that is preventing you from falling. Falling into all of that.

Now, sit on it like you're in a schoolyard playground. First, the seesaw. The stained red orange wood has captured an afternoon's sun. It's warm on your buttocks, your bare thighs stick to it. Push down with your legs, and you're up, suspended. To get down, think weight. Breathe in heavy air, lower your shoulders, relax until your torso has taken on new density. Unsuccessful? Ask then. Request that your partner let you down. You'll know the best tone of voice: polite, playful, commanding. Strike a deal? Say it's your turn.

Now, we're on the swings. You grip the chains so hard the blood runs out of your fingers. Start slowly and the wind against your face is like you're being painted with brushes made of squirrels and pussywillows. Then you pump your legs in front of you and faster, faster: you're exhilarated and soothed at the same time. Your stomach catches with fear and pleasure as you kick your legs out, the arc getting wider and wider. You fly up face forward into the sky before you're taken backwards again, rhythmic rocking: one, two, three, four. If you choose to jump off, mid-air, you will learn flight, excitedly clawing and scraping at the air. There's soft sand below you, and children can fall without breaking bones.

KEVIN HUNTER

Ya, Boy

Walking through the sauna, I see a man stroking his thick, six
-inch cock just ahead of me. He is just over six feet tall, 160
pounds of starting-to-flab, thirty-year-old muscle, firm pectorals—
not overly muscular, thick-set legs, and a sprinkling of blond fur all
over his body. His hair is bushy and blond and doesn't quite suit him.
He is certainly not turning me on at the moment, but his intense,
raunchy look makes me pay a certain amount of attention.

I try to walk by but he doesn't let me pass. He leans into me, his
cock poking against me. "How about sucking my cock?" he asks.

"No . . . thanks," I reply.

"You want it," he says, and to my astonishment he presses his
body heavily against me and drives his tongue into my mouth. I don't
know why I allow this for so long, but ten seconds later I break free
of him and repeat, "No thanks," and scamper off.

I find a place to sit and watch all the boys go by. Then I feel a
presence behind me. I turn to face it and see that same stubby dick
being stroked in front of my face. "You just want a taste," as if trying
to hypnotize me into agreement by the rhythmic stroking of his cock.

"No," I manage to say, not understanding why I'm playing this
game with him.

"Just a taste," he repeats. His cock, now pressed against my lips, urges my reluctant mouth open so I taste. I give it a few slurps and enjoy it. It gets very hard. He pulls it out, confident I am now his. "Come to my room," he says softly. I do.

Once inside the tiny room I freely touch his soft, hairy body as he does with mine. Both of us stare into each other's eyes, almost romantically. He reaches up and firmly grasps the back of my head and kisses me. I give in to him, savouring the taste of his mouth. Feeling almost exhausted from his kiss, I go down on my knees and suck his sweet dick.

"Yeah, you like that, boy," he purrs.

"It tastes so fucking good," I moan.

"Good boy. You're a good boy," he says, repeating it over and over as I suck that cock that fits so well into me. I can easily take it all the way down my throat and I like that. I like how it feels there, how it tastes so far down my throat—the constant drool of pre-cum his cock feeds me.

He lays down on the bed and points his cock upright. "Come on boy, taste some more." He spreads his legs and I cradle myself in them. I keep stroking his cock, slick with saliva, and he keeps repeating, "Ya, you're a good boy." This excites me so much. I caress his body and tweak the smallish, hard nipples and their protruding centres.

"This cock'll do anything for you, boy. It'll piss for you, come for you, play with your hole. . . . " I stare at him in anticipation. I want its piss but I'm too shy to ask. I keep sucking harder than ever now. He sits up again but my mouth never leaves his warm dick. He pulls me up to kiss him. "Ya, that's it, boy. Mmmm. . . . "

I stop and look into his eyes. "Can . . . " I get the courage to say it, slowly and carefully: "Can it . . . piss for me?"

He smiles, "Ya, my boy needs some piss. Go on boy, drink from it." I crouch down again. His cock has gone slightly limp. My tongue cradles his dick and soon a strong, warm flow begins to drain into my mouth. I go fucking wild at this. I spit a gulpful back onto his bush. "Yaaa," he says. I make sure I am covered in the liquid—my hair and my face. My eyes sting from it. I am close to coming but I stop myself. "How'd you like that, boy?" he asks.

"Fucking tasty," is all I can muster.

He lays back down, spreading his legs again but this time revealing his pink hole. I salivate for it. I can't resist it and dive down to it.

"Ya, lick my hole. Give it kisses. Soft kisses," he tells me. I do so. I start with one slow, soft kiss right over the hole, then tiny, soft kisses around it.

"Ya, like that. Give it one long lick." I do this carefully, as if it was to be my only taste of his hole. I start from the bottom, before the crack begins and lick all the way up to the base of his nuts. One long, clean, wet stroke. One great taste of his furry ass.

"Ya boy, now french my hole. French it like you're frenching my mouth."

I do as I'm told, licking wildly all over the puckered hole, with lots of spit. "Go on boy, french that hole. Go all the way down it's throat." I do so, burying my tongue deep into his fleshy, sweet-tasting asshole, savouring each musky breath I inhale from it.

"Ya baby, I'm gonna come."

Immediately, I go pay attention to his cock again, the cock that is to feed me. I suck madly and then he says, "Ya boy, I've got something for you," and out spews his creamy load. I get a blast of it down my gullet before I remove my mouth and it shoots spastically all over my face. I've tasted him now—really tasted him. Sweat, musk, cum. It didn't take me long to shoot. Finally, when it was all over, he said, "Ya boy. How did you like that mouthful of cum?"

"Fucking tasty," was all I could say.

ROYSTON TESTER

Naked Night

*very second Friday was "Naked Night" at Brighton's "South Coast
Sprawl," a fag guesthouse off Cannon Place. One of Randy's haunts.
It was September; seven airless, sticky days and nights. I was getting antsy,
so I went alone with him, nutbar as he is.*

*"Doing anything besides working your ass off at the Pavilion?" he asked
as we stripped down in the cloakroom along with three older men.*

"Nah," I said. "Pretty knackering."

"Gotta put yourself about, Billy," he said as we walked into the bar.

*He gets all this shit from Major Chubb, our housemaster. I'm out of
Chubbsy's "transition home" in twelve months.*
Then I'll really get sorted.

SECRETARY OF STATE, HOME OFFICE, WHITEHALL.
H.M. DETENTION CENTRES. CADCUSE PARK.
REGULATIONS.
WASHING, SHAVING, AND HAIR-CUTTING

*I tried not to look, but Randy was hung like a mule; black tattoo crawling
out of his groin.*

77. Arrangements shall be made for every inmate to wash at all proper times.

There were thirty or so men—and only men—in the bar. And a fair number walking about. Even the two barmen were cockproud all right, leaning over the counter. All dicks and balls. I couldn't believe how natural everybody seemed. Outside, on this really dim terrace, there were more nude men in groups or strolling under the trellises. It was difficult to see. I guessed there was action out back; it was a fruit hangout, after all. And I knew Randy turned tricks for a fiver or two—how else could he pile up so much dough in his room? But he didn't seem in much of a mood for trade tonight.

to have a hot bath at least once a week

We strolled out back. It felt odd being starkers, especially with all the checking-out happening, but Randy was cool. He nodded to one or two people but never stopped to talk; all very serious. Randy never smiles anyhow. Glances took in glances. The owners had strung up lights over the few bushes, and although there was conversation out here, it was more subdued. I was kind of enjoying the inside-out feel to the Sprawl—a "fuck you" garden party—men urgent and easy at the same time. As we wandered deeper into the garden, Randy shut up altogether. Thank Christ. The chat around us had stopped, too; turned into stroking and kissing.
One man knelt at the feet of another.

and for male inmates (unless excused or prohibited on medical grounds) to shave

Four or so men were jacking each other off. And you shuffled past them, kind of glad they were having such a hot time. I wondered if Randy really was queer like them or whether he was getting about, as he says. I couldn't work him out. He hesitated, then leaned against the wall. Somehow he looked quite different; as though he was scared or something, in a hurry. I stared at him.
"Suck me," he said.

or be shaved when necessary

Randy's cock looked thicker than ever; he pulled the skin back so I could see more.

69

"Not into it," I said.

Two guys were nuzzling in on another guy's armpits.

"I'm paid up, Billy boy," he said.

I tried to look confused. "Eh?"

"The forty quid. See you been in my room again."

I looked at him some more.

"You wouldn't want Chubbsy to know. Eh, Billy?"

"What're you on about?"

"Suck, or I talk."

He slapped his hard-on against my thigh—once, twice—and grabbed my shoulder.

"You're full of shit, Randy."

"You like that Detention Centre up north?"

"I didn't touch your stash."

"Sent back to Cadcuse Park, Billy boy. Plenty of room up there. Suck. We'll say no more about it."

"Fuck off."

He grabbed at my cropped hair and pushed me down hard onto his dick. How to make friends and influence people. It tasted cheesy and sour. But I worked him over good, like a kid with a pacifier the size of an arm. Could smell the chip shop on him, too. I licked his massive balls. Randy started necking with one of the guys next to us. Maybe he is a fairy. Who knows. Or maybe it's just like Cadcuse: no bloody choice. As I see it, I'm just part of the scenery, anyhow. What do I care? I sucked his huge dick.

Yes, sir. Thank you, sir.

Randy's ribs flickered above me; he shot into my mouth. Forty quid for a mouthful of hot juice. I gagged and spat the cum into my hand, smearing it down my own cock like a rubber. I knelt at his feet and wanked myself off while he was still at the nipple of the guy next to him. I shot against the brick.

Randy didn't seem to notice he'd come. Cadcuse Park all over again— solemn, get-it-over-with—but no lock-up or iron grilles afterwards; not the same kind, anyways.

"Let's get another pint," Randy said, pulling away from the guy next to him. I looked around at the terrace, wiping my hand on some ivy.

and to have their hair cut as required.

"See the stars?" said Randy as we ducked under some branches towards the light and the man-chatter inside. "Two pints of bitter, Jack. An' a couple of bags of scratchins." Randy led the way to some seats near the door, stark naked. Two beers high in the air.

"Now Billy . . ." But I still feel sorry for the guy. It's like he's burning-up wicked. "My forty quid back by Monday," he said, slamming the beers on the table, pointing a finger between my eyes. "You cough up or I squeal." His free hand twisted my balls.

And as my cock stirred above his knuckles, the bastard smirked. First time ever I'd seen him crack. Right there, like he was having fun.

D A V I D   G R E I G

Below the Parade

The steamy streets are filled with noisy gay activists, but I feel the need for a different kind of brotherhood. I turn the corner and descend the stairs. I enter a deeper world. A private fortress where men seek men. Where grasp seeks stubble. Where dick seeks grunt. A place in which to discover it. Discover him. Discover myself once again.

I wash my hands out of habit and see the mirror reflect my face as serene as a figure from Fra Angelico, basking in the glory of having found the gold of the Handsome Man who always calls everyone an "animal." He's known for never reciprocating, but he's finally been all over me with licking that provides a map that I use to journey beneath his skin.

When he first lifts his arm to touch me, I'm not sure if it's actually happening, or is instead an exquisite hallucination. The few times I've encountered him before he's always struck a distant brutish pose. He only lets guys suck his dick. He doesn't do anything else. That's what I've heard him say. But there's something about him. Something I sense might be inside that compels me to stand next to him whenever one of his "animals" sucks him off.

Each time, I've suppressed a prayer as I casually slip my arm like a drunken fishing buddy around the Handsome Man's shoulder and wait for him to direct me to pet the boulder-hard bulge of his curved hairy gut. Or nuzzle his densely bearded jaw. Or gaze directly into his jet black eyes that are steely but always moist.

The guy on his knees begins to move his mouth between our cocks. The guy eventually engulfs them both and makes us swell to maximum hardness. Our two average-sized wieners are pressed together into one jumbo throbbing ham. The Handsome Man then groans and in a stern, loud voice asks if I think the guy on his knees is an "animal." The bliss on my lips obstructs my reply.

Though he's never rebuffed me, he's never initiated contact. But this time I catch him off guard and he stops as we pass each other with no one around. He reaches out bashfully and gently strokes the sweat-smeared hair on my chest. When his hand lingers longer than a mere proposition warrants, I swear I can feel the person he actually is straining to be behind the gruff and distance of his façade. He must sense this because his eyes grow wary, so I mimic his usual stance back to him and do nothing but stare.

He looks hurt as he traces his finger along the silent swell of my lips. But I pull back and walk away, patient with the certainty that he really needs so much more and that probably he's just afraid. I chuckle out loud at something he mutters as he catches me up in the hall. At the sound of my laugh, his jaw drops in surprise and he lets his mask drop to the floor.

With a boy-like grin, he takes the risk and lets himself begin to trust me. To climb out of the role he's worn for how many years. The hard core blueprints that have made him act in a way that he thinks he must act. It all begins to disappear with one honest touch from his hand. His false and rusted "top man" armour dissolves into a genuinely masculine sensuousness. Blood floods his beautiful flesh and refashions him whole in my hands. He grows more authentically a man with every display of his need

As a crowd of men gathers around, he whispers that he's been looking for me. He firmly nudges them all away, then shyly relaxes. Yet I can still feel his hesitation. It takes so much courage for him to do this—to reach out to another man. Uncover his emotion. Betray his vulnerability. Become truly naked.

I look into his eyes and see him transform into the man that he actually is: little boy with brand new puppy. Now there's the prize—the marrow within the bone

Then he leans over and takes my cock in his mouth and tongues it and slurps, and even though he isn't very good at it, the fact that it's him doing it makes it feel as sweet as it ever can feel. We take turns making love to each other's dicks, then he hugs me tight and I hug him back. We lap and lick each other's beards until he roars, and pumps warm semen over my belly, and I shoot my load till it dents the wall.

He kisses me hard as if he's always been my lover, and we part with smiles, open and touching and deep. I whistle as I head for the shower, not knowing if I'll ever see him again, knowing only that his kisses and whispers were true and that he never once called me an "animal".

I shower and dress and prepare to ascend. But before I do, I pause, amazed. For I'm sure I can hear, from the door at the top of the stairs, the roars of a jubilant crowd. Coming from the other side of the wall. Coming from somewhere up above.

A L A N   A L V A R E

The Monastery

White-robed monks glide up and down the darkened cloister. The monks stare straight ahead, but occasionally eye a confessor or penitent, a celebrant or altar-server, with whom to partner for the Holy Sacrifice.

The cloister is always dark. Cell doors may be opened or closed. The Holy Sacrifice may be in the middle of enactment on any given altar. Sometimes Solemn Exposition, with the door open for adoration, may be in progress. Some cells are empty, their altars cold.

In the Great Chapel, where vapours of incense rise among the worshippers, crowds are venerating. In the Chapel of Penance, weights are lifted.

Vocations are most plentiful on weekends. There are a few novices, and a great many regular weekend retreatants, drawn by the consolations available in this house of ease. The Friars Regular are attached informally to this house, and many know each cell intimately. It's so popular that all the cells are taken, and new applicants have to wait with only a locker, until that blessèd call comes, "Locker 44, your room is now ready." Sometimes there is silence, but this is a very ascetic order, and silence has been given up, and the penance of disco music taken in its place.

Brother Maurus lies on his back in a torn towel. He is in Cell 207 tonight, and he has left the door open to receive a caller. Of course, it must be the right caller, the Messiah who is to come. Like John the Baptist, he will know the Messiah when he sees him. Tonight the Messiah will be slim and small, and under twenty-five. Last week, the Messiah had to be a fat and fully-clothed Daddy with a belt. The Messiah is present in anyone at any given time. His Second Coming never stops.

Brother Ignatius is sprawled on his stomach, wearing nothing. His cock and balls are pushed back, exposed between his legs for all those wandering down the cloister to see. Brother Ignatius is very humble tonight, very accepting, requiring only that he be able to carry another's burden. His shoulders are broad enough, his back strong enough, to carry whatever the night may bring. Or is it day?

Brother Aelred sits on the edge of his altar, having looked under the fair linen sheet to see how torn the mattress is, and wondering whether it contains things more alive than the relics of saints to be found in colder altars. He knows that the monastery could pay for new mattresses, but does not know of all the charities competing for the monastery's money.

The Abbot-General must buy drugs, and makes large donations to the political party that defends his right to be Abbot-General. Some would call this corruption. The Abbot-General calls this teamwork. He likes things with hyphens. His name is Frederick-William-Herbert-Scott. Working underground in World War II, he had a sin-gle-barreled name, Michel Auger, but he didn't like it. Short names now bring up memories of clip-clopping down the street in awkward heels to escape the Gestapo, and the labour of drawing stocking lines on the back of bare shaved legs.

Cloister Garth is the monk who never leaves—the phantom of the vapours. Some says he lives here. Some say he's a ghost. Some say the Phantom of the Opera was based on Garth. Some say he's the owner. Some say he's the real abbot. Some even say he's the Pope. Cloister Garth is none of these things. He just likes the monastery, and can afford to be here daily and nightly. He cannot afford to be anywhere else.

There is a holy well of swirling, healing waters. Brothers Paulinus, Maximilian, and Lucius sit there. Their toes touch. All three have underwater erections. None of them will expose tonight. They are playing Hard To Get, which after a time means Left On A Shelf.

Brother Januarius is also in the swirlpool, and is about to give caring ministrations—a hand job, as they call it in the world—to Brother Lucius, when an angel glides by. The Laying on of Hands is delayed. The angel in question, or in vision, is a blond boy, by which in this heaven is meant a young man, perhaps twenty-two, like Brother Januarius himself. His hair is clipped short enough to look like a halo. His smile is shy, as if the knowledge of his own beauty, like the psalmists knowledge of God, was too wonderful for him to contain. The angel's arms and legs and ass and tits are muscular. He is a very tough-looking angel, with a single undecipherable tattoo on his right arm. He wears a loincloth. There is a very human imperfection in this angel, which Brother Januarius only notices when he is racing hard after the angel down the cloister. The angel's wrists are badly scarred, vertical strips of old wounds.

Brother Januarius follows the angel to the refectory and buys a hotdog. He's English, a cockney, to be exact, a word that has always excited Brother Januarius. No wonder Pope Gregory used to go to the slave market to see these creatures being sold, and no wonder he noticed they were angels. In Gregory's day, the Angles/Angels had not been missionized into hating sex. Original sin, an evil-smelling soap concocted by Augustine of Hippo, and liberally lathered up by the imperial hierarchy, had not yet been exported to Britain. That was to be Pope Gregory's mission. This much Brother Januarius remembers from Church history classes.

Brother Januarius, like any monk, dreams of approaching angels. He approaches this one, and asks some stupid question about the time. Even as he asks it, he wonders why. The angel smiles, shakes his head, and looks away to the refectory's TV screen. He is clearly there for the duration. With an awkward and spiritual shrug, Brother Januarius trots back down the cloister, barefoot, barehanded, and bare-assed. He has taken off his simple towel habit in anticipation of a shower. He does not notice other monks beginning to jerk themselves off as he passes their cells.

Brother Januarius returns humbly to his cell. He climbs on the altar, with its thin mattress, and waits for the future to expose itself to him. Meanwhile, he exposes himself to it, coyly arranging his towel to reveal his balls and the bottom of his cock.

PAUL VALLANCE

Backroom

With deeds of loving kindness, I purify my body.

He's going to stay down there all night if I let him, but it's three o'clock in the morning and the club will be closing soon and then they'll start flashing the house lights on and off, like they do on the 253 bus when they want you to get off, and you're left thinking, but I haven't reached my destination yet, what about me? and you think well I must be one mega desperate slut to still be here at this hour and you count the change in your pocket and realize you don't have enough for the cab-fare home, and isn't bottled beer expensive, and you remove the cock ring from your swollen genitals which are turning blue, and your jeans are still soaking wet, and suddenly they switch the music from something hardhop and tripno like Uberzone or Fatboy Slim to something classical and baroque like Handel's *Water Music*, and before you can say "Pavlov's dog" the entire club puts its cock away and buttons up, it seemed quite funny the first time you heard them do it, but now it just seems downright cruel, and the promoter says, "Come on, you're not in Amsterdam now," then finally the lights come on full, the dry ice disperses and you realize how absolutely filthy fucking dirty the place really is and you watch the sweat dripping from the ceiling and spunk trickling down the scuzzy black walls, and men emerge from behind the camouflage netting and oil-drums looking lost and confused, like the survivors of a road traffic accident waiting for the emergency services to arrive, and you realize you're one of them too.

With open-handed generosity, I purify my body.
I squeezed his nipples tight and pulled him up to level with me. He was trembling slightly and unsteady on his feet after crouching for so long, or perhaps it was the amyl—for a while we'd lost the lid. He was younger than I imagined, early to mid-twenties.

He had a great body, perfectly proportioned and muscular in an understated, swimmer's kind of way. His face was kind and strangely serene, without a hint of beard, and the fineness of his features, his long, slender nose, wide, finely arched eyebrows, soft, relaxed mouth lent him a slightly androgynous air. He wore his long shiny black hair in a thick braid, coiled up, coming to a peak, like a pointed crown. It gave him an exotic appearance, but at the same time there was something strangely familiar about him.

I tried hard to think who he reminded me of. At first I thought it must be a pop-star, or perhaps one of the presenters on MTV? Then it dawned on me who it was. He had the face of a Buddha, albeit a paler-skinned, occidental one. A Buddha in ripped jeans and Reeboks.

With stillness, simplicity, and contentment, I purify my body.
I pulled him closer, rubbed my hands up and down his broad wet back, and as our naked chests pressed together, felt his heart beating fast, and, felt a little sad. I placed my sticky hands on either side of his beautiful head and drew his face closer to mine until I felt his long eyelashes brush my cheek.

Our mouths moved closer. I could smell my cum on his face, although I guess, looking back, it could have been anyone's. I took a deep breath and covered his mouth with mine, and we shared each others breath until we reached the edge of suffocation. He pulled away first and we gasped and panted like deep sea divers coming up for air, and then we were back in that shithole of a club and I could hear a guy nearby moaning and groaning theatrically to climax and smell someone fist-fucking in the cubicle next door and I felt separate again.

With truthful communication, I purify my speech.

Suddenly, for the first time in the twenty minutes we'd been together, he spoke.

"There's something you should know." He sounded American. My heart sank.

"Your cock," he said, still slightly breathless, "tastes really great."

I squeezed his bum affectionately.

"No I really mean it," I said. "It's just I think it's real important to let people know, 'cause, well, you can't taste your own cock, can you, and unless someone tells you, well, you'll never know."

Maybe the new kid on the block wasn't quite so innocent after all. Now that's what I call rejoicing in merit, I thought to myself. Thank you, Bodhisattva.

I wanted to say something witty but couldn't think of anything so I just bowed instead, adding rather lamely, "Your cock tastes great, too." He smiled brightly and that gloomy backroom closet seemed to lighten. Then someone started rattling the door, demanding to know how much longer we were going to be in there and his smile vanished and I thought *I've got to get out of this place.*

With mindfulness clear and radiant, I purify my mind.

I was just thinking how nice it would be to invite him back. I could light some candles—the orange ones—burn some Japanese incense, roll a nice fat spliff or two, play some Miles Davis: *In a Silent Way*, or *Kind of Blue*. Then later we could go for a walk down by the river and I could show him where the herons nest. And then it occurred to me that I didn't know his name and I was just about to ask, when still buckling the belt on his jeans he said, "I've got to get out of this place. I'm supposed to be meeting some friends at Trade."

He pecked me on the cheek and as the door closed behind him they started flashing the lights on and off.

ALEX F. FAYLE

Morning Choice

Andrew stands in front of the bookcase, one hand half-raised. He reaches for *Pride*, but decides against it. *Pride* is a heavy book and stiff to open. He doesn't feel up to *Pride* today; he's not interested in that much work. His eyes and hand shift three books to the right to hover over *Lust*. Just looking at its spine stirs up a familiar feeling in his groin. Even though he won't choose *Lust* on a workday, he can't resist pulling the book off the shelf.

He flips through the book, scanning the tabloid font, smudgy pen and ink drawings, and clear, sharp photographs. The text and images together describe everything from the sharp memory of the beautiful stranger on the subway when he was thirteen, to the drug-filled blur of a party in Montreal last October. He lingers over one of his favourite and most vivid passages. It describes a party he went to a couple of months ago. He reads the text and lightly runs a finger over the glossy, high-quality pictures. He savours the feel of Tim, Eric, Gary, Jack, and several other men, all nameless and eager.

Andrew snaps the book closed, shutting off the memory before he loses the willpower to put the book back and choose another.

He ignores the bottom shelves where basic books like *Hunger* and *Sleepiness* sit. These books span several volumes and Andrew only ever reads them when he thinks they are filling up and need new volumes added. Everyone's usual ten books fill the top shelf. His godparents gave him the first seven: *Pride*, *Sloth*, *Gluttony*, *Lust*, *Greed*, *Envy*, and *Wrath*, while the other three: *Faith*, *Hope*, and *Charity*, came from his grandparents. The rest of the shelves hold a wide variety of books, in all sorts of shapes and sizes. Some, like *Childish Spite*, are as small as the palm of his hand, while others, like *Shocked Outrage*, are oversized, almost too big to fit on any shelf. He runs a finger along the shelf, scanning the titles. He wonders if he really needs so many different books.

Need? Close, but not quite.

A gap in the books catches his finger. He stops to figure out which book is missing. *Intimacy* and *Despair*, the books on either side of the gap, offer no hints. He pokes his finger into the gap, trying to pick up any residue left by the missing book. Nothing. Poor book, all alone somewhere. The thought triggers his memory. Two nights ago he was wallowing in *Loneliness* in the back bedroom. He remembers dropping it behind the bed when tears filled his eyes and he couldn't read any longer.

He pulls his finger away from the gap. He's not tempted to go get the book now that he remembers where it is. *Loneliness* is much better off where he left it.

On the shelf immediately above *Loneliness'* usual spot, Andrew spies a thin book he has never noticed before wedged between *Love* and *Hate*. He pulls it out, careful not to touch its neighbours. *Love* and *Hate* are intense books. They often suck him in and hold him prisoner for weeks at a time and he has no intention of giving in to them today.

The thin book he pulls out is new, but he doesn't remember getting it. He probably got it as part of one of those package deals he is forever being talked into. The book is slightly larger than most paperbacks, but smaller than the average hardcover. It doesn't have a regular cardboard cover either. Instead, someone has crafted the cover from handmade paper, predominantly pale blue, but with strands of sea-green and white fibres pressed into the mixture. The pages themselves are made of creamy tissue paper and are almost thin enough to see through. A dark blue silk ribbon finishes it off, binding cover to pages.

All the pages are blank, which is unusual. Most new books have something written in them, have a description of some emotion he has experienced without realizing it. His eyes flicker down to *Excitement* two shelves down. He recognizes the flutter in his stomach and knows there will be a new passage waiting for him the next time he opens that one.

The title is written in a graceful gothic script, in the same dark blue as the ribbon. The letters form the words *Melancholy & Longing*. He thinks about Greg, the new guy in the office with the great body and devoted lover. The guy who flirts, teases, and touches, but won't take it any further.

Andrew puts the book down on the coffee table and finishes getting ready for work.

Melancholy & Longing. Perfect.

R . W . G R A Y

Freighters

Six freighters anchored in the bay today. All facing south. The sky splits open and the rain falls all absent-minded, keeps falling while the sunlight slicks it all so the whole world starts to melt. On the bus last week you told me how you fall in love with bus drivers—their hands. And then you confessed that a poem you have already given me is about my lips. My lover's hands, too. I confess to you that my lover's hands seem like monkey paws, like in *Gorillas in the Mist*. Wise hands.

You and your lover are opening up your relationship. You use words from manifestos: "experimental," "counter-culture," "radical," "anti-oppressive."

I tell you that my lover and I are trying to keep a closed relationship. That in the face of so many gay couples arguing for "openness" and "liberation," it seems radical to just stay monogamous. And I wonder, I ask you, why do you get to use words like "open" and I get words like "closed." Seems unfair.

We are like two sheep licking each other through the electric fence. How's that, you ask. Like lamb chops? Like two hand puppets on a weird woman's hands. Sounds like divine intervention to me.

I remember now, we were going to buy de Sade's *Justine*, 'cause we were both going to read it at the same time. We do that, you and I. Read the same books. It's a form of flirting for us.

The next day, now, and we are walking along the bay. I have asked that we walk on the sand, 'cause my lover has told me not to. It's his job to sweep the apartment and he hates it when I track sand in. There are eight freighters facing north now. I am telling you that what I miss most about being single is the threesomes. Seems funny, that I would not want an open relationship, yet the place I have most enjoyed being is sandwiched between some people. Guess I just like the attention, and the freedom to leave when I want to.

Why did the wind change last night, suddenly come from the water, not the mountains, and bring thunder and those tropical showers? All the queeny boys who had done their hair just right and hadn't brought their new raincoats had to laugh off their disarray in the coffee house. Cavalier, almost butch. Last night as we talked in the coffee house I wanted to hug you, say it'll be alright. "It" being the fact that we are both in relationships where we asked for the full meal deal and didn't get what we ordered. Or, perhaps more accurately, we keep repeating ourselves at the drive-thru window, and don't feel heard through the damn speaker. Analogies are always disappointing.

And it all smells of when I was a kid and my parents would be having one of their tear-down-the-house fights, and my brother would sneak into my bed, shivering with fear, and how I would hold him and tell him, "It'll be alright," and how telling him almost made me believe it. And I want to tell you right now, "It'll be alright."

And sometimes when we read to flirt, I want to read you, get a cup of tea, hold you in both hands, with good light, and I won't even mind when my mind wanders and I find myself reading the same line over and over. A type of lingering, the repetition of you. And I might sneak a peek at what lies beneath the surface, hold you up to the light like parchment when no one is looking.

Only three ships today. Never seen so few. In the afternoon I watch you at the gym and watch you furious with your body, remaking it, making it new, and I am both envious and jealous. I am afraid to remake myself that way. And I am suspicious of why you are doing it. To be beautiful enough to circulate on Ecstasy nights. I worry, 'cause you seem less comfortable in your body than when I first met you, like a cat licking itself. Now you seem anxious, like someone who now multi-tasks sensations and never has enough.

Perhaps that's the way Ecstasy reconfigures you. . . . Perhaps it not only increases your threshold for sensations, it demands that you increase the sensations, makes you feel idle when there is not enough.

And I feel all contained, all Tupperwared compared to your explosions, your frenzy. And I wonder if that's true. Why "closed," not "open"?

I told you once how I feel drawn to the freighters in the harbour, how they turn like synchronized swimmers with the tide changes, all facing south, all facing north, all with their backs to us, leaving but not moving. Suspended in motion.

My lover is afraid that if he left me I would get together with you, and I'm afraid that if I keep grinding my teeth at night they will break into shards and pieces, and it seems it would be the worst thing in the world, to be here without a smile. The way people who think they have bad teeth don't part their lips for the camera.

And you wrote a poem about my lover's hands, the strength of them, "Paws," you said. And I wonder how you separate that from the knowledge that he hit me that night, backhanded. But it wasn't his stupidity that bothered me, not the suddenly articulate well of his angry marrow, but the appearance of it all. And I want to call my mother and say, "I am the woman you never let yourself become," for she kicked my father out before he could hit her, though sometimes words leave larger marks.

And he'll never hit me again, so maybe it's best that we got it out of the way. I wonder if I flinch more than usual, or whether I will ever admit what I really thought when the back of his fist connected. That it was a relief, that all I could think was "There, now we got that out of the way." Context is everything.

It's just before dark and the four freighters in the bay all face elsewhere. Confused between the tides, they hunker down solemn behind slack lines. Somewhere between glass half full and glass half empty is a place I call quiet, where there are no questions, just the blind path of the day to day. And I never knew this place existed, and never knew that I would get a taste for it, the way things go good when you don't think about it. There are no pictures of these times. I want to wait and see the ships pull back together, but the rain has started to fall again and I promised I would walk you halfway home.

S A M   S O M M E R

Watching Jared Sleep

I stand by his open door, watching him sleep. Jared is naked. The white cotton sheet, tangled about his legs, seems to glow in the reflected moonlight. A warm breeze coming in through the window blows across his body, innocently disturbing the soft brown hair on his chest. He stirs. I hold my breath until he's once again still.

Jared lives in the house that I share with three other men for the summer. I've had a major crush on him since the day he arrived. He doesn't know this.

His hair is sun-bleached and slightly long. It softly curls about his face and pillow. His lips are full and pale, nearly the colour of his skin. I visualize his dark, sparkling blue eyes, the colour of lapis— pure blue, with just a fleck of silver. There's a small bruise on his chin. A souvenir from yesterday's volleyball game on the beach. His hand momentarily flexes. Something in the house creaks, and is then silent. We're alone here—the two of us—my housemates still cele- brating the weekend's infancy.

I peel off my shirt, damp from dancing, and let it slip to the floor. My heart races, my palms are moist and cool.

Jared's chest rises and falls just slightly with each breath. His lean, defined stomach and small waist almost move me to tears. His dick and full ball-sac caress the inside of a thigh. I think how wonderful it would be to simply cup them in my hands. His skin is golden bronze. The room smells of salt water and Jared's own sweet body odour. I inhale deeply, and close my eyes, committing it all to memory-to take back with me to my bed.

I've removed all my clothing now, and stand naked by his door, my manhood hard upon me. I run my hand over my chest, teasing a nipple to erection. My breath is short and shallow. My heart beats rapidly.

Jared stirs again, this time rolling over onto his side. His firm ass, pale and round, torments me. I take one small step into the room and stop. He sighs and rolls over onto his stomach. I can't believe how beautiful he seems to me, how incredibly beautiful.

Jared has always been friendly to me, but somewhat distant. I find it difficult to talk to him. He prefers his silence. He reads, avidly, consuming the books he brings with him each weekend. He drinks vodka gimlets, unfazed by quips of how passé they are. He goes out, dances, laughs with all of us, but always returns early, long before the rest of us creep back to our beds, wilted and spent. Some nights I watch him from afar, wondering who he really is, what makes him tick.

I fantasize how he feels, each night before I go to bed.

I came back early tonight to be alone with him—to watch him sleep. Jared stirs, sensing something.

"Who's there?" he asks, his voice scratchy from sleep.

"It's just me, Jared," I say. "Go back to sleep. Sorry to disturb you."

"Jeff?"

"Yes?"

"You alone?"

"Uh-huh."

He adjusts his pillow, and squints at me standing in his doorway. "You okay?" he asks.

"Sure, Jared. I'm fine. Go back to sleep."

"Good night, Jeff."

"Night."

I hesitate, pick up my clothes and walk down the hall to my room. Jared will be with me all night—in my thoughts.

I shower, jerk off, and still feel frustrated and confused.

There are a few weeks left before we close the house for the summer. I fall asleep holding onto that thought.

eddie james

The Unravelling of Twine

I thought I was only fucking him. That when he went down on me as I sat behind the wheel of my Mustang, struggling to concentrate on the road ahead—him kneeling on the floor boards of the passenger side and me in the driver's seat, seat pushed way back, feet barely reaching the pedals—I thought that it was all just wild sex that we would smile about later in life whenever anyone talked about the "head room" of their cars. I thought it would quickly fade the night he tied me to his rickety futon, spread-eagled, using the cotton twine he'd stolen from work, wrapping it gently around my wrists and ankles and then tightly knotting the fraying ends to the futon's wooden frame. When he poured chocolate syrup over me, and ferociously licked it off, and when his adventurous tongue explored the depths of my ass or slid over my eyelids, and when his strong, calloused hands gently ran down the length of my goody trail, I thought each of these acts was just another technique of stimulation and satisfaction that he'd learned from other guys he'd fucked.

To me, the day we ditched work and lay in bed taking photos of our naked bodies was just another crazy idea. He initiated it early in the morning, caught me in a mess of sheets with the comforter wrapped loosely around me, my hair a matted mass, and a sly, satisfied look on my tired face. He got me again at breakfast—which he delivered to me as I sat up in bed—and again later in the shower, my wet hair clinging to my scalp, my eyes barely able to see the flash of his Polaroid camera through the steam, water, and shampoo.

I thought that his incessant probing into my background, and into my likes, dislikes, and attitudes, that his listening to what I had to say, were just his way of keeping the conversation going between fucking. Once, in the middle of conversation, I reached over and grabbed his belt. "Come here," I said, pulling him closer. "Come here and fuck me." He said nothing, didn't move. I didn't mean anything derogatory by it, but I knew he objected to the crudity of the words. I meant, "Come here, and hold me. Come here and make love to me. Come here and . . ." but he didn't understand. He got up off my couch, *Mr. Smith Goes to Washington* still playing on the VCR, and slammed my apartment door with a loud, "Fuck you."

He came back half an hour later, saw me crying and asked if I wanted my ass eaten, asked me to suck his cock, asked me if I wanted to be fucked long and hard up the ass. I told him "Yes," and he reached over and drew me into his arms, began slowly kissing my eyes, licking the tears away.

He destroyed the photos I'd taken of him. He went through them all one morning, pointing out imagined flaws and complaining that his penis looked much too small. I tried to stop him, reassured him that he looked beautiful, sexy, but he'd already retreated as he absent-mindedly tore each Polaroid picture into ten identical pieces.

After our final afternoon of making love, in the afterglow of light, panting and with glistening foreheads, as we not so much held each other as got further entwined in each other's body, I whispered, "I like you, a lot."

"What?" he asked.

"I like you, a lot," I repeated, my head resting on the soft cushion of his chest, staring at his toes.

"Oh," he said. "I like you, too. You're a really good fuck."

WARREN DUNFORD

Seven a.m. on Miami Beach

It was Monday at seven a.m. and Thomas was walking down the beach alone.

He'd come here on vacation to relax, to catch up on sleep—to finally get over what had happened with Simon. But he'd awoken at six-thirty, just the way he always did at home.

Grant was lying face down across the other bed, snoring quietly—still in his white tank top and Versace jeans, still reeking of cigarette smoke from last night.

Thomas pulled on the khaki shorts and t-shirt he'd worn yesterday. He dug in his suitcase and found the flask of tequila. He slid it into his front pocket and left the room, closing the door gently. Grant didn't notice a thing.

He walked the three blocks from their hotel to the beach. Yesterday, Ocean Drive had been jammed with fashion models and muscle boys, but this morning it was nearly deserted.

He took off his sandals, hooked them around a finger, and set out across the wide expanse of sand. The dawn sky was yellow with a heavy murky blue at the horizon.

He passed a white-haired man and woman, walking rapidly, swinging their arms like pendulums.

He passed a teenage girl in a baseball cap, sitting cross-legged in the sand, eyes closed in meditation.

Just before the shore, the ground fell away in a sharp slope and Thomas took careful sideways steps down to the water's edge.

The surf was warm and bubbled around his toes.

He walked along the beach and thought about Monday mornings back home in the cold. If everything were normal, he'd be rushing to the office by now. He'd have already kissed Simon goodbye.

Last night, Grant had insisted they go out to a club—do some Ecstasy, have a good time. Before shoving his way onto the dance floor, Grant had listed off the clichés: "Life is for the living. It's time to move on. Simon wouldn't want you to do this to yourself."

Thomas nodded and went to the bar. He ordered two shots of tequila.

Simon had been sick for so long, trapped in bed for eight months. Everyone understood why he took the pills. They didn't know why Thomas couldn't accept it, too.

Thomas went to the washroom. As he stood at the sink, he found himself staring into the mirror. Staring into his own eyes, wondering what he was seeing. When he broke away, he realized he was being watched by the man beside him. Fashion-model face. Shoulder-length, straight blond hair. Shirtless with a perfect, smooth body.

Thomas turned away. He went back to the bar, found a place against the wall. The music blared and dulled his mind.

Then he saw the blond man again—in the crowd on the dance floor with a dark, hairy-chested man in black leather jeans.

They were necking as they danced, their bodies pressed together, their fingers digging into the flesh of each other's back. The blond man tilted his head and caught Thomas watching him.

His eyes not leaving Thomas' face, he licked the dark man's cheek. Thomas focussed on the sensuous glide of his tongue. Then the blond man broke from the embrace and crossed the floor to where Thomas was standing.

"I know you," he said.

"From where?"

"From the toilet." He smiled. "I saw the look on your face."

"What look?"

"In your eyes. Like something inside is eating you alive."

93

Thomas stared at the man's mouth. Thick, curving lips.

"I don't know what you're talking about," Thomas said.

"Guilt is bad," the man said. "It can hollow you out. Chew you up until you're totally empty."

"I don't know what you're talking about," Thomas said again.

The guy laughed. "Just fucking with your head."

Thomas stared.

"You want to dance?" the man asked.

Thomas paused a moment. "Not now."

"Anytime you want. Come find us." And he kissed Thomas on the mouth, his teeth biting hold of Thomas' lower lip.

Then he was back in the crowd, grabbing the man in leather, turning him around, kissing him, his eyes never leaving Thomas' face.

In an instant, they were swallowed up in the mass of dancers.

Thomas realized he was trembling, shivering all over, like one of those fits Simon had had near the end.

He took a cab back to the hotel, gulped a mouthful of tequila, and dropped to the bed.

He had no idea what time Grant came home.

He looked out at the ocean, concentrated on the soft roar of the waves. He measured his distance by the pastel row of hotels over on the street.

Up ahead, on the crest of sand, Thomas saw a figure lying asleep. As he drew closer, he could see that it wasn't one person, but three. Three men, lying pressed together, stomach to back. A large white towel was spread across their waists, but the towel had been pushed away from the man at the rear. He was naked and he was fucking the man in the centre. The third man—the man at the front—lay still, as though he were asleep.

Thomas kept walking, kept watching.

The guy's ass was muscular and round, no tan line, pumping in a steady motion. His head was a swatch of wheat-blond hair.

Thomas knew right away who it was.

When he stood just below them on the slope of sand, Thomas stopped. The guy flicked his head back to shake the hair from his eyes.

He saw that Thomas was there and he smiled. He smiled and he kept on fucking. He smiled like they were together in some kind of conspiracy, like it was all a joke, like he knew what Thomas had done—that Simon had had no idea he was taking all those pills.

Thomas started walking again, but every few paces he looked back over his shoulder. The guy was still watching him, still smiling, still fucking.

JOE LAVELLE

Playa del Ingles

End of the night at Kings Bar. I've done nothing but stare again. Cock from all over Europe paraded in front of me, but I spoke to no one, except bartenders. *"Una gin con tónico, por favor."* I watch men come and go. Young, tanned, big, small, English, German, Spanish, Scandinavian. Some hover in doorways, then disappear into the darkness. I've never been in a backroom. Fourth night spent standing in this exact same spot. Sixth G and T. One life. It's now or never.

I hear sighs, whispers, and the sound of flesh being slapped. I smell sweat. It's too dark to see. Invisible hands caress me. I reach a wall and lean against it. Someone stands in front of me. There's the faint smell of brandy then a kiss on my cheek, a hand on my thigh, another on my shoulder. I tremble. My cock stiffens.

"I'm . . . I'm nervous," I blurt out into the darkness.

"Me llamo Juan." A whisper.

Someone laughs.

"¿Cómo te llamas?" A whisper again.

"Joe."

"¿Inglés?"

"Yes."

"Joe! *José. ¿Sí?*"

"Yes."

He kisses me. I taste brandy, feel the stubble on his cheek. His tongue, warm, moist, probes my mouth. His hand is now on my crotch. Fingers undo buttons, slide inside my jeans and into my CKs. I place a nervous hand on his bare arse. His flesh is firm, smooth, pneumatic. I knead it. I move my other hand down the contours of his chest. Definition without bulk. My ideal. My hand stops at his crotch. I feel a fat, erect cock. It throbs as I caress it. He kisses me. I slide my fingers up and down the shaft of his cock, touch his heavy, hairy balls. I move to the side and, with my other hand, trace a line across the cheek of his arse then down his crack to his wet, tight sphincter. He inhales deeply. I close my eyes, move my hand from his arse to the back of his head and push his face into mine, only . . . only our lips do not meet.

Eyes still shut, I sense brightness. I open them. The lights are on. I am alone. I look around the backroom. In another life, it was a women's toilet. I button up my jeans, make for the exit, slipping on cum as I leave.

Afternoon. Dunas de Maspalomas. A sea of sand, crests, and hollows, sensual like flesh. An azure sky. A single white cloud defying the sun. Men, some naked, wander through wispy vegetation. Several look at me. I smell their cologne, their sweat, their sex, and I look back, take in pecs, abs, semi-erect cocks, arses. They're blond, pasty-skinned. Scandinavians? I move on.

The sun is fierce, unrelenting. I sit on the ground and swig water from a bottle. I stand, strip naked, and lay face down on my towel. I gaze at the sand in front of me, then close my eyes, imagining what Juan looks like, what it would be like to fuck him or be fucked by him.

I wake to the touch of cool hands on my back.

"*¡Hola José!*"

"Juan!"

I attempt to rise, but he is on my back, naked, pinning me down. He kisses my neck. I feel his fat, rigid cock against my arse. He rubs it up and down my crack, drooling pre-cum. He says something. I don't recognize the words, but I understand.

"Yes. Fuck me."

He wastes no time, lubes my hole with spit. I relax beneath him. As he spreads my cheeks I turn my head toward him, but the sun is in my eyes. I face forward again. He enters me. His cock is shorter than I expect. I remember the writing on the cottage wall at the Curzon: "Long and thin goes too far in, but short and thick just does the trick." And it does! I feel pleasure-pain as he penetrates my gut. I raise my arse, digging my elbows and knees into the ground. He thrusts into me, groaning. He slaps my arse cheeks, chews my neck, groans into my ear.

Grabbing my hair, he pulls my head back and nibbles the side of my face. I glimpse his face: dark skin, stubble, heavy lips, short black hair. Then he pushes my face into the sand. He thrusts deeper, faster. I raise my head again. He bites the nape of my neck. I grind my body against him, raising my hungry hole to meet every thrust. He bites harder, thrusts even deeper, groans louder. His body stiffens.

"¡Estupendo!"

He comes and so do I. He collapses on to me, lays panting a while before withdrawing, then climbs off. I turn to look at him, but he is gone.

Centre Stage. My last night. I sit alone. The crowd watches a Shirley Bassey video playing on a TV set located high on the wall. Shirley launches into "Hey Big Spender."

"Oh, cheer up! You're on holiday."

I look at him, middle-aged clone: bushy, grey moustache, bald head, wrinkled skin, checked shirt.

"Piss off," I say rudely.

He stares back, startled.

I leave.

I'm drunk when I reach Kings. In the backroom I hear sighs, whispers, and the sound of flesh being slapped. I smell sweat. I can see nothing. Hands grab at my crotch, stroke my arse, undo buttons. My exposed cock stiffens, but I do not want them.

A kiss annoints my lips.

"Juan!"

A hand covers my mouth.

"Shhhh."

I embrace him, but his body somehow slips through my arms. I think he has vanished, but my cock enters the warm, wet pit of his mouth. Lips slide along its length. I fall back against a wall, throw my dick into his face. Each shove takes my dickhead further into his throat. His nose touches my pubic hair as my cock rides in and out of his wanting mouth. I lose control, emptying myself into the back of his throat, only . . . only there is the faint thud of my cum hitting the floor.

I stand alone.

"Adiós, José."

Then silence.

J . R . G . D e M A R C O

Arriverderci?

Sebastian wandered around the ruins of the Roman Forum aching with indecision. Leaving Rome after two years of teaching was difficult, yet he could find no excuse to stay. He had found neither love nor real friendship in the Eternal City. The sultry, dark, and sexy men he saw every day made him crawl with desire, but few of them had ever graced his bed. Those who did were either married or mamma's boys.

He didn't want to leave and admit defeat, but he had given himself a deadline and it had arrived with no binding ties to keep him here. Stumbling, he steadied himself against a ruined temple wall. He sighed, wishing to be as permanent as this ancient place. His hand caressed the wall, seeking some connection with Rome's past. The stones were moist and green with patchy, thin moss.

Wiping this bit of Rome from his hand, he looked at his watch. Today his university friends were giving him a farewell send-off and he dared not be late.

In the subway, he bumped against lumpy American tourists padded with cash belts and backpacks. He felt a dank breeze wafting in from the tunnel. Behind it came the train, electric eyes glowing. Doors clattered open revealing rush-hour throngs mashed against one another. Sebastian sighed, slinking his way between over-heated bodies. When he stopped, he realized he was face to face with the most beautiful young man he had ever laid eyes upon.

He mentally named him Flavio. His hair was light brown as were his eyes, which were set off by luxurious eyebrows, making him seem mysterious and sensual. Sebastian caught his breath. Flavio's wide mouth and red-pink lips were full and wet and set just below a perfect nose.

Sebastian's chin itched but he tried to ignore it, not wanting to move his hand which rested against Flavio's bare arm. The itch worsened. He slid his arm up; slick sweat allowed his flesh to glide easily against Flavio's skin. It was electric. The itch gone, he moved his arm down. In doing so, however, his hand now lay palm forward on Flavio's crotch. On his cock actually, fully recognizable through the thin, grey cotton running shorts.

Flavio stared at him nonchalantly, as if a stranger grasped his cock every day on the subway. Sebastian did not want to remove his hand. He remained still, determined to enjoy it as long as Flavio permitted. The train lurched and his hand swayed with the movement, massaging the dick which began to stir in his palm.

A bead of sweat trickled down Sebastian's forehead into his eye, causing him to wink it away. Flavio winked in return and Sebastian felt his heart flutter, his breath became short. He looked into Flavio's eyes but there was merely blithe insouciance. Sebastian felt disturbed in the midst of ecstasy.

Flavio's cock continued to swell; Sebastian yearned to squeeze and pull but he contented himself with just holding. The intense heat of Flavio's body burned into Sebastian like desire and he wanted to scream at the exquisite frustration.

Flavio's cock felt so good, so familiar, in his hand that Sebastian didn't notice as the train pulled into a station. *"Stazione Quintiliani,"* the tinny voice blared from a loudspeaker. The train's motion pushed Flavio hard against Sebastian. The doors pulled open. More people got on than off. Now, he and Flavio were pressed together more completely. Still Flavio offered no facial expression; the swelling of his cock was the only indication of his feelings. Sebastian was transfixed.

Acutely aware that the next stop was his, Sebastian felt the stirrings of a great dilemma. Should he exit or go on with Flavio for an uncertain rendezvous? Was Flavio merely toying with him? Could he miss a party in his honour? Flavio seemed everything Sebastian thought he wanted, perhaps even the great romance he craved.

Looking into Flavio's eyes he saw pure gold, but was unable to read what lay just beneath the surface. Was it only fool's gold? As Sebastian searched those eyes, Flavio seemed to move into him; it was subtle, perhaps caused by the train's motion. Sebastian bit his lower lip. Was this the signal he had been waiting for?

Flavio's cock was hard now, and hot. Sebastian could feel a wet spot forming on the running shorts. His own dick was hard and pulsing, but Flavio made no attempt to touch him.

The train pitched and rumbled and Sebastian knew that decisions had be made.

"Stazione Tiburtina." The voice stabbed him through the heart.

A halting shudder shook the train forcing him up against Flavio. The doors rattled open but no one moved. The moment was his alone. Sebastian glanced out the door then at Flavio. He felt that cock once more and hesitated an instant longer.

At the last possible moment, he pried himself loose and stepped out the door hoping against hope that Flavio would follow. Sebastian stood on the platform and stared, willing Flavio to join him.

Instead, as time stood still, Flavio's expressive eyebrows drew themselves up in a quizzical expression. His luscious lips moved to form a word. Sebastian concentrated. Flavio mouthed the word, *"Perché?"* "Why?"

Sebastian watched in horror as the doors slid shut—like a curtain closing on his future. Slowly the train began to pull away. He stared at Flavio's face, the expressive eyebrows still knit questioningly, the red-pink lips still pursed around an Italian "why?"

Then he was gone.

Sebastian savoured the lingering warmth of Flavio's cock on his palm. Rubbing his fingers together, he realized they were wet and sticky—and all he would ever know of Flavio.

DALYN A. MILLER

You Can Wait Forever

Y ou can wait forever for the E train," he says.

"Yes," I say. "Forever."

It's eleven-thirty p.m. and the black man standing next to me in the cavernous, empty subway station is beautiful. I have never seen him before, I think, and will never see him again. I am surprised at myself as I pretend to stare at a billboard about unwanted pregnancy only to be able to see him better out of the corner of my eye. Catches you by surprise, the advertisement says, as a pregnant girl stares frozen back at us.

We are waiting for the E train and I am waiting for more. I am waiting for the man next to me to turn, gaze into my eye and say, "Last train of the night." The man checks his watch and then looks at me and smiles.

"That's right," I say. I look around us. "Do you take it often?"

"The E train?"

"The last one."

"No," he says. "Just tonight. And you?"

"Just tonight." I want to think of something clever, something amazing. Instead I grasp at the loose change in my pocket and count it by feel. A dollar and nineteen cents and an extra subway token. My hands squeeze and relax in nervous anticipation. The man's lips part and then close again, a distinct moment of decision not to speak. I turn to look at him, but look beyond instead at a toothless woman huddled in the corner wrapped in a dirty blanket. She holds a paper coffee cup up to me half-heartedly and gives it a quick shake.

"You can wait forever," the beautiful black man repeats to me and the homeless woman puts her cup down again. Transient.

Behind me I hear a woman scream out: "Get them coloured kids away from this house!" It is my grandmother screaming at my cousins who are waving sticks and chasing two frightened boys down the dirt road. On the boys' tiny dark faces, tears and snot mix with dust as they run as fast as they can away from my family and my home. I sit in the yard as my grandmother looms above me on the porch. I am crying and she thinks I am afraid of the boys, but I'm afraid of her. I wait eleven years and then I run away, too.

The black man balancing on the edge of the platform waiting for the E train, the last one of the night, pulls a cigarette from a pocket on the inside of his coat.

"Do you mind?" he asks me, even though I am standing more than four feet away. I shake my head no. He lights the cigarette and offers it to me and again I shake my head. Slower.

"No respect," the transient woman spits at the man who turns to her, waits a moment, exhales, and then holds the pack up. The woman extends a grungy glove towards the man and he carries the pack to her and lays it in her palm.

"Keep warm," he says.

"God bless," she says and he flips a book of matches at her as well.

In my grandmother's hospital room, I watch as her respirator rhythmically pushes air into her ruined lungs. I imagine I can see it through the opaque tube, breathing artificial air into her as it moves her life forward second by second. At the foot of the bed stands my cousin, who holds his own breath as if willing my grandmother's to stop. He waits for death so he can move outside of the hospital room and keep going. In my grandmother's last moments she refuses to let a black intern help her sit up to ease her death and dies miserably uncomfortable.

In the giant tube, which is the subway station, air is pushed through by an oncoming train. It is going in the opposite direction. I wonder, then, if it is breathing life out of us on the platform waiting for the last train of the night.

"Damn," says the man. "I thought we would get lucky."

The transient woman laughs and all I say is: "Yes, I thought so, too."

"You can wait forever," says the transient and I wonder how long she has waited already.

Air approaches in front of the E train. As it stops and I move toward it, I pass the transient woman on the platform and flip the extra subway token into her paper cup. "Keep moving," says the black man behind me. I don't know who he is talking to, but I feel his breath on my neck and his hand gently on my back as we enter the train together, the doors close and we begin moving slowly forward.

T O M   L E V E R

Mehmet

Even on a cold winter's night in Berlin, there's always something to do - or should that be someone? All the usual faces in
the local backroom bar. Wall-to-wall men, yet no one who captures
my interest. Every time the bell rang announcing a new arrival, all
eyes turned towards the door. *"Frisch Fleisch."* Then I saw him come
in. Him? Here? Well, why not?!

I'd seen him regularly working the bar at a gay Turkish event. He
was a hard act to miss with his stocky, tan figure, close-cropped hair,
thick bushy moustache, and handsome face. I had desired him. But he
appeared aloof, disinterested. Maybe a Turk who, like so many others,
had problems with German reserve. Maybe I should let him know I
wasn't reserved? Maybe, I should be the one to make the move?

He didn't bother to order a beer, his thirst was for something
else entirely. Negotiating the crowd, looking neither left nor right,
he passed quickly through the heaving barroom and headed directly
downstairs into the cruising cellar.

I shot after him like a bullet from a gun.

Downstairs was even more crowded than the bar above. Men
shuffling along the narrow passageways, hands and eyes reaching
out.

He stood in the entrance to one of the private cubicles. His shirt open to reveal a thick mat of hair, one hand tucked inside lazily toying with a nipple. He caught my eye and beckoned me towards him with a jerk of his head.

Locking the door behind us, a calm settled. The rest of the world shut out. Standing close to me, I could smell him. The sweat of a working day mingled with his aftershave. Looking at him intently, I reached out to run my finger across his face. He smiled.

"Mehmet," he said.

"Tom."

"*Deutsch?*"

"*Irisch.*"

He grinned again, the whiteness of his teeth illuminating the darkness. Then he leaned forward and we kissed. I ran my tongue over his lips, his moustache, slipping it into his mouth. Feeding hungrily on him. Our bodies locked together.

It was no time before I was on my knees before him, struggling with his zipper, and releasing his swollen cock and balls to my willing mouth.

I reached around to cup his ass cheeks in my hands. He grunted. Almost disinterested, but his balls were telling me something else. That, and the swelling of his cock, its head now engorged, rubbing against my beard. My mouth was full with his balls, sucking them right in, pressing my mouth against his body, extending my tongue to lick between his legs towards his hairy cleft. His body arched up to meet me.

Turkish cock slipped down my throat, my copious spit easing its passage. I could feel every ripple of its surface, taste the sweat and feel it throb. Mehmet stood over me, moaning as I pulled the shirt free of his waistband and ran my hands up under it to grip nipples buried in hair. His cock grew even fatter as his excitement increased.

He withdrew slowly. Every inch of his stiff prick glistened with saliva. Then, plunging it back in, he began to pump, while I gripped his ass cheeks. Sucking on his meat, wanting to drain every drop of juice from his fertile balls, but not yet.

Pulling away, I turned him around, bending him over. Sticking my tongue between his hairy ass cheeks elicited a series of groans. He pushed back. I dove deeper. The cheeks parted to reveal his puckered hole—pink and juicy—waiting for me. I teased it, pressing the tip of my tongue against it. His entire body quivered, and the hole opened a little, allowing me access.

Standing up, I took out my own cock, already dripping pre-cum and ready to fuck.

I ran the head of my cock between his ass cheeks, wet with my saliva, and teased his hole by pressing my cockhead against it. More pre-cum oozed out, lubricating the entrance.

His moans were the only encouragement I needed. I pressed and his muscle relaxed, welcoming my cock while he reached around to guide my length in.

"*Ohhh . . .*" sounds much the same in any language. "*Ohhh . . .*" he moaned, as my balls slapped against his hairy ass.

I began to fuck him slowly. Looking down as my cock slid deep inside his hole, and then watching it as it withdrew until the pink head was showing, and then plunging it back inside. His body shuddered at each thrust. His ass muscles gripped tightly, not wanting to let my cock out.

Mehmet reached back to pull on my chest hair, tugged on my nipple ring and twisted.

"Oh, ja!" I growled, slowing the pace of my fucking, and bending Mehmet right over until he was almost touching his toes. His legs were spread and he was wanking furiously.

His ass was well lubricated by this time—a mixture of sweat, pre-cum and ass juice. I was close to coming.

"*Ich komme gleich, Mehmet.*"

He just moaned. My thrusts grew longer, more violent. Plunging into the heart of him. Then it began. The tightness in my groin, the grip on my prostate. The rush of spunk, oozing out of my balls and rushing with increasing velocity until it was spraying the inside of Mehmet's ass.

He thrust back, impaling himself on my still pumping tool, his cum shooting over the wall of the cubicle.

"*Oh Oh Ohhhhhh . . .*" sounds just as sweet in any language. "*Ohhhh . . .*" he groaned, as my balls nestled against his hairy ass.

HARRY MATTHEWS

Landmarks

I s that Central Park?"

"Well, no. We're looking south, so that's Madison Square."

"Then where is Central Park?"

"It's on the other side of the building, to the north. It's the big dark expanse you see beyond the brightly-lit towers."

When a group of tourists first sees New York at their feet, they tend to lose their orientation. Tired of the obvious questions, though, most tour guides skip the ride to the observatory, favouring a local sports bar or coffee shop instead. But I always get a charge out of the view, all the more dramatic at night.

"Are those shooting stars?"

"No, those are planes lined up to land at LaGuardia. Watch for a few minutes, and you'll see one follow another all the way to the airport, over there. If you look off to the west, you'll see the same thing going on at Newark Airport. And those tiny lights off in the distance, moving from right to left—they're planes landing at JFK."

"Do you come here often?" Hardly the usual tourist's query, but when I turn around, I realize it's no tourist. It's Ben, a fellow guide. We spent an hour that morning camping it up on Liberty Island with other members of the guide "sorority."

"Come here often? Are you kidding? You'd have to pay me to come here!" We both laugh, though I have to ask, "Shouldn't you be watching the ball game in the bar?"

"But I saw you taking a group up the escalator." His answer catches me by surprise; he doesn't sound like he's joking.

"Give us a big kiss!" Just down the railing, a friend is taking pictures of young newlyweds. The woman struggles against the wind to hold a small veil on her head, while the man accepts the photographer's invitation to press his mouth tightly against hers. The flash goes off, but it doesn't seem to distract them in the least. Another flash. "Got it, guys," the photographer calls, but the couple's attention is focused entirely on each other. A sudden gust seizes the veil and carries it through the railing and off toward the East River. "Marcy, your veil!" Clearly, she has more important concerns.

"Are they gonna make it to the hotel, or will they wind up in the john?" Ben asks.

"The john?" I don't get his point.

"Come on! You know and I know that they only have unisex toilets up here, both large enough to accommodate a wheelchair—or some space-consuming activity."

"But who would come all the way up here to have sex?" I thought it was a rhetorical question.

"I would!" he grins. "Care to join me?"

I take it as a joke and laugh. I know Ben and his lover only recently split up, and I imagine that he's horny as hell. But me? Low-keyed, grey-haired me?

But he's definitely serious. "Come on! We've got twenty minutes before these folks will be ready to go back downstairs."

He prods me inside, past the gift shop, and we join the line for the can. We help the Japanese man in line ahead of us deal with the lock and wait for him to complete his business. "What will people think if we go in together?" My Puritan grandmother would be proud of me.

"I can be a man with a disability who you're helping," Ben suggests.

"What kind of disability?" I ask, looking at his lanky, well-built body. "You're all too clearly a blond, blue-eyed distance runner."

"What if I were blind?"

"Why would you spend seven bucks to see the view?"

"You are so damned practical!"

Our Asian friend emerges. "Look, there's room for two!" Ben announces loudly, grabbing my hand and pulling me into the room. He slams the door, turns the lock, and wraps his arms around me. I never realized how much upper-body strength a runner could develop. As we tumble to the floor, I wrap my arms around his hard, tight chest and send my tongue on an answering expedition to his lingual invasion.

"This is insane," I say when we pause for breath, even as my cock begins to swell in response to the pressure I feel growing on my thigh.

"This is as close as I'll ever come to the mile-high club," Ben gasps.

"You're 4,000 feet short. This building is only 1,250 feet or 381 metres tall." I can't help it! Some figures pop out without thinking.

"But that's to the top of the tower," he replies breathlessly. "We're only on the 86th floor."

"It's visited by ten million tourists a year." At this point, the door handle rattles vigorously. "Including one who's desperate to pee." Suddenly, we both start to giggle. The scene is utterly ridiculous: two grown men, fully dressed, rolling around on a cold tile floor surrounded by hundreds of blissfully innocent tourists. If only they knew!

"Central Park has 843 acres," he intones, "including five artificial lakes."

"My apartment has 640 square feet," I reply, "including a bed."

"Are you proposing a private tour?"

"I'm free after four o'clock tomorrow." I give him one of my business cards.

"'Discover new excitement in New York,'" he reads. "Now there's an offer I can't refuse!"

BRIAN STEIN

The Occidental Tourist

The boat's P.A. system jolted me awake. I looked out the cabin window and saw the ripples on the brown, silt-filled river. We had come aboard in Chongqing the night before following our flight from Beijing. This was my first view of the Great River, as the Chinese call the Yangtze.

The dining room was already full when I arrived for breakfast. Our group had a table reserved for us.

"Morning," I said.

"Little foggy out there," someone piped up. In the time it had taken to shower and dress we had moved into an area where it was difficult seeing the shoreline.

"As long as we can see when we enter the Three Gorges," I said, taking my seat.

A tall, slightly-built waiter was standing beside me. He was handsome, with a thatch of black hair, smooth skin, slender fingers, and no discernible beard.

"What would you like to drink?" he asked softly.

"Some black tea, please," I said, and then noticing the small nametag on his vest, added: "Oliver."

"Okay," he said sweetly, elongating the word. He poured the

steaming tea from a clay pot, smiled, and then moved on.

The first morning we were treated to a history of the Yangtze by the boat's resident guide, but I soon got bored by his youthful erudition, and could barely wait for lunch to be served so I could see Oliver again. He couldn't have been that beautiful, I mused.

Since arriving in Beijing, I had been intrigued by all the attractive young men I had seen in the Forbidden City, at the awesome Great Wall, at the Ming Tombs, men to whom I might never have given a second glance to back home.

"Wow, this stuff is really good," someone said from across the table as Oliver poured some local beer. His eyes caught mine briefly.

The second morning began at six o'clock when we congregated on the deck for our entry into the Qutang Gorge. A cold mist was swirling around the peaks. Men on both banks were fishing, and occasionally a junk glided past, a poignant reminder of another time.

Later, as breakfast was served, I tried to appear nonchalant before Oliver, but I was sure he knew I was intrigued. I wondered if the same kind of coy, flirtatious games we played in Canada were common in China.

About midway through the gorges, we went on an excursion up the Shennong Stream. Willowy young trackers with bamboo ropes harnessed over their shoulders dragged us through the rapids in sampans, small, pea-pod-shaped boats. The trackers, sometimes singing, sometimes grunting, were flimsily clad in jockey shorts that hung loosely around their muscular thighs. One man steered the boat, another kept it from crashing into the cliffs with a long bamboo pole. As the trackers clambered over the banks, straining and pulling, all I could think about was how their naked flesh stung in the cold waters and how I suddenly longed for the touch of Oliver's warm flesh.

The final night of our cruise, the waiters and crew, outfitted in colourful costumes, performed traditional songs and dances for our group. Oliver appeared in two numbers wearing an outfit cut to expose his golden flesh. Afterwards, I found Oliver and handed him an envelope with a thank-you note and a large tip of my remaining yuan. I had a drink in the bar and then returned to my cabin.

Later, while writing in my journal, there was a faint knock on the door. I grabbed my robe and opened the door. It was Oliver.

"I have disturbed you?" he asked haltingly.

"Of course not. Do you want to come in?"

He looked nervously up and down the corridor. "I shouldn't." He paused, then said: "Okay," in the same sweet voice that had touched me when he took my order that first morning.

My cramped cabin was not meant for entertaining. He felt awkward by our proximity and clearly wanted to make a quick retreat.

"Can I give you something?" I asked. "A soft drink? Some fruit?" I wanted him to stay awhile.

"Thank you, no. I came to say goodbye."

"Not hello?"

Oliver giggled. I touched his arm.

"You are very kind."

"You were very attentive. *Xièxie.* Thank you." I leaned closer and boldly kissed his cheek, uncertain what his reaction would be. He remained still, as if my move had not been unexpected nor unacceptable. Then his hand reached up behind my neck and he pulled me closer to him. He deftly opened my robe and pulled it from my body.

"You are very hairy," he said ingenuously.

"You're very smooth," I said, fingering the buttons of his shirt. "Why don't you get undressed?"

"Okay."

Surely I was dreaming. For four days I had imagined such a moment with Oliver. And here we were, this beautiful young man standing naked in front of me, in full control of the situation. My tongue traced circles on his warm chest. His skin felt like silk and tasted of anise and sesame oil. We moved toward my bed and he pulled me down on top of him.

Our love-making was gentle, like Oliver. He was considerate, remarkably adept, even adventurous, always trying to please me. A simple movement like my touching his cock produced muffled squeals of joy.

So this is why two friends back home had taken Asian lovers, I thought, as I began to drift off.

I must have loosened my grip of his body as we slept, because he was gone when I awoke. At breakfast, there was no sign of him. Had someone seen him enter my cabin and reported him?

We finally docked at Wuhan after our inspection of the mighty dam that would soon change the course and the history of the river. We were to be played off by a band of uniformed waiters. I felt a tap on my shoulder. I turned. It was Oliver.

"I thought I might not see you again. Are you okay?"

"For you," he said, handing me a folded piece of paper. "Wuhan is my home."

The crush of passengers began to move, carrying me with it. I could no longer see Oliver, but I knew he was watching me as I stepped aboard the waiting bus. I opened the paper. He had written down his name and a phone number.

SANDIP ROY

Prolonged Exposure May Cause Dizziness

It's 12:25. He never comes in before 12:30 but I just wanted to be sure. Just in case, you know. The bench is hot on my bare butt and I wiggle around trying to avoid the nails. The sauna smells of stale towels and trapped air. Someone left a newspaper inside even though the sign explicitly says, "No newspapers." The pages feel dried to a crisp. I glance at them—the sports pages, oh well. I spread my towel on the bench and sit down and wait. I have been watching him for days from behind my book on the Lifecycle.

The other day I almost got him. He was looking at me in the shower. I soaped myself in what I hoped was a languorous gesture. I leered suggestively, trying to look sexy and get the soap out of my eye at the same time. Then I wrapped the towel carelessly around my waist, and walked over to the sauna. Just before I went in, I paused theatrically and glanced back. He turned away quickly but he had been looking. After a while he followed me in. I smiled at him, casually touching myself.

That was when the white guy came in. A thirtyish guy with blue eyes and bulging pecs—and the biggest dick I had ever seen. He was always parading around the locker room with a half hard-on. He usually did not even notice me. But that was okay. I much preferred this other boy with the nutmeg skin and slim, tight figure, and average-sized dick.

The white guy put his towel down and parked himself between us. We shrunk into our corners and fell to examining our toes. I gave the white guy the why-don't-you-leave-us-alone look. But he just leaned back, spread his legs, and started to stroke himself. I wondered what he would do if someone walked in. He wouldn't be able to hide that thing under his little white towel. Maybe he'd make a quick tent with the sports page. I gave my lover boy the let's-ignore-this-monstrous-exhibition-and-do-our-boys-of-colour-bonding look.

I wondered if it was polite to walk past this blatantly aroused man and make out with my man. It seemed kind of rude and I just wasn't brought up to be like that. So I stretched and walked to the door ostensibly to look at the clock. Now it wouldn't look so obvious if I went and sat next to my guy instead of returning to my spot. I turned around to walk towards him and stopped short. He had moved closer to the white guy and was feeling his dick. I stopped, unsure what to do. The object of my affection did not even glance at me. Forgetting all our telepathic messages in the shower, he started blowing the white guy with great gusto. I stood there, stranded, towel in hand, while his head bobbed up and down. The white guy closed his eyes and said in a throaty, bad porn star voice, "Yeah, baby, suck that big cock." It was so cheesy. I felt bad for my lover boy. He deserved better. But he just made a slurping noise and tried to open his mouth wider. I should have left right then. If I had, the white guy wouldn't have had the chance to open his eyes, look at me, and ask, "Would you mind watching the door?"

But that was then. Today it will be different. My friends would say I am pathetic but I am willing to give him another chance—as one person of colour to another. I have also checked. Monster dick is not in today. I am horny and determined. Afterwards I will explain to him about racism in the gay community and why we boys of colour must stick together.

I glance at the clock. 12:35. I start reading about college basketball.

12:45. The sauna is getting really hot. I am getting a little dizzy. I rub the sweat across my chest.

12:47. My throat is parched. I should have brought some water.

12:52. I guess I could hop into the shower and come back. But what if he poked his head in right then and seeing no one, left?

12:57. Getting hungry now. An old man comes in, stretches, and leaves.

1:02. I am thinking about this Thai restaurant that serves the best *tom ka gai* and iced tea with sweet condensed milk.

1:05. I am thinking basil and lemongrass and iced tea refills. My stomach grumbles. I am almost about to go when the door opens. I freeze. My beloved pokes his head in and seems startled to see me. I uncross my legs and look him in the eyes. He hangs his towel over the coals and then quickly steps back out, shutting the door behind him. I wait, thinking maybe he was taking a quick shower before coming back. He returns five minutes later, fully dressed, and picks up his towel. This time he does not look at me. Now I feel like I can't even leave the sauna until he is gone from the gym. I don't want him to have the satisfaction of knowing I was waiting for him and him alone. I watch him outside drying his hair.

I close my eyes and think of Thai food. I think of Combination Lunch Number 5. I wonder whether I'll get it with tofu, chicken, beef, or pork. Tofu would probably be healthiest. Fuck that. I am getting pork. And maybe even some of that creamy coconut ice-cream. And fried rice instead of steamed rice.

He's still in the lobby when I leave. But I don't care. I walk past with my head held high. I smile. I can almost taste Combination Number 5.

JOEY SAYER

Magda Says

Everything is planned to perfection. Magda says the ambience has to be just right in order to suitably impress the object of one's desire. I worship Magda, she has never yet led me astray, and I plan to follow her every word of advice.

I've gone out on a couple of dates with this one guy, and he seems to be everything I want in a man and much more. It was all I could do to physically restrain myself from pouncing on him and schtupping him on the spot when we first met. But Magda says that one should refrain from sexual relations until at least the third date, in order to have him prove his desire is true. One must avoid the TCTF Syndrome—too close, too fast—for this only leads to broken hearts and prematurely stained sheets. Magda knows everything. She's so wise.

Thus it is now our official third date: a romantic dinner at my apartment. All prepared according to the rules. Magda's rules. It should be flawless. The preliminary dates over with, I plan on (close your ears, Magda) fucking him raw.

He arrives fifteen minutes early, while I'm still preparing the noodles for Magda's suggested boeuf sauvignon. (Actually, Magda suggested boeuf bourgignon; unfortunately, bourgignon was a wee bit beyond my price range.) I take his jean jacket (I must work on his fashion sense so that it will meet with Magda's approval) and seat him at my perfectly appointed table, having ditched the kitschy Elmo placemats for lit candles and matching flatware. He's gorgeous: dark, thick hair, trim goatee, piercing almond eyes, olive skin. I am so in lust.

I hustle to make sure the dinner will meet Magda's exacting standards. I dim the lights and put on a CD of Lotte Lenya croaking out soft jazz renditions of Kurt Weill standards. Perfect.

I serve the initial course of Caesar Salad with homemade dressing and freshly made buns. I seat myself, and gaze coquettishly into his eyes. As we eat, we discuss light, innocuous topics (Magda says definitely no politics at dinner!) and I laugh at all his jokes, and casually ignore his occasional belch and odd scratching. Everything is going according to plan, so I start in on phase two.

I begin leading our discussion about the TV sitcom *Will and Grace* into an increasingly sexual banter, comparing him alternately to actors Eric McCormack and Sean Hayes, attributing their individual best features to him. While doing so, I subtly slide my chair closer to his, and brush up against his shirt while supposedly reaching for the wine bottle. All is in readiness for the big move: romantic candlelight, a full stomach, blue balls from not having put out for two dates and a dinner. Magda would be proud. Making it seem completely unrehearsed, I lean forward and gently kiss him on those full lips of his.

He reciprocates: the last of my lingering doubts flicker away as the Gods of Testosterone grace us with their carnal gifts. He begins removing his shirt.

"No, wait!" I stop him. "You're not allowed to do that!"

"Huh?"

"Magda says that, in order to make the first magical, shared intimacy perfect, I should be the one undressing you," I offer.

"Who the hell is Magda?"

"Magda Stoddart, of course! The doyenne of domesticity! The guru of etiquette! You know, the one who writes all those books, like *Magda's Rules*, on how terrible we would be without her advice?"

"Oh, her. She's a bit much, isn't she?"

"Please, I adore her."

"But I'm not into threesomes." With that he grabs my head. A pulsating liplock ends the discussion. I decide not to push it. There's always time to educate him.

Slowly, tantalizingly, I begin the process of leading him away from the dinner table down the hall, to where Magda's next suggestion lies in wait. By the time we reach the end of the corridor, we are both gloriously naked and caressing each other in areas designed to further inflame the fires of our passion. He begins to pull me to the bedroom; I resist, trying to coax him towards the bathroom.

"Please," he groans, "I want you in bed."

"But the bubble bath is next," I counter.

"Bubble bath?"

"Magda says that intimate relations, in order to achieve their zenith of fulfillment, should be preceded by a relaxing bath, delicately perfumed with a rich, vanilla-scented bath oil. Cleanliness, after all, simply cannot be ignored."

"Jesus Christ, man, I just wanna get laid!"

His logic irrefutable, I allow him to lead me into my bedroom. I pray that Magda never finds out I broke the rules.

We land on the bed in a bonfire of desire. We roll around, each vying for the perfect position to begin. I'm thinking that we must look fabulous, and that I should have installed ceiling mirrors, even though Magda would consider this the height of tackiness. He struggles to squeeze a hand between my back and the bed. He pauses for a moment, and then pulls out a rose petal.

He holds up the red floral offering. "Why are there flowers in your bed?"

"To underline the romanticism of this special evening of passion, of course," I reply. "After all, Magda says. . . ."

"Oh, fuck Magda!" he cries, as he wrestles me off the bed and onto the floor, leaving our midnight Malmaison behind us. He takes me in his mouth, engulfing me, and reaches to attack my nipples. Every time I begin to say something, he roughly kisses me and swallows my advice from Magda. We suck, we caress, we lick, and we massage each other throughout the night, bestowing upon each other our most personal intimacies. We fall asleep on the floor beside the bed, in each other's arms.

The following morning I pull a Fahrenheit 451 on Magda Stoddart. As he walks into the kitchen for a late morning breakfast, the last page of *Magda's Rules* is engulfed in flame.

ROBERT THOMSON

Bad Emotional Risk

Gay men are fascinating creatures. They can be sexy and sly when you first meet them, and then, when you go on a date with them, turn into icy prudes.

"I've always told you that you weren't built for dating," my friend Ronald says over an extremely expensive cup of coffee.

"Oh, so you think it's my fault that I only date ridiculous men?"

"It's all in your perceptions, Brian. There's something wrong with you. I just haven't been able to put my finger on what it is."

"You've put more than your finger on what usually gets me in trouble." I smile.

"Yes, and never again, as the saying goes."

Ronald is an ex. An ex-whatever. We had sex a couple of times, went out for dinner once or twice, and then realized that we'd taken things about as far as they could go. As soon as the pressure was gone to perform or to be on our best behaviour, a frighteningly honest friendship developed.

"Who said I was offering?"

"You know, for somebody so critical about other people, you are remarkable blind to your own faults."

"Yes," I said. "I'm a human being. Gloriously flawed. Take it or leave it."

"I have and I did," Ronald says, smiling into his coffee cup.

"Do you want to hear about this guy or what?"

"If it'll make you feel better, go ahead."

"Last Monday night I was working at the restaurant, and this guy and this older woman come in and sit on the patio. He's tall and a bit skinny, but boyishly cute, you know? Throughout the course of the evening we exchange glances and somehow I get involved in their conversation. As they're getting ready to leave, he goes downstairs to the bathroom. She pays for the bill and asks for my phone number for him.

"I tell her that I usually don't give out my phone number, especially when the person isn't brave enough to ask for it himself. She's embarrassed and says she's just trying to help. She says that he's shy. So I write my number down on a slip of paper and give it to her. He resurfaces from the bathroom and they leave. When I get home that night there's a message on my machine from him. His name is Jeff."

"Did he have a big dick?" Ronald interrupts. He thinks I'm obsessed. "That's what this whole thing is about, isn't it?"

"No, it's not another big dick story. Be patient, would you?"

"So what happened?"

"We arranged to go on a date."

"Uh-oh. He had it coming then."

"Shut up! So we go on this dinner date. He's cocky, you know? He's condescending to the waiter, which does not impress me, and there's this almost combative tone to his conversation all the way through dinner. Like he's got something to prove. It's kind of amusing for a while, but there's an edge to it that gets really annoying. Anyway, I drink too much wine, of course, which literally translates to take me I'm yours. So we go back to his place. He owns this nice condominium down by the lake and he puts on some soft music and it's all very romantic. But when I start to look around the place I notice all these Barbie dolls everywhere. And then he starts to show them to me. He tells me he's a collector. Oh my god, of all people, I've gone home with a man with a Barbie fetish! I think I might have laughed at the collection, which wasn't very nice, I know, but just imagine a condominium filled with Barbie dolls and this cute, masculine guy. Oh yeah, and he smokes."

"Eeeww."

"I know. So we're in bed and you know, we're having sex, and all of a sudden he stops and says that he'd really like to fuck me. I just look at him and say, Yeah? Well, I'd like to fuck you. I'm just mocking him when I say it, you know? And he just kind of smiles and tells me again that he wants to fuck me.

"I said, I heard you the first time. And he says, I've got condoms and lube and you're ass is so hot. . . ."

"Porno talk," Ron interjects.

"Yeah, you know, which is really only appropriate coming from a television set and not a real live human being. Anyway, I say to him why don't I fuck you first and then you can fuck me. And he says no, he only gets fucked when he's in an intimate relationship."

"Are you serious?"

"Yes! Only when I'm in an intimate relationship. An intimate relationship! And this is where I lost it. So I go, Oh! It's alright for you to fuck me and we've just met, but I can't fuck you? And he says yeah. I can't believe my ears. I ask him if he realizes how stupid that is and how hypocritical and he says that he doesn't think so. He says that anal sex is something very intimate and is appropriate only within a trusting relationship. And I say, Yeah, but it's alright for you to go ahead and fuck me? You wouldn't actually be involved in the proceedings? It would be kind of like me sticking a dildo up my ass, right? Except he's the dildo. Like I'm the whore and he's totally innocent and not involved. This makes no sense at all. And then do you know what he says to me?"

"What?"

"He says, I should have known from the fact that you're a waiter that you were a bad emotional risk."

"What?" Ronald can hardly contain himself.

"A bad emotional risk he calls me. Because I'm a waiter. I mean, my god! He's an insurance salesman who collects dolls! And he doesn't think he's really there when he fucks someone! What does that make him, a good catch?"

"Where do you find these men?"

"I have special skills. I'm a bad emotional risk."

"So then what? Did you leave?"

"No. We finished having sex."

"Because he had a big dick?"

"Of course. Then I left."

"You're so distant and cruel."

"I'm a bad emotional risk, what do you expect?"

"Have you heard from him since?"

"Yeah, he kept calling, asking to go out again."

"Did you?"

"No. I haven't returned his calls. Think he'll get the message?"

"Why not tell him the truth?"

"People don't want to hear the truth, Ronald."

"They don't?"

"No."

"Is that why you don't want to see this guy again, 'cause he called you a bad emotional risk?"

"Maybe. Or maybe it's because he said that and still wanted to go out with me."

RICHARD HAGGEN

Thirty-Six Seconds

He pushes my arms over my head. With his left hand he grabs my thumbs and pins my arms behind me. The humidity inside his bedroom is mirrored by a drizzling fog outside. His scent is intoxicating. Sweet kisses make me forget the vulnerability of my position. He kisses me lightly, first on my nose, then on my cheek, making his way towards my ears. He bites my earlobe and whispers, "I wanna fuck you."

Fuck me?

Fuck you!

My mind recoils.

Around him I choose my words carefully. Around him I am on my best behaviour. We've seen each other for only a short time, but I know it is more than it is less. Still I remain hypervigilant.

I banish the thought of intimacy. The implications of him inside me fill me with anxiety and dread. Definitely no pleasure for me. And for him, would he feel pleasure? Or once inside would he know I feel like a warehouse gutted by a four-alarm fire? I am hard pressed to recall when I haven't felt this way. Much like I have difficulty remembering a time when all my friends were alive.

I am jarred into the moment when he asks "Please?" I look into his eyes, he into mine. They shine with promise and assurance. Do mine betray my fear? I lay beneath him and am aware we're breathing in sync. He releases my thumbs and I clutch him tightly. Our bodies are wet with warmth. I pull him closer, he feels oddly delicate.

My thoughts drift to last Saturday and this puny little boy who joined my nephew and me in our sand castle construction. After introductions he announced, "I'm seven and a half." He smiled and chirped, "Mrs. Alice is my math teacher. I can add and take away." Pleased with himself, he looked at me in that penetrating way children do. I smiled weakly, stood up, and threw myself into the ocean.

The candle on the nightstand flickers. I too can add and take away. It is my privilege to trust him and let him into my life. Much as it is my prerogative to subtract this experience, to shut down. I begin to tremble.

A L A N   M I L L S

Damien

The bedroom is beautiful, and the whole house is beautiful, and brad is beautiful as he shuts the door behind him and locks it, looking at me with a disarming smile curving one side of his lips, and i sit down on the bed, waiting for his next move, which is equally charming as he walks around the bed and starts a fire in the marble fireplace that dominates one wall, and even though the fireplace uses gas logs, they are really nice ones, and it's hard to tell the difference between them and real wood, but that isn't really important anyway, because brad is here with me, and i have been wanting to be alone with brad, in this way, for quite a long time, but that always seems to be the way that relationships go with me, or at least, it has been my experience that whenever i really, really want someone, they never seem to have any interest in me whatsoever, and that's usually okay, because i've made it a point to not expect anything good to happen in my life, but brad is a good thing, or at least i pray that he is a good thing, because what i really need in my life right now is a good thing, and brad comes over to where i'm sitting on the bed just across from his new fire and kneels right in front of me to unbutton my shirt—the fire becoming a burning halo around his dark auburn hair—and i look down as his hands travel the blond coat on my stomach and chest, the tiny hairs glowing like burning embers, and i reach down to pull off his black shirt, and when it slips over his head, i feel overcome by the sight of his stunning body, which isn't necessarily perfect, but is instead more normal or natural, like my own body, but everything about him is stunning to me because of who he is, and, over time, i have truly grown to like who he is even though i never expected to be given this opportunity to be so intimate with him, being that, so far, i've only known him through friends, or rather acquaintances, that i see on occasion at the small neighbourhood gay bar which hides somewhere between our two separate homes, and even though we've talked numerous times about the empty topics that characterize bars, i've never had the courage to tell him how attracted to him i've been, until this evening when, through some accident, we both showed up at what was supposed to be a friendly gathering but is, instead, a bacchanal feast, and through this same accident, it turned out that each of us, with the exception of our elusive host, was the only person here that the other one knew, but i feel extremely appreciative of accidents and chaos and random occurrence when brad stands up, kicks off his shoes, undoes his fly, and lets his pants drop to the floor, and i remove my shoes and socks, stand and let him open my jeans and push them down so that we both stand naked as the fire casts a glow on our skin, and it is then that brad kisses me, for what is now the second time, and it feels like a first because now the clothes are gone and his lips and body and genitals press against mine, and when he first kissed me, i was caught off guard, having never been expecting him to feel about me the way that i most definitely felt about him, and so it was to my surprise that he leaned over and touched his lips to mine while we sat uncomfortably on a sofa surrounded by sex, but then his tongue touched my lips and my tongue touched his tongue and we opened our mouths the way we open our mouths right now as brad runs his hands down my back to my rear, pulling me toward the bed, and we fall together onto the soft mattress, still locked in an embrace, and he rolls me over onto my back and kisses me passionately as his cock and balls rub up against mine, sending waves of stimulation up through my spine, and we kiss, rolling back and forth, touching and kissing skin while our erections press firmly against each other until the pleasure grows to a pinnacle of ecstasy which makes our breathing become laboured and causes us to groan, as if in pain, until the friction makes us come, spreading our semen across my stomach and thighs and his stomach and thighs as he continues to rub against me, and, slowly, our breathing returns to something that could be considered more normal, and he looks into my eyes and smiles, and i instantly wonder if we're ever going to do this again, only because i have always wanted to be close to him whether or not sex is involved, and now i feel afraid even through i also feel hopeful, and i lie here, looking back into his eyes, waiting to hear what he has to say, knowing what he says might change everything or might leave me where i've always been. . . .

S H A U N   L E V I N

Making Meringues

I'm inside my boyfriend, Timmy, when he says, "James, how did you make those meringues?"

Our guests have just left and we're on our bed. Tim's on his back and I'm on my knees between his legs. I take a swig from the bottle we brought into the bedroom and I kiss him, wine running into his mouth. Tim's referring to the meringues that held the strawberries and ice cream.

I say, "Get your ingredients out first."

"Yes?" he says, caressing my chest with one hand, the other behind his head.

"You're so gorgeous," I say.

Timmy's long black hair is spread out on the pillow. His blue eyes unmoving from mine, his succulent lips shining with kisses and wine. And his armpits. God, his armpits.

"So gorgeous," he says, grinning, clenching his arse around my cock. "And you're so drunk."

"Two eggs at room temperature," I say. "A big bowl, a smaller one, sugar."

"That's better," he says, taking his hand from my chest, kissing two fingers, bringing them back to my lips.

"Now comes the delicate part."

"Delicate?" he says. "So soon?"

"Separating the eggs."

"Ah," Timmy says, his eyes closed, moving his arse in circles, smiling, the walls of his insides pressing against the head of my cock.

"Crack egg number one on side of small bowl," I say. "Then let white of egg slide out. Pass yolk between shells until all of white is in bowl. Make sure yolk doesn't break. No specks slipping out with the white."

"And if it breaks?" he says, pulling himself up and taking the tip of my nipple between his teeth.

"Oh, fuck, Tim," I say, holding onto his back, him onto mine, pushing into him as far as I can go.

"Tell me," he says, my nipple still between his teeth. "What if the yolk breaks?"

"That old-fashioned cookbook . . . the cookbook says . . . it says . . . it says the best way to . . . the best way to remove bits of . . . bits of yolk is . . . Ow!"

"What?" he says, his tongue flicking the tip of my nipple. "What does it say?"

"Wet a soft piece of linen, squeeze it dry, then dab out the bits of yolk."

"Good advice," he says, lying back. "Tell me more."

"Both whites of eggs should be in the big bowl by now," I say. "Take out hand whisk and start whisking whites."

Timmy smiles at me, brings one leg over, pushes his bum into my groin, keeping me inside him. We manoeuver our bodies so I can fuck him from behind.

"Whites of egg need to be stiff," I say. "They need to peak."

"I love stiff egg whites," he says, on all fours, turning his head around to be kissed.

I lift the curtain of dark hair from the side of his face and bring my lips to his. I run my tongue over his gums. Strawberries and dry white wine.

"It's so warm inside you," I say, slowing down so as not to come.

"What happens when the whites are stiff?" he says.

"Timmy," I say. "Do you really want to know all this?"

"You know I do," he says. "Keep talking."

"Take half a cup of caster sugar and pour, gradually, while

whisking whites."

"That's a lot of sugar for two eggs," he says.

His shoulders are speckled with freckles. His skin is beach-sand from a distance, his vertebrae a range of windswept dunes. His waist as narrow as perfection, like polished driftwood.

"You don't have to worry about that," I say, holding on to him from behind, stroking the soft hairs on his chest.

"I want pink meringues," he says.

"With hundreds and thousands?" I say, close to his ear.

"Of course," he says. "Hundreds and hundreds and pink."

"Some red food colouring then," I say, lifting my chest off his back, fucking him slowly.

"How about blood?" he says, doing that circle motion with his bum. "We can use blood. Two drops. One from me and one from you."

"Oh, Tim," I say, almost coming right there and then.

"Then?" he says, pushing into me and pulling on his cock, his face in the pillow.

"Spoon mixture onto greaseproof paper on baking trays. Flatten mounds with back of spoon. Leave overnight in oven on low, low temperature."

"Then?" his voice muffled.

"Then, while they're turning into meringues," I say, cupping his arsecheeks, looking at my cock going in and out of him.

"I think I'm going to come," he says.

"Oh, fuck, Timmy, oh, fuck," I say.

"James," he says. "My James," he says, and comes.

I do, too, inside him. I kiss the top of his back and his shoulders and lower myself with him onto the bed. We ease our legs out behind us. I am on his back, still inside him, going soft, stroking his cheek and kissing him. I'm hugging hard earth, peering over the edge of a cliff. I have been here forever. I slip out of him and curl up at his side. Tim's breathing slows down and he wriggles his head under my arm, nuzzles up against my chest.

"What should we do with the yolks?" he says, letting sleep take him.

"Make mayonnaise," I say.

"Oh, my lovely pink meringue," he smiles, lips against my skin.

"Ah, my sleeping beauty," I say, kissing him good night.

IAN-ANDREW McKENZIE

You Inside Me

I am naked and you wear a pair of jeans as you put your arms around me and gently push me onto my back on the bed. You come to rest on top of me, and we kiss. I feel your moustache on the corner of my lips as you push your tongue deep into my mouth. You have a hand on my throat, and when I inhale you force your breath into my mouth.

My head swims, and the weight of your body makes my breathing more difficult. You move your hand from my throat to my cheek, and you hold my face and kiss me. Then you push a finger into my mouth while your tongue still probes and pushes at my lips. I suck at your tongue and fingers hungrily.

I grab your broad shoulders with both of my hands. I try to pull you closer, which is practically impossible, as you rest atop me. I feel you pushing your denim-clad crotch into my hip as you grind your body into mine. With your free hand you grab my arm from your shoulder and pin it down on the bed, over my head. Your fingers encircle my wrist firmly. Knowing how to play this game, I try to free my wrist, but you tighten your grip and I am unable to move.

You remove your other hand from my face and place it back on my neck, squeezing one time in a power play. I nod slightly, to tell you I have surrendered for the time being. You move your hand down to your jeans, where you begin to unzip them and pull them off. Your shoulder presses into my chest and I cannot breathe, but I remain still.

You back off me for a moment. While you remove your jeans I admire your smooth skin and strong arms. I watch the muscles move in your neck. When your pants are lying beside the bed, you grab your cock and say, "You wanted a man; you got a man." I look down at your big cock, and my body instinctively arches itself towards it.

You grab my thigh and tell me to turn over. I roll onto my stomach and listen as you apply lube to your dick from a tube on the stand by the bed. I hear you opening the condom, and I savour the anticipation of having you fuck me. My back is still arched, and you push your lubed fingers into my crack, rubbing at my waiting, eager hole.

You try to push a finger in, but it hurts and I move away. You push down with great force between my shoulders with your large, strong hand, shoving my face into the pillow. Again you try to stick a finger in, and again I move further up the bed. Though I want you, I am aware that it will hurt. Part of me also wants to tease you, to make you take me, make you work for it.

You move your free hand to my shoulder to keep me from moving further away. I finally relax, and a finger goes in. You pull it out slowly and put it back in, repeating the motion. I expect you to ease another finger in, but you surprise me by removing the finger quickly and trying to press the head of your cock into me. I jump away fearfully, but you throw your body onto my back and grab my wrists in your hands.

You guide the big head of your cock into my hole. It's a searing, tight feeling, and I try to tell you to take your dick out, but you have my face pushed into the mattress.

"Shut up," you command. "Shut up and take it." Your angry tone makes me tense up, which I know you feel, as you stop forcing your big meat into my ass. You lean down and whisper into my ear, "Come on, baby, take my big cock. It's your man's cock. It needs you."

I try to relax, and you caress my shoulder lightly. Slowly, you resume your hips' movements, and I push my butt back to meet your thrusts. I can feel your body fall into the pleasure, and I raise my ass up more eagerly. After a few slow strokes I lift my butt and feel you push all the way in, where you rest. "You got it all," you tell me, and I can feel every inch.

You pull your pole out until just the head is inside, then you slide it back in all the way, letting my hole get accustomed to your size. You do this several times, each time more quickly until you are slapping your balls against my ass cheeks. I grow used to the rhythm, and begin to move my ass in small circles and tighten my butt around your cock.

Again you surprise me, as you pull all the way out, and I can feel my ass close like a door. But then you push yourself in again like a jealous lover bursting into a room. You do this several times, and each time I feel a delicious anticipation of the re-entry.

You pull out one more time and tell me, "Get on your back." I do as you say, and you grasp my legs and put them over your shoulders. I feel you press into me again. Once more you push inside. You roll me back onto my shoulders, so you can slam yourself into me with maximum force.

"Here's where we make your ass sore tomorrow," you say. I am thinking that I am already sore. I try to ask you to slow down, to let me catch my breath, but you cover my mouth with your hand and bend and kiss my ear. You whisper, "And here is where I get what I want." With your hand still on my face, you fuck me faster and harder. My hands are on your shoulders and chest, pushing against you, but your weight, desire, and momentum overwhelm me.

You fuck my ass with total control until I feel you press deeper than you have before, and you breathe in quickly and hold your breath. My ass grabs at your cock as it seems to double in width. You continue to punch your rod deep into my gut three or four more times, knocking the wind out of me. I can feel your cock radiate heat as you come inside me.

The heat and penetration trigger something inside me. I clutch onto your shoulders and look into your eyes, and I feel myself shoot all over my chest and stomach. I'm not even touching my own cock. You take your hand from my mouth and nod to me, saying, "That's right. That's good."

For the first time since we came to bed, my spine relaxes and my muscles go weak. You rest on top of me, your heart still madly racing. You pull your dick out and pull the condom off. I don't know what you do with it. I am too busy concentrating on catching my breath. I bite your shoulder lightly when you ask if I'm okay. I feel so close to you, ready to drift off to sleep, but you speak in a low growl. "Baby, when you bite my shoulder that way. . . ." You don't finish your sentence. The increasing pressure of your growing cock against my hip says it all, and I realize that there is no intermission between scenes one and two.

The ass you just fucked tightens almost instantly, and I try to crawl out from under you. But you pin my arms and tell me, "You're gonna let me in again."

GREG WHARTON

Love

He stands with his smooth back to me. His legs are firm under him, feet secure on the hardwood floor, arms stretched out in front of him, large hands flat on the edge of the table.

Beautiful.

His skin is shiny. He is taller then me, his shoulders wide, neck and arms strong, waist small. His round ass cheeks are red from the slaps I gave them when he first stripped down, my emotions taking control immediately. His thighs are muscled, his feet long. He is strength in perfection, willing to give up control to another with calm and trust.

Grateful.

I walk up and grab his ass cheeks, pulling them apart to expose the hairy pucker. I want to lap at it with my tongue and I groan, letting the sight ignite my desire. I smell it and reach around him to grab his cock jerking the foreskin while forcing him against the table with my weight. I push his head and shoulders until flat on the tabletop and his weight lifted forward. I quickly place the plastic bag over his head and pull the edges tight around his throat, making a handle as I grab my slippery cock and force it up into his ass with one swift shove.

Desire.

He gives little resistance as I pull the full length out and force it back in fiercely, banging against him with all my weight and rage. His asshole clenches tightly around me and I feel him shove back despite being off balance, his feet barely touching the floor.

I keep a firm grip on the bag, pulling it snug around his throat as I fuck him hard and fast. I know I should be careful not to push him too far but I am quickly out of control and can't think of consequences, only the final release. My heart is pounding wildly and my vision blurs. I'm numb. I grind into him, wanting to split him open.

Doubt.

I pull him upright just as the pressure in my balls tighten to the point of exploding and pull the bag off. I clamp my mouth on his shoulder and bite down, yanking his head back sharply by his long sweaty hair.

He cries out and I feel his ass clench tighter, literally jerking me off with its force. He sprays across the table while the muscles in his ass pump around my hardness.

Release.

He leans his weight against me while his lungs breathe deeply the air they had been denied. I continue to stir in him as I stroke his still stiff cock. I start to cry. He closes his eyes and moans my name softly. I pull his face around and explore his tongue with mine, tasting my tears as they fall down my cheeks.

Fear.

I pull my cock out and gently lay him on the table again. I put my mouth to his asshole, tasting my sperm mixed with his ass juice. I lift his legs up and under as he kneels on the table for me, ass splayed. I brush my lips on his cheeks.

I slap him hard, as hard as I can. He forces back against my face and I accept. I place my hands on his hips and put my mouth to his hole. It opens up as my tongue slips in and I lap at it hungrily. Wetness drips down my chin and I place a finger right at the opening to rub along with my tongue. The smell of his ass ignites me again.

Anger.

The lights dim abruptly and the ground shifts under my feet. I bite at him, catching hairs with my teeth. I close my eyes to make it stop. I pull my finger out and immediately replace it with two. My cock slaps against the table as I back away, dripping both from my chin and cock.

I drink my beer and watch him in silence. He hasn't moved. I step closer to him and press the lip of the bottle against his ripe, swollen ass lips. It slides in and out easily. I smile, then drink the last of it.

Thirst.

"Sit on it," I tell him. He shifts position and quickly swallows the first half of it. I jerk him by his hair so that he is upright on his knees and grab the bottle. "Harder." I kiss him on the back of his neck.

Tenderness.

He screams as he forces himself down onto the glass. I turn him around by his hair to face me and pull his head to mine. "Tell me you love me," I say as I grab his cock.

"I luh . . . " I slap him and grind on his cock.

I feel the room spinning. I yell, "Say you love me!" and jerk on his rock hard meat sliding the tight skin off the head over and over.

"I love you!" he shouts back as he sits down hard on the bottle. I see just the bottom inch sticking out. His nipples are hard and I grab them both and pinch. I pull his face to mine and force my tongue into his warm willing mouth. He moans and I feel the tightness pulling on my balls again.

Pity.

I growl and grab at the back of his neck, yanking his head down so his chin is against the tabletop. I ejaculate against his lips, then force my cock into his mouth and shoot again. I fuck his mouth, hitting the back of his throat over and over.

I lift him up by his chin and lick his bruised wet lips. I kiss his neck, chest, nipples. I kiss his belly. I take his hardness into my mouth and reach for the bottle. I close my eyes.

Love.
I love you, too.

DAVID MUELLER

Cheating on Mark

Keep in mind that all this happened in the eighties. The hair was much bigger then, the shoes pointier, and the sex was absolutely deadly. I don't think anyone was sure there'd be a faggot left by 1991.

It was a terrible time to be twenty-two and horny. I felt like a luckless new initiate to a species headed towards imminent extinction. And, horrific as it is to say, what shocked me ten years later was not how much death there'd been in the interim, but how many of us seemed to have survived.

But as far as I could tell, horny twenty-two-year-olds never stopped having sex. Though we lied about it more, because in 1986, despite the miracle of latex, almost everyone still acted like the virus had morals—bad ones.

I had a lover then, and now I can see that I wasn't in love with him. He was my cover. He made me seem safe and clean and, ironically, fuckable.

His name was Mark. And I'm not even sure where he is anymore. I ran into him once in South Beach, each of us too messed up to give a shit about the other or to convey any real details about the eight years intervening. It was fitting. But we got in a few laughs about the last time I'd cheated on him. With nearly a decade gone by, it had finally become funny.

I'd been on a train. And I don't know if it's like this in every city, but in San Francisco the trains are as cruisy as a sidewalk sale on New Year's Eve. I don't think AIDS ever changed that much. It might be eight in the morning, and still, it seems like at any moment the entire car might strip and continue the commute in a slowly lurching knot of mass BF-ing—or break into a Gershwin medley.

But I was on a train going home—a very crowded train. And I found myself wedged firmly between a large, somewhat bewildered, tourist from the Midwest and a young local around my same age and orientation. The latter was almost two inches shorter than me. His hair was dyed black and the fumes from his mousse were making my heart pound. He was facing away from me with his ass jostling against my crotch.

I started to get hard, and he must've noticed, because he began taking advantage of the motion of the train, grinding into me as the car pitched and jerked around, elaborating the bouncing ride down the track with his own movement. By Church Street I was ready to blow, and with one more sudden stop, I half-came in my khakis as the doors opened at Castro and the car abruptly unloaded.

I followed him into the crowd, but somewhere among the grey and blue flannel I lost him. My hopes for infidelity already abandoned, I climbed up to the street, only to find him standing there, smiling.

"So are you coming?" he smiled.

"Yeah," I said.

"Do you live around here?"

"Well, yeah. But we can't go there." And he didn't seem surprised by that.

"So we'll go to my place," he said. "It's just on 18th. And my name's Jim, by the way."

I hadn't really seen him from the front before and I was pleased to find out that he was just as cute facing me. We got to his apartment, and I doubt he'd even shut the door when I attacked him. The two of us stumbled up the stairs entangled.

His room was full of moving boxes. A mattress on the floor was strewn with eyeliners, and there were Death Rock cassettes scattered everywhere among half-empty coffee cups doubling as ashtrays.

"It's kind of a wreck," he said. "I just moved in a couple of weeks ago."

I took off my jacket and tossed it on a box labeled "Steve's." He put on some Bauhaus or something equally morbid and I slid my hand into one of the rips in his jeans, holding his bare thigh for a moment while we made out.

"Hold on," he said. "I need a cigarette."

"That stuff'll kill ya," I laughed, but he shot me a nasty look.

He lit his smoke and I knelt down in front of him. I undid his studded belt, unbuttoned his pants. No underwear. I could have guessed that. I took his cock in my mouth but he pushed me off of it.

"What?" I asked him, startled.

"Well, you know. . . . " And when I looked back at him like I didn't he said, "Nothing."

I got him on his back and pulled his pants off. He was lying there in a blue Smiths t-shirt with his ankles around my neck.

"You got any condoms?" I asked.

"Yeah," he said. "But I don't really know if I want to get fucked." Now, I was getting a bit pissy.

"You did on the train," I said.

"Yeah, but you know how sometimes you want to get fucked, but you don't really want to?"

"No," I said, "because I don't ever want to."

"Oh," and he gave me some variation on the same nasty look. "I mean, it was really fun on the train." He took a long drag from the cigarette. "I don't know. Would you, like, you know, take it slow?"

"Yeah." I said, because that was all I needed to hear. And about twenty seconds later I was watching the small muscles tensing in his back, his spine arching through the skin.

That's when I noticed, on the right of the mattress, a small piece of paper. It said "Mark" on it, and below was my boyfriend's work number, written in the same handwriting that signed my birthday cards and rent cheques.

MARK MACDONALD

The Kiss

After your call, on my way to our rendezvous, I couldn't for the life of me remember when we had last met. I remembered flashes of our lives together, the good and the bad, like our relationship had always been a connect-the-dots puzzle between explosive moments of passion and hatred. After swearing never to see you again, it seemed natural, even imperative to meet with you once more. After all this time, you still produced doubts in me, a deep mistrust of my own motivations.

I got to the parking lot of that gas station on Arbutus, your arbitrary, and somehow covert, meeting place not needing to make sense. There you were, sheltered in the phone booth across the pavement, dry in the heavy summer rain. I wanted you to have changed, to have outgrown me, but you appeared exactly the same as our first meeting years before. Thick wool sweater, tight, faded jeans, shorn head, and stubble, like some skinhead-hippie.

And the moment we made eye contact, our surroundings melted away. You stepped from the phone booth, and as we approached each other, I could have been watching from above. The warm rain coursing down drenched you in the seconds it took for us to come face to face. It was so overwhelming I can recall every detail, like

144

describing the climactic scene from a favourite movie.

We stood like that for a moment, absurd in the pounding rain. As we came together and embraced, we were left the only two people on earth. The pedestrians that ran past beneath their umbrellas, or the attendant who watched from his little gas-booth became greyer somehow, like pixilated background props. Right here, exposed in the storm by daylight, under the gaze of the crowded intersection, we kissed.

The sound of the rain pounding the concrete, the smell of your soaked sweater, congealed around us like a cocoon. Your tongue, sliding soft between your lips, tasted faintly of Drum tobacco, as always. Your unshaven face pressed against mine, the way you clutched my head and forced yourself deeper into me, it was all as familiar as the air.

The hot rain trickled down between us, sealing our lips together for a moment that seemed like years. This was our true communication, this kiss, better than anything either of us could possibly say, but with just as much significance, intent and meaning. Our bodies pressed close enough that I could feel your body beneath your denim, and I wanted it.

But at exactly the instant that I noticed your growing arousal and thought about all the people watching us, all the disapproving looks and whispers, the true meaning of your kiss became apparent. This long-needed hello, this blatant and unashamed act on your part, was also goodbye. I knew you could no longer allow yourself to struggle with the love of a man, that all these years of cheating on your girlfriends in an affair you could not justify had to end. I was horrified, shattered all over again. And yet this time I was also relieved.

Our lips parted for a moment, and we saw recognition in each other's eyes. Sad resignation in your look, a smile with tears. All confirmation, it was our final meeting. Once more we kissed, the salty taste of tears present in your mouth, and then, silently, we parted. Followed by the stares of the crowd aghast, we simply parted. Smiling, I left the parking lot. I was glad you had called. I was glad the rain hid my tears.

The kiss was complete. Clarity and perfection, reason and understanding, mean nothing to me. My life goes on of course, with its thousands of rituals and routines, but I go nowhere, I can do nothing, without that kiss. It has replaced all other memories of you, as I think you intended, and that is a wonderful thing indeed.

A. VINCENT WILLIAMS

Desire's Revenge

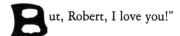ut, Robert, I love you!"

"I'm sorry, Carl, but I don't think that I love you."

Robert wouldn't look me in the eyes and it broke my heart. He just stood there with his head down and his hands in his pockets. So cute and vulnerable, I just wanted to take him in my arms and hug him. Until he opened up his treacherous mouth, again.

"I also don't think that I ever *could* fall in love with you."

"How can you know that!?" I was practically screaming at this point. I crossed my arms over my chest to hold in the pain, and to keep myself from doing bodily harm to this person that I thought I was in love with.

"I just think . . ."

"That is *exactly* your problem, you think too fucking much! Why don't you try to let yourself feel for once?"

Robert finally raised his eyes to look at me. There was pain there, sure, but it was hardly enough to satisfy me at that point.

"I know you feel *something* for me," I insisted.

"I do, it's just that . . ."

"I know, it's just sexual. You just wanted me for my body, right?"

I slowly moved my hands over my torso as I said this, and looked directly into Robert's deep brown eyes.

"That isn't true . . ."

"It might as well be," I said softly, cutting him off yet again. I had to keep him on edge, defensive and off balance.

I moved closer to Robert, my eyes never leaving his. Staring into their depths, I remembered why I had initially been attracted to him. Unfortunately, my desire had blinded me to the fact that his eyes weren't deep with emotion and sincerity, as much as with logic and thought.

"That is all I was to you, wasn't I?" I continued in the same softly seductive tone that I knew he liked. "Just a great fuck!"

Robert opened his mouth to protest, but I sealed his lips with my own before he could speak. He made a weak sound of dissent, which turned into a moan of pleasure as our tongues met and my hands roamed his body. I walked him over to my bed, my mouth on his until he was lying down, safely pinned beneath my body. Then I spread out my attack, licking and nibbling at what I knew were the sensitive areas of his neck, collarbone, and around his ears. At the same time I unbuttoned his shirt and loosened his pants.

"Please . . ." he whispered, grabbing at my hands as I unzipped him.

I held his wrists and stretched his arms above his head, holding them there. Robert struggled, weakly and ineffectively, stopping completely when I stared into his eyes again.

"Please, what?" I asked, darting my tongue out and teasing his beautiful lips. "If you want me to stop. . . ." flicked my tongue lower, over his Adam's apple, the hollow of his throat, then his lightly furred chest, all the while continuing to hold his arms prisoner while he gasped and bucked beneath me. " . . . all you have to do is say so."

I lowered his arms and continued my oral exploration of his chest. He moaned when my mouth found his right nipple.

"Oh, god . . ."

"He can't help you . . ." I informed him, punctuating the words with flicks of my tongue across his hardened nipple. " . . . but, I can. Just ask me to make love to you."

"Please . . ." Robert's voice trailed off.

I released his arms and let my fingers assist my lips, teeth, and tongue in exploring his torso. Robert grabbed my head and arched his back with pleasure as my mouth teased his belly-button.

"Say it," I whispered.

"Please . . ."

I inched lower, letting my tongue follow the trail of hair leading from his navel down his lower abdomen.

"Say it." I whispered, again.

My face was now directly over Robert's crotch. I allowed my lips to brush ever-so-lightly down the shaft of his cock, which was straining against the fabric of the white, bikini-cut briefs he always wore. He still had his hands on my head, so I removed them and raised my eyes to meet his looking down at me. I could feel the tension radiating from him in an almost palpable heatwave.

"Say it," I commanded.

There was a few seconds' pause that lasted an eternity before he responded.

"Oh, god. Yes! Please, I want you to make love to me."

I smiled and sat up.

"I can't make love to you, I'm sorry. But, you can go fuck yourself."

Robert didn't move a muscle, but I could feel his entire body recoil from me.

"Now, get out of my bed, out of my house, and . . ." I stood up so that I could look down on him in every way, and add emphasis to my next words. "Out. Of. My. Life."

If I had literally driven a knife through his heart, I do not think Robert's eyes could have expressed more pain. Without a word he got up, fastened his clothing, grabbed his leather jacket and left. He didn't look back, not once.

I did have the satisfaction of seeing Robert hastily wipe a tear from the corner of his eye as he left. But what I couldn't understand is why there were several more of the same streaming from my own.

DOUGLAS G. FERGUSON

The Growth

I did all that I could to be rid of him. A week after Jimmy and I had split up, when I'd gotten news that he'd returned to his ex-girlfriend, I dyed my hair Bitch Blonde. The second week, after a friend told me he'd seen him at the pub, looking happy and content, I got a tattoo. On the third week, after I had heard that Jimmy and his girlfriend were planning to backpack across Europe in the spring, I joined a gym. But still nothing, absolutely nothing, could wash that man outta my hair. Nothing could return my heart from the boy I'd given it to so willingly.

So I quit the gym.

What was the point of even trying to get over him when I knew damn well I wouldn't? Not as long as he was still coming over in the middle of the night, drunk, maudlin, tellin' me that he missed me. Not as long as he was still willing to fuck me during those drunken nights, leaving the sweet smell of his sex-sweat and cologne lingering on my sheets.

The boy was fucking with my heart. And why not? He owned it.

He'd done so three times, already: Come over after a night of drinking with his straight buddies. He'd get sentimental, fuck my brains out, then feel remorse over what he'd done—until the next time—because he knew his loyal girlfriend would be fast asleep at home, oblivious to it all.

Funny thing is that I actually felt sorry for his girlfriend, felt ashamed for what I was doing, until that day I saw them together, walking down the street hand in hand. They saw me, too. And, while Jimmy ignored me, his girlfriend gave me a dirty look. *Bitch!* Then as I crossed their path, Jimmy and his girl put their arms around each other, as though battling the Gay Forces of Evil with the power of their love. If only she knew that he'd just been over a few days ago and fucked me in that nasty way that he couldn't do with her.

Still, crossing their path, no matter how low I felt, was the best thing that could have ever happened to me.

That day, when I got home, I cried my eyes out. The following morning, however, something had changed.

But what had changed? Did I get over Jimmy? Hardly. But my feelings of rejection and low self-esteem had turned into an anger that boiled like lava inside my veins. And my longing for Jimmy had merged with that anger—and turned into a growth.

It appeared on the front of my left wrist. The morning I'd discovered it, it was no bigger than the size of my thumb. Still, it wasn't there the night before. It tingled at times. It even grew numb. I considered going to the doctor to have it checked out, but decided against it.

That same day, I'd received a message from Jimmy. He was breathing hard on the machine, like he was nervous or something. He apologized for ignoring me on the street, but said it was for the best; that he loved his girlfriend and thought we should never speak to each other again, even in private. To avoid any "mistakes," as he put it.

Hearing that, my rage overwhelmed me, and I fell asleep for the remainder of the afternoon and night. The following morning my growth, like my rage, was inflamed even more. It was now bulbous like the head of a mushroom.

After I had finished my shift at the comic shop, I went for beers with a couple of buddies of mine. Despite my attempt to hide the growth under my baggy sweater, they had noticed the pinkish thing.

"You should get that checked out," said one of them. "It could be cancerous."

"It's just a bacteria build-up," said the other. "Or a root. You can get it extracted. I had a friend who had one once, and she smashed the thing with a book."

"Yuck," I said. "Did she get gangrene?"

"No. But she got rid of the thing."

I decided to neither smash the thing nor see a doctor. A week later, it had grown two full inches. It became apparent to me what it was. It was half of Jimmy's prick. I knew this, not only because of its shape and smell—the smell of his sweat and cologne—but because of the way the flaccid flesh became erect whenever I thought of him. When I realized this, I took several days off from the comic store, feigning sickness. I sat in my apartment and thought about him as I stroked and tongued the thing. After a couple of days, it became a full three inches when hard. I eventually mastered a position where I could stick it up my ass, the growth only softening after I came.

That was a few days ago when I figured out its purpose.

I've been using it ever since. I can't believe I ever thought of getting rid of it, it's become such a handy lil' thing! I no longer need Jimmy's affection. I have his manhood. Don't get me wrong, I'm still not over him, but it's getting easier.

I saw him walking past the shop this morning. I didn't drown in despair the way I once did, I merely waded in it. Jimmy, on the other hand, looked gaunt and sullen, full of worry. Like he'd misplaced something. Something important.

He was also alone.

Perhaps the next time I see him I will feel nothing but pity. Until then, however, I will keep the thing, despite how itchy and uncomfortable it is, hidden under my baggy sweaters. And perhaps when he returns my heart, I will return his penis.

Or, perhaps I will just smash the thing with a really fat book.

JOHN BRIGGS

Pillow Talk

I guess I never told you: I've had twins. Only one pair, that's all, but that's one pair more than most people manage, I guess."

"Together?"

"No, not together. Separately, and months apart. Gilbert and Charles. They were identically stunning, with grey eyes and full, soft lips."

"You know, I'm a twin."

"What? You never told me that."

"It was a mistake, really. One of those monstrous jokes nature can play."

"I don't know what you're talking about."

"The doctor had me come into the hospital for outpatient surgery, to have this cyst removed from my thigh. No big deal, right? They kept me awake the whole time. Thought they wouldn't let me see them slitting open my thigh. I heard a nurse say, 'Jesus,' and I knew I was doomed. What could go wrong with such a routine operation? My pulse was racing. Sweat ran down the surgeon's temples, and he turned to me and said, 'You're fine. Don't worry. It's just a little . . . bigger that. . . .' I could already feel the sutures being drawn through my flesh as they started closing up the wound.

"When I got to Recovery, I stopped and asked him what that was all about. 'The cyst had hair and baby teeth. It happens. It's called a teratoma.' It would have been my sister or my brother if I hadn't swallowed it up in my mother's womb. I'd been delivered of the embryonic twin I murdered months before my birth."

"That's grotesque."

"Yeah, isn't it? So tell me more about these grey eyes and hot lips."

"God, I still remember the way each of them kissed. I didn't even have the chance to ask Charles if the two of them had ever fooled around as boys before he dramatically announced how offended he was by the prurient curiosity of every gay man he'd ever met. He even dared to ask about *my* own brother, if the two of us had ever fooled around. You've met Stanley. God, can you imagine? Of course, I objected. 'That's completely different,' I said. 'We're not twins. We're not identical. We're not even close.' He let my revulsion settle in, then he said, conclusively, 'No, it's just the same.'

"I don't think it's the same, at all. Imagine being that good-looking, gay, fourteen, and sharing twin beds in some overheated attic room. You hear him tossing on sweaty sheets just four feet away. You know exactly how he'd smell, the sounds he'd make, how well your parts would mesh. Don't try to tell me that it wouldn't cross your mind."

"You know, you do look a little bit like your brother Stanley."

"I do not."

"Trust me."

"We're not talking about Stanley."

"Does he like boys or girls?"

"As near as I can tell, he doesn't like either. But who cares about my brother? It's kind of hot in here, isn't it? Do you mind if I take off a blanket. Aren't you warm?

"The scrub nurse could tell I was intrigued. About the cyst. The teratoma. She was the one who suggested I take it home. 'If you don't ask for it,' she said, 'someone else will.' I guess there's some sort of black market for O.R. offal. I consented, just to keep it off the street, but then I immediately began worrying about what I'd do with it. I imagined my bathroom mirror sliding open on this demonic little kewpie doll floating in formaldehyde between my aspirin and vitamins, and some guest screaming in the middle of the night, 'What on earth? I've never seen anything so . . .you know, I think it looks a little bit like you.'"

"What did you do with it?"

"I threw it out with the garbage without even looking at it."

"Jesus."

"Yeah."

"It was a few months later, after Charles left, that I learned the truth from Gilbert. As boys, the two of them had indeed played games in bed, and in the shower, in the back of the family station wagon, and on Boy Scout camping trips, from the age of eight until they starting dating other men at university. He said at first it drove him mad to think of someone else attending Charlie's needs, someone else's lips exploring Charlie's thighs. In fact he asked me what Charlie and I had done together, and insisted that I do the same things with him.

"Of course I pretended I was outraged by Gilbert's invasion of my privacy, but you can imagine how excited I was being caught between two twins. Figuratively. Okay, I admit it, I wondered what it might be like to be caught between them, literally. Gilbert and Charles were both beautiful, but they weren't at all the same. That would have been something.

"I know. I know exactly what you're thinking. But what difference does it make that neither one of them was really making love to me? No one ever really goes to bed alone."

LAWRENCE SCHIMEL

Cruising the Clinic

I hadn't expected to be cruising the STD clinic, but then I'd never really thought much about the place before I arrived. I mean, I always practice safer sex—or at least, I thought I did—and didn't think I'd ever need to go to one of these places, although I knew they existed. But I was too embarrassed to go to my regular doctor and show him the painful red spots on my dick that had shown up just before the weekend—ruining any chance of my going out and getting laid! So before work Monday morning I'd called the hotline in the phone book and gotten the address to come here instead.

Evidently, I wasn't the only fag who'd had the same idea, although there were plenty of straights, both men and women, waiting, too. I half-expected to see someone I knew from my gym (David Barton) and was relieved to be spared that humiliation. I imagined that each of us had spent the weekend painfully examining our dicks and ruing the days or hours until the clinic opened—not to mention losing a prime summer weekend. I wondered if any of them had shares out on Fire Island, and thought how angry they must be to have had to stay celibate during their expensive weekend instead of slutting around in the dunes and after tea dance.

At least, I hoped they'd all stayed celibate, since they were in here to get treated for some STD, but obviously some people didn't feel that moral obligation, which is why I was in here a week after going to the West Side Club sauna and playing with a few guys. Everyone I'd had sex with had looked clean—it's not as if they'd had sores on their dicks the way I do now. But then, as I had just read in the pamphlets in both English and Spanish that littered the waiting room, with some STDs that means nothing. Even getting sucked off by someone wasn't safe. Or might not be, depending.

I wondered which of the guys around me had just caught something over the weekend, and what unsafe things they'd done to catch whatever they had. . . .

In a chair two rows ahead of me was a guy in a tanktop and beige shorts. He was short, overbuilt, and covered with curly black hair. I thought he looked like the kind who liked sex messy. The kind who, if he's fucking you and pulls out to change positions and there's shit on the condom and it gets on his sheets, just shrugs and says, "Shit happens." The kind who sweats a lot when he gets excited, and likes the smell of sweat. He likes to lick your armpit, especially if you're ticklish and it makes you squirm. The kind who uses a lot of lube, who wants you to rub your cum into the thatch of hair on his chest as you're lying together in an exhausted heap after sex.

I wondered what he had. I imagined him being the sort to rim someone without thinking twice about it.

He wasn't at all my type. I couldn't really imagine having sex with him, although he looked like the kind of guy who was always ready and willing, like a rutting goat. He certainly kept giving me the eye, as if he expected we could both step into one of the examining rooms and get it on, never mind the problems that had brought us here.

More my speed was the guy sitting to my right, a preppy-looking blond who was defined—his bicep filled out the cuff of his baby blue polo shirt sleeves to good advantage—but still slender. He had one of those smiles that could stop you on the street. I couldn't see it, but I hoped he had a cute round butt. He was the kind of boy you could bring home to your parents, who would bring you a long-stemmed rose on your second date, but even though he liked to go out for romantic dinners, wasn't the type to insist on getting-to-know-you before having sex. I imagined him lying on his parents' bed at their summer house where we were for the weekend. He's naked and on his back, and I'm holding his legs apart, giving me a view of his beautiful butt and his pink asshole that I'm about to plunge my condom-sheathed dick into. . . .

I almost laughed aloud, because it was so ridiculous—even in my fantasies, I practiced safer sex! It was so unjust that I needed to be here. I hated that sex was such a crapshoot these days, that it could be so dangerous. My dick was hard in my pants from my fantasies. This made the sores hurt worse as the scabs cracked. I wished that I'd been born a few generations earlier, to have lived in the halcyon days of the seventies, free to be as much of a sex pig as I wanted without fear.

The young Latino doctor came in and everyone looked up. He was definitely my type—I would've gladly dropped my pants for him, I thought, and then realized that I might be doing just that soon. He called a number. Short and fuzzy stood up and followed him away.

When I looked back, the young preppy was watching me, and I smiled. He smiled back. I wondered if I could exchange phone numbers, but then imagined calling and explaining where we'd met. . . . It seemed doomed from the start. Although if we had both caught the same thing, that would make life easier. . . . But what would we tell people? I know couples who met at the bathhouse, but this involved disclosing too much information. . . .

Nonetheless, I took one of the herpes pamphlets (since I was pretty sure that's what I had) and wrote, "You're cute. Call me—in a few weeks," along with my name and phone number, and when the tall black woman called my number, I dropped the pamphlet in his lap, and was rewarded with one of his heart-stopping smiles.

DAMIEN BARLOW

The Skin Kisser

His office is definitely perfumed. I'm not sure if it's just something aromatic in the air, or more insidiously, a sweet-smelling anaesthetic. The ghoulish decor of his walls is even more unsettling. Everywhere you look, there is a layer of former patients' skin—numerous framed photos of disconnected body parts, which from a distance create a monstrous fleshy collage.

I stare closer at his richly textured walls. Some photos are limbless or lack a head, others focus more minutely on cracked lips and oozing sores eating away at ears and noses. The skin is always freckled with moles or skin cancers or terminal melanomas. There are also unusual hues of brown and black—bubbly skin, scar red.

The doctor sits calmly at his desk. The cool ducted air keeps everything moderate and controlled. Laid out in front of him are more photos, each with a small white tag in the corner with date, client, and file number. The only photo in his office which does not double as a diagnostic aid is the one of his wife and kids. They inhabit an acknowledged yet unimportant niche on his desk.

"Well then," the doctor begins in hushed tones.

"You understand that when we are concerned with possible skin cancers or melanomas, it is essential to use a high index of suspicion when conducting physical examinations. I'll also need to take some photos for future reference."

His voice is soothing, even disarming, as he tells me to take off my clothes. The camera hangs behind him like a large vacant eye.

I start to undress. The doctor puts the camera around his neck and disappears into a small adjacent room. I am momentarily alone in his gallery of skin, and suddenly realize that the majority of these people are probably now dead, or at the very least horribly disfigured. He returns and tells me to lie face down on the bed. I taste disposable paper towel, abrasive and functional, against my mouth. I can also smell his hands, which overwhelmingly reek of photographic developing fluid. The doctor turns on a movable light that starts to heat up my back. He does not wear gloves. As his fingers trace and retrace a semicircle just above the cheeks of my arse, the doctor begins talking into a tape recorder, describing my body in a strangely poetic yet clinical fashion:

"On the lower back there is a large constellation of moles, curiously circular, forming an uneven curve. However it is also a nebulous configuration, blurring with the surrounding skin. Speckles of red-brown melanin give the overall design a cute blush."

I feel the slight pressure of his wrist on my arse, then a cold steel watchband, which by the time it leaves is flesh warm. Intrusive flashes come next, erratic clicking from behind. I start to feel self-conscious, exposed. The light is switched off.

"You can get dressed now," says the doctor.

I fumble with my clothes, successfully hiding my erection, as he writes out a reminder card for my next appointment.

"Two weeks, okay? I'll show you the photos then. Bye now."

I think his smile looks almost affectionate as the doctor again disappears into the small photographic room.

Melbourne is cast in a thick midweek smog, the type that makes your lungs tighten and sees the sunsets turn a rich fluoro red. Even the tram seems to wheeze its way through the city, past the Victorian grandeur of Collins Street with its gold-boom facades announcing the entrances to sleek multinationals. His nameplate is polished and proud, too, though it doesn't shine, as the fierce Australian sun barely reaches street-level here. For some unknown reason, his receptionist makes me fill out another form declaring my high-risk, potentially disease-carrying status. She doesn't appreciate my lack of cooperation and tells me it is a necessary legal requirement. I eventually tick the box and read a copy of *Who Weekly*.

His office retains its unsettling ambience. The pastiche of flesh on his wall seems to have changed shape and colour since my last visit, but one cannot be sure. The doctor doesn't notice me standing there and looks slightly irritated when I interrupt his absorbing study. His demeanor softens when he recognizes who I am, and enthusiastically greets me with a photo of the curved moles that reside on my lower back. The crack of my arse is also just in shot. I ask if it's cancerous. The doctor shakes his head.

"No, I don't think so. I believe they are just some unusual mole formation. But of course, we must keep a close eye on them."

I cautiously start to undress, acutely aware of my semi-erect cock. I leave my boxer shorts on and concentrate instead on the sick skin that adorns his walls. I think about death, or less dramatically, having his expensive hands make large excisions in my flesh. I imagine biopsies, skin grafts, and the egos of those who practice plastic surgery. Yet my cock still grows as he begins to stroke my back. I can feel his breath tickling my skin, and for a second, I sense the slight graze of chin whiskers. I hear him speak as if to himself, or perhaps someone else. He whispers, "Looks like the top of a lip." The doctor kisses my intriguing moles, sucking my skin. A bruising flush of blood appears. He momentarily stops, and talks to my moles as if to a lover. "Beautiful," he mumbles affectionately.

CHRISTOPHER PAW

Keeping Up Appearances

Justin got the phone call at nine as the sun was setting over the high-rise-infested skyline.

"I' ll pick you up in forty minutes," the husky voice at the other end told him. "Same scenario. You know what to do." The same voice rang once or twice every month. For the same reason.

Justin hung up and immediately filled the tub. Forty minutes wasn't long. He'd have to rush. In ten minutes, he was submerged in the scalding tub. His pores opened and relaxed with the onslaught of steaming water. Five minutes into the ritual, he rose from its depths, sat on the porcelain edge, and liberally applied half a dispenser of shaving foam to his moderately hirsute torso. He only had a small triangle of chest fur that ran from nipple to nipple and converged into a thin highway of hair from his stomach to his crotch. But it was too much for this event. So he reached for his razor.

Thirty minutes left.

The razor glided effortlessly over his chest. No nicks around his nipples. His underarms shed their protective fur without resistance. It took him ten more minutes to completely eradicate the unwanted follicles from his torso. Smooth as a baby's bottom, Justin drained some water from the tub and foamed up his crotch.

Twenty minutes left.

He was so practiced at shaving his groin that he was surprised with the deftness he demonstrated. The entire area, including his asscrack, only took five minutes to scrape clean.

Fifteen minutes left.

His legs, the least accustomed to the razor's edge, were always the problem. Justin nicked the skin, but pressed for time, he couldn't afford the luxury of a careful shave. His calves and kneecaps curved in ways that made it impossible to run a razor smoothly over them. He didn' t know how women did it. By the time he was done, tiny droplets of blood dribbled from no less than six nicks on his now hairless limbs. He still had his face. Although he' d shaved that morning, he would need to do it again. It only took a few quick strokes to remove the unwanted stubble from his visage.

Justin had dried himself and was applying the prerequisite baby powder when the caller rang his doorbell and handed him the knapsack containing his costume. Justin didn't notice his driver's lusty stare as he donned the required outfit and wrapped the trenchcoat around himself.

"Let's go."

They drove in silence to the hotel. Outside the entrance, the husky voice spoke again, "Room 605. I'll be back in an hour."

Justin nodded.

Three minutes later, Justin was at the hotel room door. He did a last minute check of the hallway, took off his trenchcoat, folded it and placed it in the carryall bag used only for this occasion, then tapped on the door.

Justin knew the man on the other side waited thirty seconds before he answered the knock. At exactly thirty seconds, the door opened. Justin was lying on the floor.

"Oh, aren't you the cutest little one?" The man gushed as he bent over and tickled Justin's chin. Justin giggled, tittered and drooled.

"It's too cold out here for you, little guy." The burly six-footer cooed, squatted down, and without effort picked up Justin and the bag in one swoop. Through the door they went into the room.

Carefully placing him on the bed, the man tickled Justin again.

Justin gurgled and stuck his thumb in his mouth.

"There's Daddy's little boy. Does uggum wuggums need his diaper changed?"

Taking the cue, Justin urinated in the Attends he had initially donned back at his apartment. It wouldn't do to disappoint the client. When the John lifted Justin's legs and removed the diaper to find the mess, he gushed his approval.

"Oh, baby did make a messy," he said, and proceeded to change Justin's diaper; wipe down, baby powder, and diaper rash cream all included. Justin grimaced knowing the cream would clog his pores resulting in ingrown ass-hairs. The client furrowed his brow at Justin's expression of discontent. "Baby doesn't like that?" He cooed and continued applying the lotion.

The next forty-five minutes were spent with the John feeding, rocking, singing to, tickling, and shoving stuffed animals in Justin's face. Justin cried, drooled, pissed, shit, smiled, and giggled on command.

When his hour was over, the man lifted Justin from the bed and carried him toward the door. Placing him, freshly diapered, fed, and bathed, on the hotel hallway floor, the john reached into his pocket and removed three crisp American one-hundred-dollar bills. Folding them once, he placed them in the pocket of the carry all and closed the door.

Justin jumped up, dug out the trenchcoat, and put it on. In the hotel lobby he met his employer, who was on time as promised.

"Weird one, isn't he?" he commented to Justin as they made their way back to Justin's apartment, once again sneaking a peek at Justin's diaper-clad crotch.

Justin grunted his response, handing over two of the bills. Sure, he knew the guy was a pedophile. Still, Justin believed the guy had found a healthy outlet for his desires. He knew the guy jerked off maniacally for an hour after he left. But wasn't that better than hanging out in playgrounds? Besides, the john was his best and most lucrative client. Justin had a fourth crisp C-note lodged in his fresh diaper to prove it.

J E F F   K I R B Y

Good Boy

I'm a tall guy, just over six-foot-three, green eyes, sandy-brown hair, shaved on the sides and back with tight curls on the top. I have long features, long face and neck, kind of a longish nose. Most of my height's in the upper half of my body. My torso is lean, smooth, just a bit of hair around my nipples and a trail down by my navel. My shoe size is thirteen. I have big, thick athletic feet. Yeah. Well-defined calves and thighs. I swim. I cycle a lot. I'm a grad student, twenty-five. I'm proud of my body, man. I'm especially proud of my dick. My dick is big. How big? It's huge. My father gave it to me. I haven't actually measured it, but I can take and hold this thing in both my hands and there's a good inch and a half before you get to the head. Yeah, real thick. I love showing it off. I love putting on a cock show. In my briefs, my jock, my Speedos, cycling shorts. My cock and body demand a lot of attention. I like to be serviced for a long time. Take time, instruct a guy exactly how to handle my meat. You up for it? Good boy.

Lay down on the floor. I'll stand right over you, my feet on either side of your face. Yeah, look up at me. Good boy. Right now all I'm wearing is a grey athletic shirt, white cotton briefs, and a pair of white sweat socks. Yeah, you like that? What's your name, boy?

Chris, you want to be my boy, don't you? I don't want your eyes to leave my crotch, you got that? Good boy.

Stroke my calves for me, boy. Feel how fuckin' thick they are. Kiss 'em for me, yeah. Do me a favour, boy. Take your hands and make 'em into fists and just pound on the sides of my calves for me. Yeah, go ahead. Yeah, feel how fuckin' rock hard they are. Fuck, man, that's nice. Yeah, you like that, Chris? Good boy.

All the time you're doing that, I'm gonna take my fingertips and just trace the outline of my big dick for you, right through my briefs. Yeah, look at that fucker tent the front of my briefs, boy. I love the look on a guy or chick's face when they first see my dick. See your eyes go fucking wide. Yeah, beg me for my meat. Yeah, you want this, don't you? Don't you? How would it be if I kneel down and bring this thing a little closer? Yeah just kneel down close enough so you can take a big whiff.

Good boy.

Show me your tongue. That's a good boy. See the power of my dick. You want it? Look at it, so fucking beautiful. Yeah, look at it twitch. I'm gonna take and shove this into every orifice of your fucking body, boy. Open your mouth. Keep it open. Keep it open. Feel the heat of my cock enter your mouth. I don't want you to touch it. You got that? Keep your mouth open. That's a good boy. Yeah, just breathe in and out onto my cock. Breathe in my dick. Don't close your lips until I tell you. Fuck, I love hearing you whimper over my cock, boy. Yeah, love to make you fucking hungry. Make you cry. Yeah! What did you say? Don't touch it! Not until I tell you. Oh, man, look at how fucking rock hard I am. Yeah, look at that drop just hangin' there. You want that? You wanna taste it? Watch me take and rub that all over the head of my dick. Get it nice and wet for you.

Open your mouth. Suck my fingers. Taste me, boy. Yeah, suck those fingers while I stroke my meat in your face. That's a good boy. Show me what that mouth of yours is made for. Take and paint your lips with the head of my dick. Pout your lips for me, yeah. There you go. Yeah. Worship my dick. Feel it throb right up against your lips. Want to touch it? Want to hold it, boy? Yeah, squeeze it man. Fuck, yes, it's a fucking dick of steel, boy, you can't hurt it. I'm just gonna wrap my big hand 'round yours. Show you how I like to stroke myself. Feel my grip boy? Feel the power of my cock? Yeah, nice and slow. Yeah, nice, long, slow strokes. Yeah, kiss it, boy. Kiss my cock. Good boy. Yeah, sniff it, boy. Yeah, smell my balls. Lay down. On your back man. I'm going to kneel down right over your face. Let my dick hang right over you, boy. Look up at me. I love seeing how much of my cock and balls cover your face. . . .

Click . . .*bzzzzzzzzz.*

FUCK!

Yeah, I'm a tall guy, just over six-foot-three, green eyes, sandy-brown hair, shaved on the sides. . . .

SIMON SHEPPARD

Only the Lonely

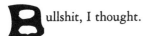ullshit, I thought.

But at three a.m., in a hotel room on the top floor of the St. Francis, you don't say "Bullshit" out loud. Not to a great-looking young guy standing a foot away, naked and near-erect. Anyway, I didn't.

When he and I had made contact in an online chat room, it'd already been one-thirty. We traded pics; his GIF, a shot of him naked, impeccable, made me drool. He had it all: the underdeveloped body, shaggy hair, and vacantly surly expression of the current year's Calvin Klein models. Too good for me.

"Come on over and let's fuck," his Instant Message read. "You can even stay the night if you want, since it's late." The whole thing seemed pretty improbable. *But hell, he's already seen my picture*, I thought, *what really is there left to lose?* So I hopped on my Kawasaki and sped through the near-dead streets of after-hours San Francisco.

I love tricking with strangers in hotels. Striding through the lobby, finding the elevator, pressing the button, rising toward some new adventure, finding the door with right number—it's the coolest thing.

In person he was as gorgeous as his picture, only more so. But he also seemed surprisingly unassuming and sweet, if it's possible for such a pretty man to pass for unassuming. He was wearing sweatpants, no shirt. We made out, tentatively. His sweats started tenting in the front. Gratifying, but even so, I knew I was out of my league. *What the hell am I doing here?* I wondered. Which didn't stop me from peeling down his pants.

His dick was as big as it had looked in the picture, one of those rare online eight-inchers that turn out to be a perfect eight for real. I sucked it. It tasted slippery and sweet. Then he returned the favour, wrapping his beautiful face around my hard-on. I asked politely if I could play with his ass. He got down on all fours on the hotel bed like a bitch, my bitch. I lubed up my gloved fingers and started to work his hole.

I had three, maybe four fingers up inside him when he suddenly said, "I don't think this is gonna work."

"What, playing with your butt?"

"No, you. This. I know just what I'm looking for, and sorry, you're not it. This isn't gonna work."

You have a fucking hard-on, I thought, but didn't say it. Sometimes I'm too polite for my own good.

I was pulling on my jeans when he told me—he was a model, not a whore-type model, but a runway model, legit, successful, in town for a convention. It was easy to believe.

I was pulling on my socks when he asked me my age. "Fifty is a great age," he said. *Tell me that in twenty years,* I thought. Sitting on his bed, I was looking straight at his nicely-trimmed crotch, his perfect dick still semi-hard.

I was pulling on my leather jacket when he said it: "You may not believe this, but pretty people are the loneliest people in the world."

Bullshit, I thought. I knew what he meant, maybe, and he was being nice enough, almost apologetic, but I suddenly got the urge to punch him in his skinny gut. Or to scream out, "What do you want me to do, drop to my knees, slice open my belly, and spill my guts on this expensively carpeted floor? Tomorrow, while you're modeling overpriced clothes for a roomful of out-of-town dentists, *I'll* be semi-desperately hunting for another trick." But I didn't.

"I'm really sorry, I'll pay for your parking and gas," he said, grabbing his wallet. Eelskin, no doubt.

I told him I'd only spent fifty cents, parking for ten hours in a motorcycle space, but took the proffered five-dollar bill, anyway; not just a whore, but a cheap whore. It was the first time anyone had ever paid me for sex, and it hadn't even been sex, not really. I was being paid because I wasn't pretty enough, just not pretty enough, and could be sent away by someone who was. I wondered if he'd ever really listened to anybody who was homely and fat, asked them how lonely they were.

Even so, he is *beautiful*, I thought, jockeying for time so I could look at him some more. But by now I was fully dressed and he, still naked, was gently but firmly urging me toward the door.

I had to piss first. The bathroom was spotless. After I washed my hands, I stole the little bottle of hotel shampoo.

"Thanks," he said at the door. "Sorry. Goodnight."

Half past three in the morning. The lobby of the St. Francis was empty, except for some homely, fat guy buffing the floor. I walked out into the night, thinking about loneliness, damnation, and a beautiful eight-inch dick. I figured when I got back to my place I'd boot up the computer, open the guy's picture, and jack myself off to sleep. The cold was making me shiver. I put my hands in my pockets. Five bucks. I headed for home.

M . V . S M I T H

The Bridge

The traffic over Burrard Street is heavy. A siren—ambulance or police—screams past and bleeds into the street noise. I'm sitting on the steps to the bridge, leaning against the cold cement wall with a line of shadow across me. It's about 2:30 in the morning.

I've been debating going home to bed or taking another tour through the little park around the stairs. My bed is warmer, but not as close. This stalemate keeps me long enough to hear your footsteps dropping down the steps behind me. I wait.

As you pass, your ass moves by my face, then your back, your shoulders, all come into view with each step away.

I'm not headed home.

I give myself a few moments then trot after you.

I come around the corner facing the park and can't see anyone around. Along the dirty concrete wall there's a trail which runs twenty or so feet, with a line of bushes before the parking lot. You step through the cover there, having gone full circle, and head my way down the path, so I lean against the wall and wait.

I like your boots, and the look on your face—a little off-guard, when you notice me. I figure I've got it made, but right away you stop. You stare into the cluster of shrubs. I take a few slow steps closer to see what I'm missing. A broad boy, faded blue jeans, colourful jersey, white t-shirt underneath, can't be more than twenty, is kneeling down in the dirt with his hands thrust awkwardly in his pockets.

My heart pounds a little harder and thumps in my eardrums. I want to fuck you, watching him, watching me.

You look up at me, so I take a deliberate step closer. You wait a second, look at the boy in the bush, look at me, at the boy, and then approach him. I'll forgive you.

The kid doesn't move. He doesn't say anything, he doesn't look away, he doesn't take his hands out of his pockets. You pull out your cock. He looks at it, and opens his mouth. You step into him.

Grabbing behind his head with one hand, you use the other to pull his jaw wider. You rub your cock back and forth against his teeth. I imagine you like the roughness, and toying with him. You slap your dick across his face and make him blink. Then you tap him on the shoulder, and motion upwards. As he stands, I catch the profile of his cock pushing against his denim. You step around him and undo his belt, then boom, his pants drop, button and zipper undone already. His cock bounces up half-way at attention. You slap him on the ass, and look over.

That's my cue. I approach the two of you. I smell beer; the boy's drunk, and breathing slow and heavy. He gives me a stupid grin.

You drop to your knees and lick between his legs.

I slide my palm under his ball sac and feel your tongue on my knuckles. I lift his balls in my hand and move my fingers like I were tickling underneath his chin, just my fingertips rubbing lightly through the hair, and across his skin.

His mouth is open. I can see his tongue. I lean closer to him, saying, "You want to kiss me, don't you?" and watch his Adam's apple jump. I think he's a straight boy, reconsidering. His ass muscles tighten around your tongue.

With my hand behind his head, I step back and pull him forward. His hands go to my hips. They're warm, like his tongue on my balls tracing a fast wet line around them.

"You're salty," he says, and you lick a long hard finger inside his ass to stop him from talking. He pulls in air and tenses up.

You're smiling at me, you bugger, turning a hand at the wrist, and sliding in a second finger. Your left hand's on your cock.

Seeing you play with his hole, the sound like warm Jell-O, I want to fuck him. I slide my cock in his mouth and push his face down on me, imagining his ass in front of me. Smooth, round, the muscles contracting around your hand, I don't know how you resist shoving your own cock in there.

Then, in sync, you focus on the guy's knotted hole, with your cock squeezed thick in your other hand. A trail of wet light runs from the tip of your head to the pucker of his ass. He's a centimetre away, then you're touching him, and you push harder from the hips and slip in. Two inches.

He's stopped sucking to make a low moan that vibrates down my shaft. We're all waiting the few seconds until he relaxes. The smell of pine needles infuses our sweat. Cool air scuttles past, tingling the hair on our legs as it goes.

Our temporary boyfriend spreads his legs further apart and nods his head so you know it's safe to push in, slowly. I wish I were you. I wish I could see him stretching around your cock or feel him swallowing you. I wish I had him by the hips. I wish I were buried to my pubes.

I'm slamming the back of his throat so I grab his hair and yank it back. "Swallow," I say and push harder, popping down his esophagus. His face is red and his stretched throat spasms as he tries not to choke. I got this rhythm going down his throat, and there you are on his other end, plowing into him, your balls swinging against him.

My eyes close involuntarily. The guy is tight and hot; his tongue is sliding back and forth against my shaft. My balls roll over and pull themselves up, they tighten like a spring ready to release, they tighten up good and hard and *bang*, I'm coming down his throat in a big shot of semen, and *bang* I come at the fucking look of you, and bang I come again.

My cock is thumping against his throat, his breathing heavy and laboured, and his body shaking with the effort of beating his meat, your face all screwed up and loose at the same time so I know you're done too.

I pull out, and his tongue looks for me to shove back in. You yank your wet dick into the open air and step back. The guy's not finished, he still hasn't come. He drops to his knees hoping either you or I will fill his face again but we do ourselves up.

I walk out of the park, up the stairs towards the lamp-lit streets, with the sun crawling over the mountains and my body already cold from the sweat of climax evaporating off my skin. You're two steps behind me, but head in the other direction when we reach the top, not looking back. I don't know your name. I look at my hands and wonder why I didn't think to reach out and touch you. We've just had sex and I don't know what you feel like, taste like. You're a body I've never had. This is how I think of you now that you're gone. This is what it means to want you.

OTTO

Nuding

It's hot. My apartment is like an oven. Naturally, I'm naked. I'm always naked whenever I can. At home, in my car, in the woods, sometimes even in the streets. Late at night. When nobody's around. Almost nobody.

I'm a thirty-six-year-old, good-looking man who has to get, has to be, naked every chance. Blond hair, smooth, lean body—like a boy's, five-eleven, and seven hard inches that's just gotta get out and feel the air. Tonight I have plans. Serious nuding plans. As I move around the place I go over them in my head. Adrenaline pounds through my body as I plan. Sex adrenaline. You know the rush. I vow to be outside naked tonight as much as possible or until I'm satisfied—as if I ever could. . . .

I'm going nuding on Mount Royal.

I drive naked through the city streets, stopping at red lights and all, windows open. I don't care who sees me. I want them to.

I park the car on the edge of the mountain. I jump out the passenger side and leap into the woods and pick my way through the black forest along a trail I can hardly see. Hot, humid air coats my sweet-smelling body like a second skin. I caress my chest and shaved balls, all sticky from sweat. I have to cross the brightly lit road that climbs up and over the mountain. My heart races as I fly in front of an approaching tour bus. Once safely in the woods on the other side, I glance back at the bus. "Peter Pan" is written on the side. That's me, I think, as I scamper up the side of the mountain to where I know there are other boys playing.

I arrive at the cruising area and wander along the maze of paths, looking for playmates. I emerge from the darkness of the woods into a clearing where night stalkers cross to and fro. I stand still for a moment to let the hazy moonlight illuminate my body. I caress my chest again and pull at my swelling dick. Out of the corners of my eyes I watch the men stop and turn as I proudly stroll past them. One whistles faintly, involuntarily, under his breath. Fuck, whispers another in awe. A guy wearing an elastic body strap gropes my cock. I pull gently at his. After a few moments we split—he's not naked enough. Besides, I want more and more men to see me.

I wander up a path, exploring the playing field. The men thin out; one brushes past. Another materializes out of the darkness. As he gets closer I see he's shirtless. Closer. My heart skips a beat: he's not just shirtless, but naked—like me. I stop. His cock and bush float toward me, then his ass as he passes by. I reach out to caress him, one naked man to another. He pulls on my cock, smiles, but keeps on his course. He's after prey he knows is his—the clothed man who just passed me by.

Noiselessly, on the balls of my feet, I step down a gravel lane. A part of the lit-up cross atop the mountain appears through a break in the trees. Soon I discern a form by the side of the lane. A man. I pull on my dick. I approach. He's dark, his shirt is open. Thick hair all over his chest. He runs his hands up and down my sweaty torso and groin. The hot night air hangs heavy in the trees. Men's shoes snapping twigs and crunching on gravel make the only sounds we hear above the dim hush of the city below.

He kneels before me. He needs to worship a naked man. I give him my swollen cock to take in his mouth, like a host. He adores it with his tongue and lips until it's so hard it's ready to burst. But not yet. I leave him yearning but grateful to have touched his tongue against the salty flesh of a god.

No. I have to show my nakedness to more men. My throbbing rhino horn proceeds me down the lane where more dark forms lurk.

Slowly I allow my horn to diminish until it hangs fleshy and heavy in the heat before me, ready for another starving mouth to feed.

Soon a big boy stops. His eyes almost pop out of his head at the sight of a naked man where none are supposed to be. I look back. Now his eyes are pleading. I can tell his hormones are killing him with excitement. I stop. Maybe it's time to release the store of sex that has welled up so ferociously for the last two hours of living my naked fantasies.

I tell him he must strip as naked as me. He complies and commences his worship. We play for awhile, stroking and exploring, sucking, as others pass and look. Eventually he wants me to master him, to fuck him. But a condom is clothing, and clothing I don't have. Not even a ring. I gotta be completely naked in order to come.

I fake-fuck him, plowing my dick between his legs just beneath his balls. Pounding my groin against his big ass. I come. He doesn't. His cock is shy. But he doesn't care. He asks me where my clothes are. I smile and head back through the black, hot forest to my car.

Gotta get gas. From a gas station where the cashier is male. So he can see my dick hanging down my shorts. . . .

J I M   V E N T U R A

The Park

Two-twenty a.m.

Clubs closed.

Scuff, scuff, sneakers on sidewalk.

The walk back home alone.

Hands in jeans pockets. T-shirt allowing in the warm night breeze.

Dark. Pitch . . .oozing on the sleeping city. Breeze lisps through shadowed trees, leaves rustling, through the park.

"Uhh . . . yeah . . . ohh . . ."

From the park.

He stops and listens.

". . . uhh . . . yeah . . . ohh . . ."

Someone got lucky. In the park. In the darkness. He steps off the concrete. One-two . . . Onto the grass. Along the edge of the pitch. Past silhouettes of trunks, his sneakers muffled in the grass.

Shfff, shfff. . . .

Scuff-scuff. . . . Back on the concrete.

Coward.

No more sounds. No more "uhh," or "yeah," or "ohh."

177

Watch it. He stumbles.

Unsteady. Vision unclear. Five beers?

Thicker, the trees; their crowns so full; and more whisperings of windy secrets.

Step, step—stop.

. . . .

Squint.

Light. He blinks. A solitary light. Shiny bright, embedded in that pitch, clearly in view. But off the path home. Off the sidewalk. Across the grass. Deeper into the park.

Don't leave the path, don't!

Scuff-scuff, shfff, shfff . . . muffled steps. Back on the grass. Off the path. To the light. (A signal?) The solitary light. Closer, he moves. Into the shadowed park. Blink . . . blink . . . the light winks and goes, winks and goes.

Listen.

Water. Faintly gurgling. Bubble, bubble. Louder. Closer. Vision adjusts to the dark. He squints. A stone cherub of naked spouting! Misty-mouthed fountain spray. Surrounded by a low cement wall. The pool of water spreads like tar, holds high the innocent babe, capturing the spew of shooting liquid.

Shfff, shfff, onward then, to the blinking light, near the spurting spray. A clearing in the trees. Deep in the park. He blinks. Pieces of moonlight seek spots, through shifting leaves, to shoot beams, white jets. Shoot ... a beam there. Gone. Shfff, shfff, closer. Shoot . . . shoot two more beams. Spots of light welcomed by dark places. Gone.

Almost there. The stone baby bubbles forth, spews loudly bolts of liquid, arcs splashing out and down, into the black pool.

The light, so bright, that lonely light. Blink. Blink.

There. At last. He is there. Wobbly-kneed, dry-mouthed. How many beers?

The light beams.

"Curiosity killed the cat, killed the cat . . ."

Squinting at the light, the little light. So shiny, like—

". . . killed the cat . . ."

. . . metal, like steel. And long . . . sleek . . . about the size of a . . .

What if his parents knew . . .

Ruler, an eight-inch ruler, behind the fountain—

. . . so late, in the park; so dark, in the night?

. . . behind the fountain, almost peeking from behind the naked cherub, reflecting the moonlight. Flash. Reflect. Flash.

Something stirs him; he feels himself aroused . . . excited . . . part of something long only imagined. . . .

"You naughty boy, you naughty . . ."

That silver light, that steel phallus in the dark . . . Blinking, like neon. Calling him.

". . . boy . . ."

Gurgle, bubble. Another sound?

Look around!

Rustle, Rising. Someone there behind the—where?—fountain. There! A silhouette.

Excitement. Desire. At last.

Bristle. Twitch. Something's wrong.

A hand aloft.

Run.

In that hand . . . the light.

Run!

Sharp, shiny. Reflecting. Not blinking now.

Run, run.

It seeks what it's lured.

"Who knows what evil . . ."

He turns. Muffle, muffle on the grass.

Run!

Turn, stumble, scuff-scuff back onto the pavement, scuff, stumble, scuff.

Get out of the park, get out!

Scuff-scuff, scuff-scuff.

Pant. Gasp. Hair in his eyes as he runs.

". . . *lurks in the* . . ."

Breeze cold on his sweat-covered t-shirt. Muscles taut. Blood pumping.

Look ahead, a head! A . . .

". . . *hearts of men* . . ."

. . . head. On a blue uniform . . .

". . . *of men* . . ."

. . . with a light. But different.

"*. . . Only the shadow . . .*"

So different—

Away from the shadow now.

—geometrical—

Back to the road. To the other light.

A good light.

Brighter. Closer. A star of moonlight.

A silver badge.

Away from the shadow, away from the cherub's sickly regurgitation.

"Help me."

Into the arms of the blue man.

"Hold me."

Naughty boy . . .

The light . . . the badge . . . the masculine scent of the blue shirt. And safe at last.

Sob. Muffled. Tears.

"Ofcr . . . Officr . . . Officer."

. . . you naughty . . .

Safe. Safe.

"It's okay, now. You're okay, kid."

Safe.

"Why do you boys keep going into the park so late at night?"

. . . boy . . .

"What are you, eighteen, nineteen? What if your parents knew . . . ?"

Safe.

"Get in the car, then." The police car. Hidden in the shadow. Hidden in the trees. The policeman sighs.

The doors close.

What if your parents knew?

"You don't have to go in there. Why do you do it?"

Naughty . . .

Breath, breath, face pressed against the strong blue chest.

"Come here, then. I'll protect you."

. . . boy . . .

Arms around him. Safe.

"You're safe now."

Powerful scent, against the strong warm skin, past the open blue shirt.

"Much safer, eh?—than that park."

Rustling, reaching . . . safe.

"There you go. Better? Feel better?"

Pulse rising, hands moving, skin grazing . . . at last . . .

"Go ahead. It's okay."

Older . . . wiser . . . stronger . . .

"'S that okay? You okay, kid?" Whispered.

Rough, against his young cheek. Muscles taut.

"You're fine, just fine, aren't you now, aren't you . . ."

Bodies rising, breaths quicker now . . . huh, huh . . . in counterpoint.

"Yeah, that's it, yeah, good boy . . . "

Beautiful building pressure, pounding heart oh my god the adrenaline oh my g—

You . . .

"Uhh . . . yeah . . . ohhhh . . ."

. . . *naughty boy, you* . . . " . . . ohhhh . . ." . . . *naughty boy.*

RON   SURESHA

Rubber Soul

Todd pedalled slowly through the park. The slanting early morning sunlight warmed the snug bulge in his Spandex biking shorts. His eyes scanned the bike path from side to side as he rode. He scouted for a flash of flaccid rubber, a slip of latex laying by the lawn. In this area, mostly at night, men often would stroll and troll for sex.

But Todd sought neither flesh nor fluid, not the actual meat of contact or the juice of its eventual release. His appetite that morning, as it had been most mornings for the previous so many years, was only to discover the mere leftovers of love, the scanty evidence of those random contacts. Todd's mission was to sight used condoms.

Most mornings he biked along the cruisy areas where he had himself once pursued the real thing, years back when something as insubstantial as someone's name, even his own, didn't matter. What had counted was connecting. But now it was not for him to contact anything, he thought as he crouched on his bike seat, looking down at the ground as if from a great height, backpedalling past a set of weather-beaten benches. He hovered over his bike seat, surveying the grounds with an idle gut-ache, like a wild game hunter apprehensive of coming face to face with the beast. Now it was just enough to have this coy game of hide-and-seek-the-Sheik.

He would usually spot his targets just outside the bushes where he presumed they'd been used. Thanks to the less lazy park sex players, used Trojans were often found in and around garbage bins. But they could turn up anywhere, and the odder the setting, the wilder the scenario Todd's mind would spin out about what had actually transpired: the black "Tuxedo" rubber bunched up with a pair of silk stockings; the lone red one hanging from a tree branch; two of the textured kind unrolled together over the top of a Pepsi bottle.

After years of intense observation of such clues, he became quite adept at reconstructing the scene, like some forensics expert. In particular Todd was fascinated by scrutinizing the way the rubber laid, like a lawn sculpture. Had it been flung from hasty hands? Laid like a love letter at the feet of one's new romance? Or dropped on its own from some just-receding member, perhaps just moments before the coupling went their own indifferent ways?

Today, in spite of a rising sense of desperation, he saw not a single sack o' fun. Not a one, *nada*. Why had it been so slow the night before? At other times during his searches he'd catch as many as a dozen glimpses of rubbery proof of male desire and hardly know where to start. But eventually he'd check out all of them, inspecting each for other signs of its particular encounter: beer bottle, abandoned briefs used to wipe up, empty poppers, ciggy-butts. But today not even a single cast-off rubber wrapper caught his eye. In lieu of real love now such proof provided reasonable substitution, a pseudonym for sex writ small.

In vain Todd searched for some discarded sheath, an abandoned prophylactic, to assure himself that even if he wasn't getting his yayas at least someone else was. All he needed was just to spot one solitary safe, but it was as if the morning rain had somehow washed away all trace of such erotics.

As he pumped his bike up an incline he began to extrapolate an image of who'd used the abandoned rubbers. He often did this when the pickings were slim. If a bag had been unrolled completely, it usually meant there was plenty of cock to fill it. Todd reviewed his mental inventory of used rubbers, now become so commonplace in his mind that it hardly seemed sexual: the materials, textures, colours, positions, residue of body fluids—or solids!—even sometimes.

Whose orifice had it entered and what trace did they leave upon the latex exterior? He imagined how it had been packed, from start to fulfillment of the act—from the initial surge, where the still-wrapped item was fingered inside a pocket as the other approached; the ripping open of the package and careful, but hurried, unrolling, inch by inch over the hardness, just before penetration. He imagined being the rubber itself, being inside it—being deep inside another.

Just as Todd reached the end of this idle autoerotic path of thoughts, he decided to give up his fruitless search. He'd hardly been paying attention to the bike trail ahead of him, though, when his ten-speed's front tire hit a curb, ejecting him open-mouthed over the handlebars onto the grass. He sprawled in a most undignified and embarrassed manner onto the moist green tongue of earth.

Slowly he picked himself up, getting up on all fours, his wet backside warmed by the angled sunlight. With his firm, Spandexed butt propped up in the air, he stopped short. There, right in front of his eyes, was a milky-white object lying shrivelled and shrunken like a snake's forsaken skin, an empty left-over emblem of some furtive lovers' embrace.

DOUG BROWNING

Phantom Orchid

"Wake up." Morgan gusts through the tent flaps, tapping Will's foot as he passes the first sleeping bag, tossing a wet towel onto the other. "I found something."

"I thought you were going swimming?" Will sits up, groping his way into a plaid workshirt.

"That was an hour ago. C'mon. Move."

Will groans to his feet. Morgan slips a reference book from his pack and heads back out, snagging him by the arm. Will stumbles after him, trusting the long shirt tails to manage the same coverage as Morgan's baggy, extra large t-shirt. Branches scratch his legs as he plows through a wall of currant and salmonberry to the forest proper.

It's like being under a dock; sleepy light and rough posts, silence and shadow in a gelatin layer between surging growth above and the more subtle convolution of roots below. Morgan's waiting, waist deep in a hollow about twenty feet ahead. Will picks his way carefully over a mat of forest litter bristling with dead fir needles and sharp twigs. He stops short at the edge of the dip. Morgan doesn't have to point or prompt him with glances.

"What is it?"

"*Cephalanthera austinae,* the phantom orchid." He squats beside the plant, tabling the book on his knees. "It's extremely rare."

Will hunkers down beside him. The stalk's about a foot and a half tall, a spout of liquid alabaster snap frozen as it began to break up and spill outward. The flowers could be tiny albino orcas with goiters, splashes of yellow in the throats, front fins raised in supplication.

"The conditions have to be absolutely right. They've been known to go as long as seventeen years between flowerings."

"We would have been twelve."

But Morgan's gone, wrapped up in the grand, liturgical swell. "Flowers several, subsessile in a terminal, bracteate raceme." He'd been the same way when they first met in grade seven. Only it was fossils back then. Will remembered him spooling of tongue twisting skeins of archaic English, Latin, and Greek with the solemn intensity of old wizard Whateley invoking Yog-Sothoth. "Prominent callosities leading into basal sac; column slender, terete."

There had been no obvious similarity between them then, but Will found that if he pursed his lips hard enough to puff out his cheeks with air and worried his eyebrows to a downward slant he could achieve a secret and exciting resemblance to his friend.

"Leaves reduced to membranous-scarious sheathing bracts."

Morgan's concentration allows Will to openly search his features, reaching for the same conscious empathy, preparing a dye trace from the liquefied emulsion of old photographs and infusing it beneath the skin. Successive stages of development overlap. The round-faced kid who only needed pointed ears to stand in for a garden gnome. The stretched, slimmed-down teenager with the puppy-dog eyes and the smoldering pout of a 16 magazine pin-up. The thickened, squared-off university student, barely contained energy fluttering in his jaw muscles. And Morgan Bruchner, thirty years old, married for five, appropriately softened and rounded again, filament lines around the bridge of his nose, at the corners of his eyes, and bracketing his mouth like external growth rings.

Will clamps his legs together, his erection painfully bent against its natural tilt.

Morgan hoists himself up, tendons snicking in his knees. "Let's get the camera and those foil panels. I think we can reflect enough light from outside to get a picture."

Will totters up, awkwardly hunched. His cock springs out between his shirt tails, bobbing like a suction-tipped arrow stuck to a wall.

"Hey, I'm flattered."

Will can't help grinning—he sounds almost apologetic. It's a familiar response to the odd overt sign of arousal.

Will had told him at the start of their first year of university. But Morgan had known for a long time, the intrinsic undercurrent of Will's fascination evoking an equal but quite different fascination in him. The exact physics of these balancing forces seemed unimportant. It was something in and of them alone, incompatible with the extraneous trivialities of the outside world.

Will stands his ground, determined not to drag out the farce by trying to cover up. Morgan watches his dick, as if hearing the time it beats in musical terms, tapping his lips with a thumbnail.

"Stamen porrect, slightly arcuate."

"Accurate?"

"Arcuate. Bent."

"Hey, nobody's perfectly straight."

"Nice try." Morgan's grin ripples from one side of his mouth to the other. "Shaft lanceolate, carinate, glabrous with strong venation. Head . . . " He's momentarily at a loss. "Campanulate, retuse, distal slit bilabiate, lactiferous. Scrotum saccate, castaneous."

"My turn." Will's shivering.

Morgan has one eye closed, filtering him through the lashes of the other, a corner of his mouth rising to the squint. Then he rolls up his t-shirt, bunching it around his waist.

"Deflexed. . . . clavate with costa, cucullate."

Morgan's head shifts a tic after each word, checking it with the glossary in his head.

"Scrotum pendulous, tormentose."

"Torment toes?"

"Hairy."

"Lose the 'r'."

"Tomentose."

"Not bad." Morgan looks down at his own penis. It's uncircumcised, the head vaguely outlined in a funnel of skin creased like old crumpled paper worn soft.

The rest is in dream motion, less a progression of movement than a contemporaneous juxtaposition of impetus and result; closeness tickling hairs on neck and arms, nudging contact, Morgan stretching his foreskin smooth over their two knobs.

Enclosing warmth sinks deep roots into Will. The long muscles in his legs tremble, neon midges swarm in his eyeballs. He pulls away just in time, spurting rapid, diminishing arcs. The last sigh curdles out into the mulch underfoot.

Morgan rolls his shirt down, cupping a hand on Will's shoulder as he starts back toward the tent. Will cleans himself with a handful of cloth. "Once every seventeen years."

"Not necessarily." Morgan's backing through the screen of brush. "Depends on the conditions."

TED CORNWELL

A Superior View

For once in my life I'm out looking for solitude, fresh air, and inner harmony amid the wisp of wind rattling through pine needles and the September tinge of red entering the leaves of the maples in the North Woods.

What I find, instead, is a young man with dishwater blond hair and hazel eyes propped on top of an ice box outside a Super America at the highway exit near Tolson, Minnesota, population 272. He's wearing cut-off jeans and a threadbare red tank top and looks like he belongs under a streetlight near Lowry Park in Minneapolis.

People think it's always cold on the North Shore of Lake Superior, but in truth, even a few hundred yards inland it can get pretty hot even in mid-September, so why not a young man in cut-offs so short you can see the bottom of his pockets?

He's got a can of Schlitz beer, which he occasionally raises to his lips and gulps from languorously. Maybe you could call him scrawny, but I'd say he's lithe. I've parked my car and I'm standing in front of the store staring at the headlines inside a newspaper machine and watching him as much as I can. He glances over once in a while but without any expression on his face. Still, he's got his legs hanging over the ice box and he's swinging his knees in and out from each other like someone from a hustler strip somewhere who's been misplaced on the map of northern Minnesota. There's that soft white flesh on the underside of his arms that I see when he lifts the can, otherwise his skin is that light brown, almost like pine wood, that Nordic people have in the summer. The muscles of his arms are defined with the efficient, cool curves of someone who lifts heavy things at work.

So I go into the store and buy the orange juice and muffins and granola I want to bring to the cabin I'm renting further north. When I come out, he's sitting with his back straight and his palms flat on the ice box like someone who's thinking about hopping off his perch.

I walk back to my car and put the grocery bag in the trunk. Then I step onto the grass and stare down at the vast blue of Lake Superior with its scrim of fog. I stretch. It feels like the whole world is watching me watch the man on the ice box, but there's only the girl bobbing to her headphones behind the window of the Super America, and some trucker slumbering in his eighteen-wheeler across the parking lot. The sun's reflection is too strong to see if anyone is looking out from the windows of Ruby's Cafeteria next door. That's the extent of the commercial district beside the exit to Tolson. The town itself is about half a mile inland and there isn't much traffic coming or going.

Pretty soon I've been standing in the sun so long I think I should be wearing sunblock. But he's still over there, and if I drive away now I'll never see those angular cheek bones again. Still, I can't get up the courage to ask if he wants to hitch a ride up Highway 61. As a sort of compromise, I go back over to the newspaper stand for another glance at the headlines. The girl behind the counter gives me a brief glance, but looks away with that seen-it-all nonchalance you'd expect from a small town eighteen-year-old.

He watches me walk over but still isn't betraying any feelings. He's got his feet pulled up and he's hugging his knees against his chest.

So I wander back toward my car but instead of getting in I step onto the grass again and gaze down toward the big lake with all my mind focussed on the peripheral view of my mate on the ice box then he finally makes his move. He hops down and crosses the little parking lot and veers down a dirt trail toward the woods behind the store.

The trail must lead to Spruce River, with its rapids and eddies and swimming holes all hidden behind deep brush or rocky crevices, as all the trails around the Tolson exit do. Maybe he's just stepping into the woods to take a leak. Maybe the last thing he'd tolerate is a Curious George following him.

But as he's edging sideways down the ravine, he reaches over his head and pulls the tank top off in one deft two-handed move and stuffs it into his back pocket, and for a brief moment before he is enfolded into that green forest I see the sweet glimmer of sunlight on his back. As I step down the trail behind him, I'm thinking of worst case scenarios: how long would it take the forest rangers to find a murder victim's body in the woods and would they find it before the wolves and bears? It's not enough to discourage me. There's also the thought of him paying no mind, luring me away with no ill intent—the sight of him taking off his shoes, dropping his shorts on shore, and wading out to frolic in the shallow cool water. That's the thought that has me pushing the bramble out of my face and hurrying to keep in sight of his thighs disappearing down the trail in front of me. And so I scamper into the woods, not in search of peaceful solitude and harmony, but in edgy, nervous, delirious pursuit.

J . B .   D R O U L L A R D

The Klover Grill

The smell was irresistible as I sat at the counter at the Klover Grill in New Orleans. I ordered scrambled eggs, bacon, and toast from the plastified menu. The cook turned around and grinned at me, a mere boy in his early twenties, revealing the gap between his two front teeth.

He wore a baseball cap on backwards, covered with badges and small memorabilia. He looked a little tough, but he had a cute face and a very winning smile. His compact frame moved about with an animal grace, and from behind I couldn't help but admire the way the cheap polyester navy blue pants of his uniform lovingly caressed his tight little bum.

As he broke the eggs into a tall plastic cup, I noticed what thick fingers he had on rough hands that were almost too big for his small body. He took a fork and beat the eggs furiously. The muscles bulged at the white short sleeves of his shirt as he whipped them. The fork clicked a loud, staccato beat upon the sides of the red cup.

I couldn't help but think just how very good he was at beating. He had the staying power to really make foam out of those eggs and draw things to a quick head. My improprietous thoughts strayed further and I wondered what it might be like to be a victim of his relentless beating and have my stiff dick whipped up in those hands.

"How's this for a start?" he would say sarcastically, reaching down my pants. It was very obvious right from the beginning who was in control in this situation. He didn't seem to display the slightest concern who might walk in.

"Now that I've got things going. . . . " he would say now that I was hard and firmly in his grip. He gave a little laugh as he sensed the profound effect he was having on me. He bore down even harder and faster. His clenched jaw didn't even affect his wicked smile. And from the bulge against my face through his tight polyester pants, he looked like he was getting off on it too.

"And now for the finale," he said, announcing his progress, grasping me even firmer and shaking me for all I was worth. It was as if he had read my mind. Just like he was doing himself.

He bent down and opened his mouth just when he knew I was coming. I shook violently, squirming on the turning counter stool, and shot into his open mouth.

He closed his lips and smiled ironically. Hesitated for just one instant. Then he spit the cum out the space between his two front teeth onto the hot grill alongside the hot frying eggs. The little wad of cum hissed loudly and danced violently from the intense heat.

Then he flipped a plate over and off the shelf with his right hand, while he coaxed the eggs off the grill with a spatula in his left. "There ya'll go, sir," he intoned, smiling, a gleam in his eyes. "Scrambled eggs, just like ya loves 'em! N'awlens style!"

JAY OLIVER DICKINGSON

Adidas Feet

He jogs four times around the college track, then down University Avenue past the administration building, and up three flights of stairs to my office. I wait for him as we had arranged. Barely breathing any heavier than normal, he comes around to where I am and sits on my desk. Rolling the chair back, I reach down and take the boy's right foot and place it in my lap. I am wearing my dark blue suit, his favourite. I slowly undo the laces of his Adidas runner. As I ease it off, I am rewarded by the pungent aroma of hot sneaker leather. I inhale deeply. My cock stirs. By the time I remove the other runner, I am almost erect.

I quickly undo my belt and unsnap and unzip my trousers, then push them and my boxers down to my ankles. Placing his stockinged feet, warm and damp from his jog, back in my lap, I thrill at the feel of his cotton-nylon Adidas socks against my naked thighs. I slowly roll the top of the right one down revealing his muscular ankle, the ankle of a runner. I massage the thick tendons and the protruding ankle bone a few moments and then roll his sock on over the heel of his foot. Again I pause to massage and caress it before slowly pushing the half-rolled sock further down. I finally slip it off his toes and am rewarded with the musky fragrance of a young man's foot.

As I began to roll the other sock down, he stretches his right leg forward, touching my ball sac with his big toe. He rotates it in concentric circles, causing my nut to roll in its sac and my penis to swell further. Removing the second sock, I hold it to my nose and inhale the moist and heady smell of him.

I massage his left foot, gently running my hands over the heel and along the hollow below his ankle bone. With small, concentric circles I work along the side of his foot to his toes, and then moving up to the top of his foot, I slowly work back to his ankle. Moving my hands closer, I work down to the toes again. After doing the same with his right foot, I raise it and inhale the fresh, pure essence of his maleness. I look up at him. His eyes are closed, his lips curled with a smile of pleasure. His green nylon jogging shorts are tented out.

I lower my head and begin to lick, starting with the back, running my tongue down the middle of his foot to his toes, and then reversing and sliding my tongue back up beside its downward path. Over and over I lick until his foot is coated with a fine film of spittle and my mouth is full of his flavour. As I commence with the other foot, my cock, now jutting straight up, drips pre-cum.

His foot is compact, the toes tightly pressed against each other, even his second digit and big toe. He keeps them clean and his toenails trimmed so that there is only a sliver of white nail beyond the pink. His second largest toe is only a fraction shorter than the big one. The rest taper down gradually so the smallest is half as long as the longest. I begin with the smallest, slipping my lips over it and sucking on it as I would a little pricklet. The boy squirms with pleasure and reaches down and strokes the bulge in his jogging shorts.

I slowly suck them one by one, until I reach his big toe. My tongue traces where the nail joins his flesh, along all three sides, and then the smooth edge. Slipping my lips over it, I suck on it as a man might suck another's cock.

Beginning with the smallest digit of his right foot, I slowly suck one and then the other as I had done with the left. He reaches forward with his other foot and presses his hot, saliva-damp toe against my rigid member. It jerks with excitement and a clear drop of pre-cum oozes from the slit.

Finally spreading apart his knees, I place his feet on either side of my aching cock so that it is lined up along the grooves where his toes join his feet. He presses them together, squeezing my throbbing erection tightly. Then this gorgeous boy begins to work his feet up and down together, slowly jacking me off with his delicious toes.

All too soon my cum jets out, shooting up in the air and landing back, running down my shaft in a thick stream. The second and third jets shoot in the air and run down over his toes as he quivers and gasps with his own orgasm. He continues to press his feet tight against my cock and to milk me until my flow of cum subsides. Removing his feet, he rubs them together, working my juices into his skin with his toes.

He smiles over at me as I pick up his sock and roll it back on over his sticky toes, and up his foot and over his ankle. The second follows, and then I slip on his Adidas runners. As he stands, I notice a large wet spot in his green jogging shorts where his cum has soaked through. He gets up and heads out the door without a word. As I hear the clap of his runners jogging down the hall, I pull my boxers up over my now limp, sticky organ, and then pull up my trousers. Squeezing my dick through my open fly, I stand at the window and watch him jog up the street, my sweet Adidas-feet boy.

BARRY WEBSTER

Body Symphony

Contrary to popular opinion, Tchaikovsky was not an easy lay. I had to work damn hard to get that sucker to show me his boner.

"But William, my friend," he said, "I think you are a superb fellow, but such things can not be done. Sexual feeling must no longer shake my fragile soul." He looked down. "Everything is consumed . . ." His eyes blackened. ". . . by music."

"Music? You mean it's better than cock and balls?" This was the fourth time I'd gotten him alone in my boudoir; I'd tried a different approach each time, but the bastard would show interest then stop part way through.

"William, you don't understand!" he said, collapsing into a gilded armchair and bringing his hands to his face, which was smooth as marble, the pale clear skin sloping down to his forest-thick beard. This guy was studsville!

"My music is dying!" He banged one hand on the table, the *torchère* swayed. "It's slipping from my grasp, and I don't know why! It *must* be caused by physical desire pulling me this way and that and destroying my concentration!"

"Who says your music's gotten lousy? I couldn't hear your last symphony without wanting to put my hand between my legs."

"It's . . ." He closed his eyes. "*Romeo and Juliet*. Balakirev says it should be ready now. But I'm stuck. Stuck!" Beads of sweat appeared on his forehead. "At the culminating moment where the contrasting subject must resolve into the main theme, the progression goes B-minor dominant, tonic, then . . . then what? I can't resolve it. Everything I try sounds Russian when it's an Italian story. The problem eats at my brain. I read the play daily for inspiration, some clue, some way to instinctively inhabit the story but fail!"

"I'm an Englishman," I said, unbuttoning my fly. "Doesn't that give me an intuitive understanding of Shakespeare?"

He looked at me for a minute. "Maybe it does." He turned and placed his fist against his mouth. "Yes, I think it might."

"As for Italy," I said, peeling off my trousers and removing my collar, "I'm a hairy, little fucker; my grandma's from the Veneto, a direct descendant of the fair Veronans."

He turned to me, eyes widening. "God," he cried, "maybe! . . . maybe!" He stared at me, and suddenly his pupils dilated. He tore off his waistcoat, cravat, shirt, and pants, and when he threw me naked on the bed, I cried out, "Oh Petie, play me like a piano, make my body a symphony, you raunchy horndog!"

Don't stop again you fucker or you're dead meat!

His prickly beard drove into my stomach as he began to hum and sing the opening of *Romeo and Juliet*. He mimicked the hypnotic chant of the violas, throaty wail of cellos, the furtive plink of plucked strings. His vibrating lips skidded over my chest, as sound, hot breath, and saliva exploded onto my skin. His sticky tongue lapped at my nipples; I smelled tobacco, hair oil.

"Yes, Petie, yes."

Then his great chest fell onto mine and the main theme kicked in. Tchaikovsky shrieked away as the string section propelled the melody skyward. It fell in dizzying drops, spun in ever-widening loops. His hands made a vice and my groin burned inside it.

"Yes, scratch me, Illyich, scratch me!"

When his gaze fell on a manuscript on the end table, I cried out and he was back to me. for the moment anyway.

Above my face, his mouth twisted and puckered, his tongue plucked lips for harp strings, breath squealed through his nose oboe, his hand beat at the bed frame, castanets clattered in his throat, and his entire body shook when he cried out a trumpet blast.

I gasped, my breath racing, the insane thudding of the bass violin, cymbal-crashes like lightning, a deafening hammer-blow as the tuba-roar filled the room.

A thousand pianists' fingers pressed my every pore.

Then as the strings trembled on F-sharp, I felt him holding, holding me in such suspense. It was agony.

Suddenly he flipped me over and the tempo raced, violins screamed, kettledrums pounded, Tchaikovsky's spit splattered over my back, shoulders, hair. I saw him in the gilt bronze looking-glass, eyes blazing, his right hand on my hip, the other whipping furiously in the air, the entire orchestra surged up and up to the cliff-edge of the highest precipice, and then—

He stopped.

"I can't do it," he cried.

"Yes you can," I screamed.

"No I can't."

"Yes you can."

He paused, then made a final thrust forward with his hips, singing out A, F, and D. A D-minor chord! What a surprising transition! Never heard before in the history of music!

We both cried out at the top of our lungs.

Then we fell to the bed and did a dying fugue of moans and sighs.

I said, "You fucking know how, you feisty sleazebag."

Tchaikovsky began to bounce up and down, singing, "F, D-minor!" over and over.

He threw the blanket in the air and as it drifted down to cover us, he started kissing me, "F, *D!* F, *D!* F, *D!*"

I sat in the Moscow Hall at the opening of *Romeo and Juliet*. Violin bows slashed the air, the conductor's body thrashed like a fish on a hook, and as the piece approached its summit—I couldn't help it—my head fell back, my eyeballs rolled up, and I yelled, "F, *D!* F, *D!* F, *D!* F, *D!*"

ALLEN J. BORCHERDING

Elevator Sex

When all you thought you ever wanted to do was make this one guy happy, it's hard to stop. Even when he tells you. Stop. I couldn't. So, against any vestiges of better judgment, I agreed to come to South Beach with Tim, my soon-to-be ex. "We'll do this," he said. "Have a great time, and when we get back home, go our separate ways. A nice finale to our years together."

"Sure," I shrugged. Make him happy.

But once we got there, I realized our mistake. Out from under the proscenium of home life, one thinks too much. And my thinking changed. About him, me, us, and what lay ahead. You see, *we* hadn't really decided anything. Tim said he wanted out, and determined is one generous way to describe him.

We had changed the ground rules for this trip, too, with the divorce pending. Time apart; "We'll need it," separate outings; "It'll do us good," flirting, cruising, all fair. He stopped just short of banishing me to the hotel coffee shop while the Do Not Disturb sign swung on our doorknob. Getting back in practice maybe, he thought.

He got his practice. In the nightclubs, the grocery line, and at the beach, well . . . Tim didn't lack for attention.

I moped a lot.

It was Saturday, our last full day in Florida. Again we spent the largest portion of the day at the beach. The sun seared the sand, toasting the oil-slippery, gym-perfected bodies, most clothed in less than a shred of mystery.

Fitness Nazi Tim blended in perfectly. He had packed equal tonnage of preening supplies and workout paraphernalia, toting along his entire aerobic regimen.

That day Tim somehow convinced me to wear my, shall we say, briefest swim suit. Iridescent orange, sheer. Definitely not me. After too much chlorine, stretching here, sagging there, it no longer adequately concealed and begged retirement. "But with your tan," he pleaded. Make him happy.

The walking shorts felt too grungy from an unlaundered week, so in just our suits and avoiding the arthritic elevator, we tromped down ten flights of stairs, lugging along books, magazines, music, and towels, and ducked out a side entrance, avoiding the Ladies Auxiliary something-or-other convention billeted at our hotel. Add to the starched-prim girls an aging frat boy reunion and the hotel mix fairly seethed hetero. The queer beach beckoned.

After hours of basting, basking, and dips in the surf, I went for sodas. Well, a soda for me, a non-ionic, electrolyte-balanced sport drink for Tim. I returned to a twenty-two-year-old case of sweating steroid abuse, saturating my towel. I grimaced hello when Tim introduced me to his new karmic soul mate. Already they had professed uncannily matching intellectual pursuits, spiritualities, and sported synchronously bulging "chemistries."

And would it be okay if he met this Randy for coffee later, Tim asked, suddenly delighting in the prospect of a beverage he has shunned for years.

"Sure," I said. Time to go, anyway.

Throwing a towel around my neck, I grabbed an overloaded bag in each hand and tromped back to the hotel. I was annoyed, no, pissed, by the time we arrived.

"We're taking the elevator," I announced in my best don't-fuck-with-me voice.

But indoors I felt awkwardly underdressed. I wanted to drop the bags and at least wrap the towel around my waist. But the elevator arrived, so we got on with a handful of others whom, in my state of malignant irritation, I barely noticed. The doors closed and we began ascending.

The elevator's slowness chafed me, and stopping on the second floor for an entire beer-pickled fraternity chapter further eroded my mood. They wedged in, cramming the car beyond capacity. Stuck dead centre, I stood vulnerably naked, nudged, and jabbed from every side. Drunken hilarity kept the doors from closing for an eternity. But once they did, I felt this hand.

Placed cautiously, deliberately against the small of my back, there it lay, no mistake. If it steadied some tottering, blue-haired hotel guest, I couldn't turn enough to see.

Then the hand slid, tugging down the drawstring of my suit. Or had I just not noticed its original placement? At any rate, it now commanded my undivided attention.

My attention, however, was the only thing to stay undivided. The hand crept lower and a finger's worth of pressure nudged between the cheeks of my ass. Incredulousness and offence boiled up in me, but futile as my situation was, simmered back down to mischievous curiosity.

By the fifth floor the back of my suit looped down over my butt. The fingers gently pried and teased from behind, and up front, telltale arousal swelled against the sheerness of my suit.

The hand shifted. Thumb and little finger spread my ass, and the three remaining digits caressed. Then the fingers reached farther, grabbed my balls and tugged them back between my legs. The swimsuit barely contained my leaking protuberance, now beyond fully erect.

With balls clamped, erection straining at the top of my Speedo, and arms weighted on each side with beach bags, I surrendered like a calf, roped and tied. A river poured down my back.

Another shift and the fingers tightened around my balls while the base of the thumb massaged my cleft. I could feel the thumb poised to enter me. I dipped in encouragement of the hand that sweat-polished my privacy. It plunged. I gasped an abrupt gasp that made Tim glance my way. My head lolled back and eyes narrowed as I involuntarily shuddered, careening toward a hands-free climax.

Suddenly the elevator doors parted and the clot of frat boys disgorged. Fresh, cool air and a few threads of orange nylon separated me from a foyer of Auxiliary ladies. A collective gasp arose.

The leader looked me up and down, glistening, straining, stained, and threw her arms out protectively. "We'll take the next car, girls." And the doors slammed shut.

W E S   H A R T L E Y

A Slice From a Cut Loaf

A slice from a cut loaf is never missed.
—*ancient maxim*

My torrid obsession with Perfect Nathan begins Friday afternoon at the famous nude beach just as I'm sliding out of my Speedos. My out-of-control dick instantly goes wooden when the stunning impact of Nathan's gorgeousness bowls me over and knocks my socks off.

Nathan is the most dazzling masculine archangel I've ever seen in my fucking life. Watching him frolicking naked in the surf, tossing his white vinyl Frisbee and catching it, and reclining gloriously on his beachblanket with his jutting teenerbutt pointing heavenward and glistening like a nectarine in the sunlight is almost more than I can fucking stand. I want to crawl across the burning sand and faceplant my queer bravado smack between those awesome ballooning sleek powerpeaches. But my throbbing gristle pens me facedown on my dribblestained beachtowel and certain impossible-to-deny facts put the brakes on the unspeakably perverse sex scenarios I'm plotting. Nathan is private property.

Nathan's protective zealously solicitous escort (and for sure lover) is a huge 250-pound hunk, a former university and semipro linebacker nicknamed Crusher, now the resident no-nonsense bouncer at a notorious breeder meetclub downtown. (Insider info courtesy of the nude beach queergossip network.)

Crusher (whose given name is Louie) seems oblivious to the gawking stares of us fans, and doesn't appear to notice the endless ga-ga marchpast of starstruck naked fags checking out his boyfriend's pristine male beauty. In the face of all the attention being lavished on the two of them, Louie's blasé attitude and seeming lack of concern is scandalous in the extreme. Cutiepie kept fuckboys like Nathan can readily be seduced by cash, expensive presents, and adventure. Exciting romantic sexploits and forbidden pleasures can stress out and undermine even the most rigorously constructed keptboy arrangements. This I know from long experience.

I begin to see intriguing possibilities. The risky obstacle of Crusher Louie challenges my inborn queer sense of caprice and danger and adds spice to my endless scheming. Naturally, I hate Louie's fucking guts. The thought of massive Louie on top of him mashing down Flawless Nathan and fucking him bowlegged is a vision I refuse to contemplate. Period. Tow Mister Crusher to the crusher.

I'm sure it must be the mysterious behind-the-scenes diddling of fucking Fate, working its ju-ju, that returns Nathan to centrestage Friday night. I'm convinced it must be Fate.

I'm at The Odyssey. I'm totally locked into this spinny bittersweet Nathan reverie. I'm being ground to powder by the harsh techno earpoison, feeling faggoty and gnarly and stoned, starting to think I ought to just go home and beat off, get over it, and crash out. Then suddenly, Nathan appears, accompanied by Louie, of course.

My jealous rage peaks and I feel like I'm going to fucking explode when I see maybe four hundred hideous homos in a vast "wave" of pivoting heads point the compassneedles of their collective predatory gaze in unison toward the magnetic pole of Nathan's True North.

So strong, so fucking free, Nathan's peachy allstar Canadian bacon is as far North as it gets.

I totally hate this trendy cesspool of letching faggot geeks with a lethal bitter loathing that refuses to abate. Queers are tolerable only until something perfect shows up. Then . . . fuck!

I position myself as close as possible to the table Crusher Louie has taken over and I keep my tireless gaze riveted on the fleshly incarnation of my daylong porn fantasies—Perfect Nathan, an exotic hothouse orchid smack in the middle of a rank plot of seedy annuals, persistent perennials, and noxious pushy weeds, guarded by an overspreading thorny stickerbush bristling with scary prickles.

Then, Fate starts diddling me bigtime.

Archangel Nathan, facing me across the smokepolluted distance that so cruelly separates us—Flawless Nathan is basking in my attentive gaze! Nathan is smiling at me! Nathan is winking at me! Nathan is checking me out! (Perhaps Sweetheart remembers me from this afternoon at the beach!) My rowdy dick kicks and bucks against the pantleg of my West Beach chinos and starts to leak sticky stuff down my sweaty thigh. I hallucinate violins. Then cellos. Then an entire fucking string orchestra. Mahler, I think. Nathan keeps the coquettish eyeballtease going for maybe an hour. I'm fucking vibrating like a come-and-get-it dinnerbell.

Finally, clued-out Louie goes for a quick whiz. As he disappears through the john doorway, Nathan miraculously rises from his chair (like the golden sun at break of dawn), walks across to where I'm standing, pauses a couple of feet away, and beams his glaciermelting smile on me like Teenage Apollo himself. He stands perfectly immobile for an instant (I'm holding my breath) then turns slowly around and strides regally back to his table, treating me to a slowmotion bump-and-grind of his totally incredible totally cheeky boybutt. It's the wetdream come true, the almost-answered prayer answered at last. My fucking tongue is hanging out. My boner is leaping around in my pants like a fucking poisonous snake thrashing on the hot pavement.

Crusher Louie returns from pissing, escorts his teaser trophyboyfriend toward the streetdoors, and the vast wave of stylishly coiffed faggot heads magnetically attuned to their dreamlike passage follows their progression as they make their spectacular exit.

I follow my dream out the door onto Howe Street. Louie hails a cab and I hail one, too. I tail them to a highrise on Beach Avenue, watch them go inside, and notice the floor the elevator stops at. On the buzzerpanel outside the frontdoor, I scan the tags listing the suites and propernames on the seventh floor. Bingo. Louie's name.

Saturday night. I wait across the street from the highrise front entrance until Louie The Bouncer leaves for work. I make my move as a gaggle of residents exit the building. I rise up by elevator to Seventh Heaven where my teen angel reigns supreme. Nathan is naked when he answers my feverish knock.

I pull Perfect Nathan close, breathe in the spicy bouquet of his fragrant teener pits, run my hands down his arching back, and burrow my sweaty palms between the sleek jutting cheeks of his awesome keptboybutt. I kiss him long and deep, push the heavy apartment door closed with my sneaker, and steer him across the thick shagcarpet and into Crusher's recroom/weightroom/bedroom.

The corny queerpornvideo grunting and flickering on the vast screen of Louie's home entertainment setup keeps time with my in-and-out strokes as my reamer probes the elastic capabilities of Frisky Nathan's sultry tighty boysocket.

Sexstar flexes his rowdy weeniesqueezer and romps my tofu toodleflute up and down the scales like a showoff virtuoso. Nathan The Prodigy has me right where he fucking wants me.

Trickster clenches his cheeky peaches and squirts bigtime, and the astonishing grip of his constricting sphincter throttles my turkeyneck in a crushing stranglehold that almost rips my bone out by the roots.

At the door Bad Nathan sends me off with wet kisses and his cellphone number. We don't sing the jingle but we both know for sure that a slice from a cut loaf is never missed.

B O B   V I C K E R Y

Fireman Nick

I sit in the tiller seat, tugging on the rear steering wheel as the fire engine goes tearing down the city streets with sirens wailing, and all I can think is *This sure as hell beats Disneyland.* Even a mile away I can see a glow in the night sky ahead of us. A few minutes later we come to a screaming halt and leap out. I take in the scene while on a full run. All the top storey windows blaze with red light; it's as if the tenants are all up and throwing a party. The flames roar so loud the sound just rolls over me like waves, and I can feel the heat pound down on me like a concussion. Hot damn, is this a kick in the ass or what!

We look for an empty hydrant to connect to, not an easy task since there are already two other engines ahead of us, hooked up with their firemen holding onto their spewing hoses. The searchlight units are in full operation, and the whole scene looks like a Hollywood set. My partner Tom and I put on our breathing apparatus, grab our equipment, and run into the building.

We race up the stairs, shoving past a stream of bewildered tenants clutching blankets and pets and screaming like the damned. On the sixth floor, the smoke pours down the corridor. Tom goes one way, I go the other, busting down doors with our fire axes, making sure all the living units have been evacuated. I swing my ax like Thor, the friggin' thunder god, and each time I hear the wood splinter, my dick just gets a little harder.

When I get to the unit at the end of the corridor, smoke is pouring down from cracks in the ceiling tiles; the fire must be directly overhead now. I smash the door down in three swings and dive into the apartment.

It's like leaping into black ink. I'm going by feel alone here. I find another door, push into the next room, stumble, and fall. I've tripped over a body, sprawled on the floor and still tangled in bedsheets. The adrenalin is racing through me. I heave the body over my shoulders, stumble to the windows, and smash them open with my ax. With the rush of air, the fire flares up, giving me a glimpse of a dangling arm and the naked torso of the body slung around my neck. There's a fire escape outside, and I clamber onto it. I lumber down as best I can, the flames giving me one final goose before I'm below the range of fire. It's only when I'm in the courtyard itself that I feel safe. I ease the body down, rip my mask off, and by the light of the flames above check out just who the hell I've been carrying.

It's a man, buck naked, either unconscious or dead, I can't tell. He lies sprawled on his back, unmoving, and it only takes me a second to see he's not breathing. I check his carotid artery for a pulse and finally find one, weak and fluttering. I drop to my knees, lift his chin up, cover his mouth with mine, and blow hard. His chest rises and falls once. I keep on breathing into his mouth, timing myself, twelve breaths per minute. *Where the fuck are the paramedics?* I wonder. I can still hear the flames crackling overhead and burning sparks fly all around me.

It takes about ten minutes before he finally starts breathing raggedly. He coughs and it's the most beautiful sound I've ever heard. *I did it!* I think. *I brought the motherfucker back to life!* I feel like God! The man lies there gasping and wheezing, and I'm startled to see how young he is, barely out of his teens. His body is smooth and firm, and as I stare at him in the ruddy light of the fire, all I can think of is how *beautiful* he looks.

His breathing is still shallow and erratic. I plant my mouth over his again, my left hand lying lightly on his chest. Without thinking, I take the nipple between my thumb and forefinger and squeeze, while my tongue slips into his mouth. His body stirs and he bends his left leg up. My hand crosses his chest and tenderly pinches the other nipple. He groans. I look down the length of his body and see his cock is fully stiff. I bend over and french him for all I'm worth as my hand slips down and circles his fat, soot-stained cock.

His tongue pushes into my mouth now and his eyes flutter open; he stares with dilated pupils into the night sky. I quickly let go of his cock.

"Easy," I murmur. "Lie still. I just pulled you out of the fire."

I hear a trample of feet and a team of paramedics bursts into the courtyard. "Over here!" I shout. It's only a matter of moments more before they're carting the man off on a stretcher, an oxygen mask over his mouth.

We don't get back until after midnight. In the shower the men talk about the fire; I'm the hero of the day with my rescue, and several of them clap me on the back and tell me, "Way to go!" I shrug and smile, but don't say anything.

I lie in my bunk, staring at the ceiling, listening to the snores of the other firemen. After a while I wrap my hand around my cock and start stroking. I think of burning buildings, of flames reaching into the night sky, of the feel of a naked man's mouth against mine as I breath life into him. I shoot my load into my wadded t-shirt and finally drift off to sleep. That night, all I dream about is fire.

MICHAEL LASSELL

Blood Brothers

I t is ten years into the plague. I am walking down a street in the East Village. It is early night and I am full of desire. He is leaning against a building that is covered in graffiti. He is wearing faded black denim cutoffs, small and tight, held together by safety pins and fastened around his narrow waist by a fat studded belt. His torn-off t-shirt is white with a SILENCIO=MUERTE button on it in pink on black. There is a heavy silver chain around his neck, from which something is suspended that looks like a bone.

His body is marble sculpted by a Renaissance idolater. The flesh of his torso flows around his navel like a stream around a hidden hollow. His head is shaved. On the left side, from which I approach, he has had an elaborate eagle tattooed over his ear, which is pierced at least a dozen times and glistens with silver rings. The wings of the eagle are splayed, erect; the beak is gaping; open talons reach for the meal of his frightened eye, which turns slightly to the left to meet my need. It is a mouth I remember from before, from decades before. It swallows time.

It is long-lost Bob's mouth that this tattooed boy in the East Village has turned in my direction with his eye of prey, and it is through Bob's over-red lips that he says, "My name is Luke," and invites me home, up six filthy flights in a nearby tenement. The room, like his imagination, has been furnished from the street.

As soon as the locks are secure he turns to face me. I put my hands on his bare waist, which is hot and dry. I touch my lips to his lips, push them into a kiss. He kisses back. He opens his lips slightly, I insert my tongue. He moans and pushes the front of his shorts into my cock, which is filling with blood. I fumble with his belt, get it open, put one hand down the back and caress his hairless ass. His shorts drop over boots to the floor. We do not stop kissing. I feel his hard cock on my belly. I stretch my hand down the crack of his ass and feel the coarse, sparse growth of hair. I pull up with my middle finger on the bull's-eye of his asshole. He moans again. Blood surges into my cock. I pull the t-shirt up over his head, his arms suspended in the air like the arms of a praying mantis or Sebastian becoming a saint. His body is a minefield of surprises. His hard boy's chest is white. It is the pale and neutral flesh canvas for another tattoo that covers his breast-bone: an elaborate heart, a flaming heart that drips blood the colour of stage light through cellophane. It holds my eye like an animal one comes across by accident in the wilderness. Beyond it I am conscious of his dark cock pointed straight at the ceiling, but I sink only as far as this heart and lick the tattooed drops of blood.

He is lying on the bed while I undress quickly. Naked, I bend to pull the boots off him, first one, then the second. There is another tattoo around his right ankle, a neatly symmetrical chain, somewhat stylized but cleanly rendered. I lift his leg and put the toes of his right foot into my mouth. I begin to suck. He purrs, his torso rippling like a tide, the heart floating on the crest of it in a vessel of fire. I slip my shoulders underneath his thighs and move down until his asshole is positioned directly in front of my cock.

"Do you have a rubber?" I ask, and he turns slightly on an axis, each of his ribs a perfect ridge below his arm, and turns back with a lubricant in his hand. I do not react. He rubs my cock, and I wonder if I will come before I even get inside him. Then he stops.

"Do it," he says.

"But. . . ."

"Do it."

I hesitate but slip inside him and realize I have forgotten what sex is, what my cock feels like buried to the hilt in the ass of a beautiful stranger, the red of my pubic hair meeting the black of his ass hair. He stares into my eyes and puts his arms around my shoulders.

How many years, how many years has it been? I wonder.

I feel an odd sensation in my neck. I put my hand to the spot. My fingers are covered with blood.

"Don't worry," he says, looking up at me. He holds a razor blade in his hand. "It isn't deep. It's only a symbolic gesture." Then he pulls me down and takes my neck in his mouth, sucking, sucking, pulling the blood out of me into his throat. And all the while I am pumping. It is as if I have never had sex before in my life. I am pumping and he takes the razor and makes a small incision on his own neck. His blood begins to dribble down his long hard neck like a leak through a crack in marble.

"Blood brothers?" he asks.

And I explode into his asshole, shot after shot of semen. I am groaning, and he is howling with pleasure as he shoots onto his own stomach, the milky stuff splattering the tattoo on his hairless chest, and every inch of me is finally alive as I bite down on his neck and taste the blood of him on my tongue.

DUANE WILLIAMS

Sacred and Delicious Eggs

Our eggs are sacred. In fact, they're worth a lot of money to the doctors. Two eggs each in case a girl kicks us square. Of course at the hospital there are no girls, just us guys. Hummingbirds, crows, pigeons, you name it. All kinds of birds are waiting to hatch between our legs and fly away, far away from the cold potatoes they serve at the hospital. Every night in the shower we wash our eggs together with soap so the birds'll smell nice when they finally hatch. One guy's got the eggs of an ostrich. That's Zack. They slap against my butt when he puts his big thing inside me. When he's doing it, Zack grunts and sounds like he's taking a crap, just like my dad. It hurts a little but mostly I go tingly and leak like there's an ocean of jizz inside me. Zack's my best bud at the hospital. I like his tattoos, especially the fire-breathing dragon on his chest. And Zack's eggs are delicious. Warm and salty. I told him so after I finished sucking them like he told me to. They were like pingpong balls and I could feel the little birds inside squirming around, their wings all cramped up and anxious to get free. I told Zack our eggs are sacred, that's why the doctors keep us in the hospital. He laughed. I like it when Zack laughs. He's even more good-looking, like Tom Cruise. Zack said they keep us in the hospital because we're sick ass-fuckers with fucked-up excuses for lives. Once, the nurse, he caught Zack and me. We were in the shower and Zack was pumping me good, huffing like a race horse. I was so tingly I just wanted Zack to keep going like that forever. He'd almost blown his jizz, his body was shaking like a crazy leaf, when the nurse came into the bathroom. The nurse, his name's Bob, stood there for a minute staring at Zack and me in the shower, our cocks standing straight up and pointing to heaven. Later on that night Bob came into the TV room where I was watching a show about elephants being hacked to death over in Africa. He pulled up a chair next to the black velvet La-Z-Boy where I always sit when I'm watching my programs. Bob smiled at me weird and looked around the room like he was scared somebody might hear what he had to say. Then he took a rubber out of his pocket and asked me in a quiet voice if I knew what it was. Of course I knew, but he showed me how to use it anyhow, using two fingers as a cock, which made my own go really hard, watching Bob do that with a rubber. He told me I shouldn't be doing what I was doing with Zack. Told me we'd get sick and die, but dying's not something I worry about. I know we'll live forever because of our eggs. Our eggs are protected by God. Sometimes I do worry about Zack, though. Last week he took a knife and cut up his arms. Nobody knows where he got the knife except me. I know Zack's got knives hidden in his body so I wasn't so surprised when I found him in the bathroom, bleeding like my dog Blackie when she got hit by that car. I held Zack in my arms for a while and sang to him, *Michael, Row the Boat Ashore*. That's the only song I know all the words to. I gave him a kiss on the lips, but I knew he wasn't feeling too good because he didn't smile or laugh at me like he does. Zack was in bad shape for sure, his eyes rolled back and fluttery. I asked him if he wanted me to suck his eggs, but he didn't answer. I reached down and put my hand inside his track pants. His eggs were cool and tight in their hairy nest. I held them for a while and pretty soon I could feel the baby birds inside. They were scared and very still, but I could feel their little heartbeats and I just whispered to them to hold on. "You're going to fly away soon," I said. "Won't be long now."

PAUL G. LEROUX

Waiting for Master

Evening fell, and the dying rays of sunlight faded over the horizon. The faint heat of the last warm fall day turned to cool night air.

Scott Stuart stood ramrod straight, chin up, shoulders back, feet apart, hands clasped behind him, waiting patiently for Master Sam Goddard.

So long since we were together, he thought. *Be good to see him again.*

Scott had been there since nine this morning, but didn't find the time long. He loved waiting for Master.

"You are to wait for me, no matter how long it takes. Understand, boy?" Master had told him once, in his early days as a slave. "The longer you wait, the more you'll miss me, and the more you'll be eager to please."

So Scott waited. It was so peaceful and quiet here. Hardly a soul passed through all day, rarely the sound of another human voice, only the cheerful twitter of birds. Around him stretched acres of parkland, groves of shade trees, well-manicured lawns dotted with marble statues.

Apart from his t-shirt and jeans, Scott wore the insignia of a slave. Head shaven, smooth as his crotch, balls and ass. White cotton jockstrap, clean, well-mended, indelibly marked with Master's initials in caps above his own in lower case. Steel ring binding his cock and balls. Grey woolen socks, red band around the calves. Black leather boots, polished daily to a glossy shine. Leather vest, with a constellation of pins testifying to the runs he'd been on with Master. And, of course, Master's chain-link collar and padlock around his neck.

In his right back pocket, freshly ironed, neatly folded in even squares, layered on top of each other so the colours and borders showed, were four hankies. Each was a gift from Master, to remind Scott of the duties and services he performed.

Grey for bondage—the literal, physical restraints of rope and cuff, blindfold and gag, duct tape and shrink wrap, and the emotional tie between Master and slave, the contract signed and sealed in their blood.

Black, for the floggings Scott had received to strengthen his endurance, subdue his will. Scott recalled the red welts that crisscrossed his back in thin stripes, the bruises on his ass that faded from dark blue and deep purple, to light brown, green and yellow. So long, too long, since he felt the caress of hand, belt and paddle, crop, cane, and whip.

Yellow. Scott always kept the fridge at home stocked with ice-cold beer. When Master had emptied a bottle, he would nod to the boy kneeling expectantly before him, granting him permission to take Master's soft cock in his mouth. Scott would wait for the sudden shock of that first flood of salt-sour piss. It would build to a steady stream, subside to a trickle. Scott wouldn't spill a drop of the golden nectar. To him, it was as precious and sacred as consecrated mass wine. He worshipped and adored everything that was Master's.

Last but not least, red. Scott valued that hanky more than all the rest. It had taken so many months, cost so much pain and effort to earn. But his boyhole had finally been broken by the hard, protruding wrist bone of Master's broad-palmed, long-fingered, latex-gloved, Crisco-slick hand. Scott had abandoned any remaining vestige of resistance and control. He had become fully and completely Master's slave. Afterward, Scott had cried a long time, tears of joy and surrender, his cheek against Master's powerful chest, Master's strong arms around his shoulders wracked with sobs.

All of these things he had done to please Master.

Wish he were here, Scott sighed as he waited. *Need to feel his cock and fist in me again, smell the raunch of his piss on my skin, feel the crack of his whip on my back.*

The sky took on the soft black of Scott's leather jacket, and the first bright stars glinted like metal studs. Night came early now.

A few steps behind him, Scott heard the familiar jingle of keys.

A thin, blue-veined, liver-spotted hand, smelling of earth and dried autumn leaves, with dirt under the fingernails, gingerly touched Scott's shoulder.

"Six o'clock. Closing time, son."

"Thanks for letting me wait, sir," Scott replied politely as he had been trained. "See you in the morning, Mr. Gardiner."

"Good night, son," the caretaker gently replied.

And Bruce Gardiner watched in wonder while Scott slowly walked down the path, as he had done every night since spring, out of the cemetery, away from Master's grave.

NORMAND FRANCOIS

Blue Movie

I am sitting in one of the last straight porn theatres in Montreal. I was eighteen when my father introduced me to my first porn flick. Back then there were at least seven or eight blue movie houses. Now there are only two that I know of, and both are very poorly attended. The movie now playing is a pastiche of lesbian love scenes. Not exactly what I'm here for, but I decide to sit it out and wait for the second movie.

The theatre is mostly empty. Down the aisle, I can see the silhouette of a man. He is masturbating. On the screen, one of the two women straps on a dildo. She is big-breasted and has a tattoo of a green dragon on her left shoulder. She positions herself to mount a small-breasted blonde woman. Both smile vapidly, pretending to have a good time.

I turn around to check out the back of the theatre and see two silhouettes against the dark red wall. I decide to join them. As I pass beside the first man I examine him closely. He is in his late sixties, with a very wrinkled face and white hair. He is tall, over six feet, and slim. He smiles at me, but I pretend not to notice.

The second man looks like a labourer in his mid-forties. He has thinning black hair and a mulatto complexion. He is about five feet eight inches and is quite heavy for his height. His large belly hangs over faded blue jeans. He is also wearing a denim shirt and a denim jacket. He hands are behind his back and he looks straight at the movie screen. He appears unaware of my presence or of the older man a few feet to his left.

I lean against the wall several feet to the labourer's right.

On the screen, the lesbian love scene continues. The blonde woman has a silver stud in the middle of her tongue and a ring through her lower lip. It looks painful.

To my left, the older man has edged himself closer to the labourer. Within minutes, he is standing right next to and slightly forward of him. With his right hand he kneads the bulge in the labourer's jeans. I look down at the labourer's matte, pointy black leather boots. His gaze is transfixed on the dildo which is sliding in and out of the lesbian's pussy.

I hear a zipper open and the older man's hand disappears into the labourer's pants. Then, with the dexterity of a dancer, the older man spins around and drops to his knees, pulling out the semi-rigid cock and stuffing it into his mouth, the entire movement taking less than a moment.

My eyes are on the live sex act. The older man stops for a second to wipe his mouth, but I suspect that he is removing his dentures. I can hear slurping sounds, the white head bobbing back and forth. On the screen, the butch lesbian has removed the dildo, and is positioning herself to lick the blonde's asshole, which is pink and hairless. The blonde has a large, wide bottom and a tiny waist. She has taken the "doggie" position. She is wearing red high-heels.

The labourer is breathing heavily and the older man quickens his pace. Eyes never leaving the screen throughout the act, the labourer whimpers quietly, then sighs. Having seen this performance in movie houses before, I know it is over. A noisy spit of saliva and semen confirms it. I make a mental note of the area so as not to step in the discharge.

The labourer, eyes ahead, zips himself up and heads for the exit. The older man, looking down, heads for the men's washroom to rinse and re-insert his teeth.

I head back to my aisle and pick a seat.

M . C H R I S T I A N

On the Screen

On the Screen:

Harry Hammer, in one of his earlier films: the same ribbed chest, though missing his later softer, fuller curves. The same gently-rolling brown locks, though obviously without his later flecks of grey. The same tight, strong ass—pumping hydraulically, sweat rolling finely down a muscular back—but just a tad tighter, stronger. Even through scratched film transposed onto cheap videotape and projected onto a stained screen, it's obviously Harry—his cock still a Hammer, still a rhythmically acting piston, a long arm of dick going into, coming out of, a clenched asshole, widely-stretched lips and mouth. An older tape, but there is something age could never take away from Harry—his tremendous, glorious, powerful, cock.

In the booth:

Watching, eyes mesmerized despite the grain, the smears of old fluids, trying to see everything yet not see his own reflection in the horrid glass. Smells: urine, very old cum, generations of man stench— pure rutting aroma, mold, mildew, and a faint bite of ozone . . . that could only have come from very, very old equipment. Sounds: the muffled groans and voices from the tape, Harry Hammering at a rosebud anus, stretching the rosy tissues with each in, each out; the sharp electronic chimes and the screeches of mating modems from the distant cash register; the baser background sounds of the other men in the booths of the Studline Palace. Soft sounds mostly, but the man in a nearby booth moans and bellows like it's him on the receiving end of Harry's fleshy bat, and not the young kid in the vid.

On the screen:

Harry's tool pops free, leaving behind an enticingly puckered asshole—a yawning pink mouth shaped for the tiniest of moments like the shaft of Harry's dick. Grease, nothing but reflections in the old-style lights, make his cock look chromed, polished, buffed, and the kid's asshole like a gleaming socket. Harry's hand descends, youthful and plush, to grip his magnificent tool, and with long, confident strokes, he loves himself: shaven balls to big circumcised knob, veins squeezing out around strong fingers, pearl of pre-cum white at the fat tip.

In the booth:

He nods, rubbing his own cock through his jeans. He's hard. He's very hard. He rubs his cock, lost in the swelling rise of pure rut—feeling his own head through the fabric *good, but not as big as Harry's*, relishing the shaft *not as long as Harry's*, and the tightness in his own small, but very hairy balls *not as big, or smooth as Harry's* and it's good—because looking, watching, he's lost, adrift in a grainy paradise of strength, length, assholes, cocks, and balls.

On the screen:

In the paradise behind the glass, all things are possible—nothing like reality intervenes. The kid licks Harry clean: puppy-tongue wrapping around iron-bar shaft, teasing veined skin, following the ridged contours of the corona, and teasing, tempting, touching the tiny mouth, the vertical smile at the very tip, coming away with a finely reflecting thread of silver cum. The kid is lost in the act, his hairstyle of decades ago impossibly not moving as his head pumps back and forth, lips stretched wide, now, as he swallows the impossible length of Harry's Hammer.

In the booth:

Not as big, maybe; not as smooth, perhaps; but it feels good so he's doing it: out in the too-warm air of the place, a straining mimic of the great cock, the tremendous cock, of Harry. On the screen, illusion of distance, he almost seems as big as the Great One—a dream that he embraces: the lips, the asshole, the enthusiasm, the desire to be touched. Hand around *hand so rough, cock so smooth* he strokes, not even feeling the coarseness of his fingers.

On the screen:

The kid's cock is not Harry's—but then, whose is? Harry's is the master dick, the dick by which all others should be measured: Is it half Harry, and thus impressive in its own right, or a more common third? While not right up there with the cock of cocks, the kid's is still mighty in it's own right: half, but not half bad.

The kid strokes himself, sliding long-fingered hands up and down, from hairy patch at the base to the pointed tip, veins bulging past as he strokes. And, as he does, he hisses and moans, legs twitching as he loves himself, as he pushes himself up that incredible hill, that ecstatic peak.

In the booth:

In his hand—there in the smelly, ugly booth—he pumps, a blur of action that burns his mind with erotic sensation. The film is there, with him, as flicking images of cock, lips, assholes, thrusts, swallows, and happiness—and yet it is not. . . . His excitement, his fucking turn-on makes following the action impossible. They are just disconnected images, but they are fucking sexy images, and that is all that he needs.

The come is a quake, a pleasurable tremor. It rocks him forward until his forehead rests against the cool glass of the screen. He smells salt, perspiration, and other things unidentifiable. Pleasure is a wave, a breaking force within his body, an escape, a brilliant smile—for just a moment.

He pants, his heart a trip-hammer in his ears. He straightens after a moment. He puts his cock back into his pants, still sticky with pure white jizz. The pleasure still making him light—he more floats than steps out into the hard reality.

On the screen:

Harry looks back, over his shoulder, out towards him—winks and smiles.

Stadium Full
of Flesh

Seeing Elizabeth Taylor in *Butterfield 8* did not exactly change my life, but it sure fucked up my dreams for a while.

"Mama, I was the slut of all time!"

Four decades and many revolutions later, Hollywood still doesn't usually allow its stars to get within a hundred yards of such a line. Jessica Lange was a big cocktease in *Blue Sky*, but she only screwed one guy behind Tommy Lee Jones' back in the course of the movie. Big deal. Laura Dern was a hot bottom in *Rambling Rose*; she put the make on every guy in sight. Thing was, there weren't that many guys around, so the numbers never really added up.

Elizabeth remains in a class all her own.

She not only pees in *Butterfield 8*, she reeks. The smell of her dripping cunt billows off the screen in great clouds of female endowment. Her tits could not be more in your face even if the director had used the 3D snifforama technology of the 23rd century. She's totally human, too. Not an alien bitch in heat, like that *Species* action doll. Nor an ice-veined murderer using sex to get what she wants, à la Sharon Stone. Sex *is* what Elizabeth wants. And sex is what she gets.

A different man every night. Money, thank goodness, has nothing to do with it. She's not a whore with runny mascara, and she doesn't pout outside of Tiffany's. A fur coat doesn't mean shit to her, because a fur coat can't come alive between her legs. The only thing besides men that Elizabeth desires is french fries. "Hey, bring me some more of those over here," she barks, with a heaving bosom. Food and dick. Not, however, in that order.

Forget the "she-only-needed-the-love-of-a-decent-man-oops-her-past-makes-that-impossible" second act which spins the movie into the world of 19th-century melodrama. Forget the slap which prompts her to say: "Oh Mama, if only you'd done that sooner," as if one whack across the face could change this character's life. Forget everything, but the moment that unattractive, alcoholic businessman says, ". . . you could fill a stadium with the men she's had."

In that moment, all distance collapsed. It was me up there on the screen. Me, and about two hundred other gay men in the audience. The laughs that line got were nervous. The image was too clear, the connections too obvious.

You want to fuck the football team, you've got to have the *largesse*.

It was just so easy to imagine that stadium full of flesh. Men, men, and more men: each one somebody I had fondled, fucked, and forgotten. A swarm of raw muscles, stony faces, probing tongues, "me-me-notice-me" baskets and pumped-up buns. Very sporty. And the smell of all those sweaty balls slapping up against all those well-oiled assholes rose thick as the heat of a day in Hell.

It was hard—*hard* to know where to shove this image. So I did what I always do. I swallowed it. Sat on it. Buried it deep inside. I took it in and let soft tissue solidify all around it. Scar tissue, in time, walled it off from my heart.

Then I cheated on a brand new boyfriend. Then the next one, too. And the next.

I started having this recurring dream.

Me and a couple of hunks on a football field, cavorting. In the blink of an eye, we're down to our jockstraps. We play grab ass, we wrestle, our cocks just naturally slip out. Now we're in a frenzy of sucking, fucking, slurping, and pumping. A few young bucks from the other team join in. The orgy rages on. More guys jump into the action, and I start to recognize one or two or three. Hey, that's the guy who fucked me in the parking garage back when I was eighteen. There's the motorcycle dude who grabbed me while my parents were shopping in the next aisle over. Him—he was the first drunk I ever fell in love with. I looked around and I knew them all, and the stadium was boiling over with men.

Young, hung, handsome boys-next-door, cocky sailors, dreamy surfers, hitchhiking straights, gray old men, skinny teenagers, hard-ass rockers in leather, beach bums, bus depot trolls, peep show derelicts, sex club tricks, a real cowboy here, a marine on furlough there, here a top, there a bottom, cocksuckers everywhere, all looking less and less like men with appetites, and more and more like hungry ghosts.

One of them suddenly takes a bite out of my thigh. Another chomps on my shoulder. A tall stud chews up my ear. A little dude starts munching on my balls. There's no blood, no pain, but I am horrified, looking around and seeing the tens of thousands of men, all hungry, all determined to get back their due.

A smooth blond swallows my left nipple as if it were an oyster.

"Don't feel pregnant," he whispers into my ear. "It's just your turn."

A dazzling black guy gobbles up the head of my dick.

"Don't worry," he agrees. "There'll be plenty to go around."

No fucking way.

But they go to town on what's left, and I wake up in an evil sweat.

Until one day, not long ago, after ten years of being single and seven years of studying the Bhagavad Gita and Vivekachoodamani and various Upanishads (and enough tricks to choke a horse), the dream was reborn.

"Just how big are you?" one of my eaters asks.

"What is it you are made of?" another stud inquires.

It isn't like the fishes and loaves, not a miracle of multiplication, but there is more than enough of me for everyone. And when one creamy punk eats up the last tiny vein in my chest, he too whispers into the spirit of my ear.

"Like it or lump it, everything you did was for love."

And I wake up, feeling like Elizabeth Taylor. On a good day.

CHRISTOPHER WITTKE

619 Words About Post-Coital Silence

Silence is so accurate.
— *Mark Rothko*

At the end of it all, you look around and let your vision adjust as you survey what's left, and what's left is your heaving chest as you suck in oxygen and the smell of sweat and seminal fluid and most of your field of vision is obscured by his shoulder, which you love, since, all things considered, it's the part of him your eyeballs get closest to most often. You're up so close you can see the pores and the freckles and the hairs and you kiss it and see it and lick it and run your hand over it when he is on top of you, when he is grinding his crotch into yours, before and after he kisses you, sometimes when he is inside you, and now that shoulder shifts slightly as he tightens his arm around the front of you and slips his hand and forearm beneath you in an embrace.

You remember saying to him, "I love looking up at you," and you hear him breathing and sometimes groaning and his lips smacking as he delicately kisses parts of you and you feel the kisses like the air near a hummingbird's wings so softly on your chest and your neck and your chin and your beard and your lips and you taste his tongue and his spit and you see two miniature versions of yourself reflected one each in his pupils and you feel a small electrical charge in your abdomen when you realize you aren't being looked at but are being seen and you want him to see himself reflected in your pupils but not in miniature, bigger than life, because you've heard it said a million times that the eyes are the windows of the soul and that would be the vision of him your soul would create.

And you feel slippery and spent and at the same time filled up with a sense of expanding possibilities, like you're a sponge taking in more and more and more than you can believe and for the first time you can recall you feel a confidence that you are able to squeeze some back out to give to him and this point stands out for you in its shining silver newness and you don't ever want to forget the sensations as you smell the sweat and the semen and you feel your heartbeats finally begin to slow down and you remember that this train of thought began as you were surveying the space around you "at the end of it all," but that isn't quite right because you have learned many times that the end is the middle is the beginning is the start is the encore is the coda is the finale is the overture is the top is the bottom is yesterday is tomorrow is now.

And somewhere in your consciousness, because you are you, you hear an old R.E.M. lyric, "I want to turn you on, turn you up, figure you out, I want to take you on . . . ," and you take his chin in your hands and you pull his face towards yours. He smiles, you kiss him, you look for words, they don't come so you kiss him again. You try harder for words and again they don't come. You kiss him again, he pulls back an inch and smiles and arches an eyebrow and cocks his head a bit to the right when for a third time the words don't come and then, for what feels like the first time in your entire fucking life, you try to find a way to just keep breathing and let the silence say it all.

Contributors

Alan Alvare was a well-loved Vancouver writer and grief counsellor, formerly paid by the Catholic Church to preside in damask on Sundays. His poems, stories, and articles have appeared in sundry places. An earlier version of "The Monastery" appeared in the *Sodomite Invasion Review* in 1990. Alan passed away in December 1996.

Damien Barlow lives in Melbourne, Australia and currently teaches in the School of English at La Trobe University. His work has appeared in various Australian publications, as well as *Queer View Mirror 1* and *2* and *Quickies*. He is also an active supporter of the Aboriginal boycott of the Sydney 2000 Olympics.

Allen Borcherding lives, works, gardens, and tends to his (friends and) companion rabbit in Minneapolis, Minnesota. His work has appeared in *Queer View Mirror 1* and *2*, and *Quickies*.

John Briggs writes poetry and short stories, sculpts wood, and takes long walks from his home base in the West End of Vancouver. His poems have appeared in many literary and gay periodicals, and his short stories have appeared in *Christopher Street* and *Quickies*.

David Lyndon Brown's short stories have been published in the U.K., Canada, and New Zealand. He has won several literary prizes and many of his stories have been broadcast on NZ National Radio. He is presently working on a novel and collaborating on a play. He plays around in Auckland.

Doug Browning currently languishes in his hometown, Victoria, B.C. Between extended bouts of chronic inertia, he produces the odd tale, even odder poetry, and sporadic chunks of a likely-to-remain-unfinished novel. His short story "Helping Hand" appeared in *Queer View Mirror*.

M. Christian's stories have appeared in such books as *Best American Erotica, Best Gay Erotica, Erotic New Orleans, The Mammoth Book of Short Erotic Novels*, and ninety other books and magazines. He is also the editor of the anthologies *Eros Ex Machina*, *Midsummer Night's Dreams, Guilty Pleasures*, and (with Simon Sheppard) *Rough Stuff*. He also writes regular columns for www.scarletletters.com and www.bonetree.com. His collection, *Dirty Words*, will be published by Alyson Books sometime next year.

Bob Condron's first novel *East Money* will be published in November 1999. His short stories have appeared in the likes of *Bear* magazine and anthologies such as *Bar Stories* and *Chasing Danny Boy*. He lives and works in Berlin with his husbear of four years, Tommy.

Ted Cornwell grew up in Minnesota and is now a journalist living in New York City. His poetry has appeared in a number of journals, including *Christopher Street* and *SpoonFed*, and his fiction appeared in *The Ghost of Carmen Miranda and other*

Spooky Gay and Lesbian Tales (Alyson, 1998).

Billy Cowan is a writer of films as well as fiction. His new film *Blue Slug Redemption* will be shown at this year's Edinburgh Fringe Festival. Other films have been shown at London Portobello and North by Northwest Film festivals in the U.K. He has completed a play entitled *Smiling Through,* about being gay in Northern Ireland at the *fin de siècle.*

J.R.G. De Marco lives in Philadelphia. He has written for *The Advocate, New York Native* and *Philadelphia Gay News.* His work appears in *Black Men, White Men, We Are Everywhere, Gay Life, Quickies, Men Seeking Men,* and *Hey Paesan!* among others. He is working on a novel and a non-fiction book.

Jay Oliver Dickingson is a dreamer, a lover, a teller of tales. He can be anything he wishes, and anything you want him to be.

J. B. Droullard (a *nom de plume*) is a professor at a Florida university after five years at a university in Montreal. While he has three academic books to his credit, this is only his second publication of 'creative writing.' His first, "Contact," appeared in *Queer View Mirror.*

Warren Dunford is author of the novel *Soon to Be a Major Motion Picture* (Riverbank Press, 1998) and the forthcoming *Making a Killing: Major Motion Picture 2.* He makes his living as a freelance copywriter in Toronto.

Jim Eigo's erotic fiction has been published in *Stallions, Best Gay Erotica 1997, Butch Boys,* and *Best American Fiction 3.* As a model he's appeared in *Honcho* and *Visionaire.* Recent essays on sexual rights have appeared in the *New York Blade* and in publications from *Sex Panic* and GMHC.

Alex F. Fayle has previously published folk tales in *Garm Lu,* a Canadian Celtic Arts Journal, and is a member of Toronto's Moosemeat Writers. He would love to quit his day job and write full-time, but is too comfortable receiving a regular paycheque.

Douglas G. Ferguson was born in Saskatchewan in 1971, and currently resides in Calgary, Alberta, where he is a social worker. His work has appeared in *The Evergreen Chronicles, Poetry WLU,* and *Quickies.* He's currently seeking a publisher for his first novel, and is in the middle of writing his second.

Dave Ford is a freelance writer dedicated to a life-long search for true love, world peace, and really fabulous skin care products. He lives in San Francisco with his fire-breathing cats, Dash and Comma.

Michael Thomas Ford is the Lambda Literary Award-winning author of numerous books, including *Alec Baldwin Doesn't Love Me* and *That's Mr. Faggot to You.* His short stories and essays have appeared in anthologies including *Generation Q, Queer View Mirror 2,* and *Best American Erotica 1995, 1997,* and *1999.*

Normand François lives in Montreal and has had several erotic stories published in *Canadian Male* magazine. He is presently working on a novel. In addition, Normand François is a photographer and has had two exhibitions of the male nude.

David Garnes' work has appeared in a number of anthologies, including *Quickies, A Loving Testimony: Remembering Loved Ones Lost to AIDS, Liberating Minds:*

The Stories and Professional Lives of Gay, Lesbian, and Bisexual Librarians and Their Advocates, and *Telling Tales Out of School: Gays, Lesbians and Bisexuals Revisit Their School Days*.

R. W. Gray's short stories and poetry have appeared in journals and magazines such as *ARC*, *Absinthe*, *Event*, *The James White Review*, *Dandelion*, *Other Voices*, and *Blithe House Quarterly*. He also writes for film and television and is currently completing a Ph.D. in literature and psychoanalysis. He lives and writes in Vancouver.

David Greig is a Toronto writer and artist whose work has appeared most recently in *Quickies*, *RFD*, *Bear Icons*, *Orchid Mouth*, and other publications. His poetry chapbook, *Bone Meal* was short-listed in the League of Canadian Poets' 1999 Canadian Poetry Chapbook Manuscript Competition. His forthcoming poetry chapbook is entitled Without a Trace. He is also the author of numerous books on adult literacy.

Darrin Hagen is a freelance writer, composer, broadcaster and drag *artiste*. His book *The Edmonton Queen: Not A Riverboat Story* is currently in its second printing. Darrin was recently voted "Sexiest Man in Edmonton." He is the first drag queen to hold such a title.

Richard Haggen is a third-generation Californian of Mexican and Norwegian ancestry, currently living in San Francisco. He is a painter and a writer who freely mixes media and metaphors.

Wes Hartley is a Vancouver-based queer elder stoically approaching his sixth decade, a longtime member of The-First-Sunday-of-the-Month Queer Writer's Group, and a frequently anthologized taleteller, Classics scholar, translator, playwright, and poet. His most recent queer stories may be perused in *Contra/Diction* and *Quickies*.

Matthew R.K. Haynes teaches at Boise State University in Idaho. He has been published in *Queer View Mirror*, *Quickies*, *Cold Drill 1999* and has a chapbook, entitled *16 november 1996*, in the New York City Museum of Modern Art. Matthew's first novel, *Moving Towards Home*, is due summer 1999.

Kevin Hunter lives in Montreal with his two cats Nico and Durk. He is the manager of a prominent landmark bookstore. His dream in life is to become a high-paid escort. His spare time is devoted to photography.

George Ilsley was born and raised in Nova Scotia, and now lives in Vancouver. His short fiction has appeared in the anthologies *Queeries* and *Contra/Diction*, as well as in *The Church-Wellesley Review* and elsewhere in Canada and the United States.

eddiejames is a storyteller and web architect who lives in New York City. He is the 1998 recipient of the Randy Shilts Award for outstanding achievement in gay journalism. His writing has appeared in the *Baltimore Alternative*, *Oasis Magazine*, *The Miami Weekly*, and on the Baltimore Sun's website, *Sunspot*.

Jeff Kirby's been published in *Best Gay Erotica 1999*, *Quickies*, *Queer View Mirror*, *Stallions* and *Other Studs*, *Queeries*, and a multitude of zines and chapbooks. He's into underwear, jock straps, Speedos, socks, baseball caps, big, thick, fucking powerful, jock cock, and cock worship and can be reached in Toronto at 416-968-6974.

Kevin Knox made his debut in *Quickies*. Since then he has been writing an advice column for the internet, trying to finish reading *The Decameron*, and spending far too much time on Wreck Beach. He lives in Vancouver.

Michael Lassell is the award-winning editor/author of ten books, including *A Flame for the Touch That Matters* (poetry), *Certain Ecstasies* (short stories), and *Men Seeking Men: Adventures in Gay Personals* (essays), all from Painted Leaf Press. He is the co-editor of the forthcoming *The World In Us: Lesbian and Gay Poetry Enters the 21st Century* (St. Martin's Press, 2000).

Joe Lavelle lives in Liverpool, England. His writings have appeared in *Queer View Mirror 1* and *2* (Arsenal Pulp Press). He is currently writing a novel and looking for a place to call his own. Playa del Inglés is a resort on the island of Gran Canaria.

Paul Leroux lives in Ottawa, Canada. His experiences in the local leather/SM community, and in a MASTER-slave relationship from 1995 to 1997, provide the inspiration for his short stories, poems, and essays. He seeks to explore beyond the physical to the emotional components of leather/SM and gay relationships in general.

Tom Lever's work has appeared in *Quickies*, *The Bear Book* (1 & 2), and in various other anthologies. He lives and works in Berlin with his husbear, Bob.

Shaun Levin is a South African living in London. He teaches creative writing and runs No Holes Barred, an erotic writing workshop for gay men. His stories have appeared in the *Queer View Mirror* anthologies, *Bad Jobs*, *The Slow Mirror*, *Mach*, *Stand*, *Kunapipi*, and *The Evergreen Chronicles*. He is soon to be published in *Indulge*, *Venue*, and *Best Gay Erotica 2000*.

Mark Macdonald is an early-aging alcoholic who lives with his boyfriend and cat and ten million house plants. Having sold books for over a decade, he has now decided to start writing them and thus profiting twice. He lives in Vancouver.

Harry Matthews is just what you'd expect from his story: a professional tour guide with an active fantasy life. Walking tours have helped him learn more gay history, and a variety of activities—from writing book ads to running a small international educational programme—have paid the bills. He has lived his entire adult life in Brooklyn's Brownstone Belt.

Tom McDonald is an artist and writer living in his native Brooklyn. His most recent work appeared in *Quickies*. He is currently putting together a collection of short stories and is finishing a new novel.

Ian-Andrew McKenzie, whose work appeared in the anthologies *Queer View Mirror*, *Bar Stories*, and *Men for All Seasons*, lives and works in Atlanta, where he enjoys driving fast, two-stepping, and going on dates with really butch guys.

Dalyn A. Miller writes both fiction and plays. He previously appeared in Arsenal Pulp's *Queer View Mirror 2* and his first full-length play, *Low Flying Aircraft*, will be produced in the spring of 2000. He lives in Boston and, shamefully, almost never uses the subway.

Alan Mills is the editor of *In Touch*, *Indulge*, and *Blackmale* magazines. When not taking advantage of his Masters education by reviewing gay porn or going to Hollywood parties, Alan can be found hiding out at poetry readings throughout Los

Angeles.

David Mueller is a twelve-year resident of sunny San Francisco. His work has appeared in *My Comrade* and *Quickies*.

Steve Nugent was born in Dublin, Ireland. He lives in Toronto, and has contributed to *fab* magazine, the *Church Wellesley Review*, *Eye Magazine*, *Lambda Book Report*, and *FAB National*.

Otto would love to swap naked stories with other hot, naked guys. You can e-mail him at *otto@st-donat.net*

Christopher Paw's aspirations include writing the bubble blips for *Pop-Up Videos*, watching a Jerry Springer episode he actually doesn't relate to, and having group sex with the Teletubbies. His plays have been produced in Toronto and Halifax and his fiction has appeared in several anthologies and numerous literary magazines. He lives in Toronto.

Gary Probe's work has appeared in *Queer View Mirror 2* and *Quickies* (Arsenal Pulp Press), *Acta Victoriana* (University of Toronto), *A Queer Sense of Humour* (Q Press), *Blithe House Quarterly*, *The Church-Wellesley Review*, on CBC Radio; and in a variety of fine newspapers and magazines. He writes and lives in the east end of Vancouver.

Andy Quan, currently in Sydney, Australia, is originally from Vancouver, and has spent time in London, Brussels, and Toronto. His story from the first *Quickies* was chosen to appear in *Best Gay Erotica 1999*. His fiction and poetry have been published in a number of reviews and anthologies, including *Swallowing Clouds: An Anthology of Chinese-Canadian Poetry*, which he also co-edited with Jim Wong-Chu. *andyq@unforgettable.com*

Sandip Roy grew up in India but now lives in San Francisco. His work has appeared in *Men on Men 6*, *Q&A*, *Queer View Mirror*, *Quickies*, *Contours of the Heart*, and other anthologies. It can be occasionally seen in magazines like *A Magazine*, *Trikone*, *India Currents*, and *Pacific Reader*. When not meeting writing deadlines he has been known to enjoy Thai food.

Joey Sayer is a Calgary-based writer whose work has appeared in Quickies, *QC Magazine*, *Clue! Magazine*, the *AGLP* and several other magazines. His monthly column, "Thank You and Good Afternoon," ran for over five years. He is currently working on various prose, lyric writing and comic book projects.

Lawrence Schimel is the author of the short story collections *The Drag Queen of Elfland* and *Bien Dotado* and the editor of more than twenty anthologies, including *The Mammoth Book of Gay Erotica*, *Switch Hitters: Lesbians and Gay Male Write Lesbian Erotica* (with Carol Queen), and *Things Invisible to See: Lesbian and Gay Tales of Magic Realism*, among others. He won a Lambda Literary Award for *PoMosexuals: Challenging Assumptions About Gender and Sexuality*, co-edited with Carol Queen. He lives in Madrid.

Simon Sheppard is the co-editor, with M. Christian, of *Rough Stuff: Tales of Gay Men, Sex, and Power*. His work has appeared in numerous anthologies, including the 1997 and 2000 editions of *The Best American Erotica* and the 1996, 1997, 1999, and 2000, editions of *Best Gay Erotica*, as well as the first *Quickies*. He lives in San Francisco.

M.V. Smith writes about sex because it sells. Still interested? Look for his dirty little poetry collection *What You Can't Have*, and his novel, *Cumberland*, full of tasty material. He's earned an MFA, a BA, and a couple STDs.

Sam Sommer is an actor and writer living in New York City. In the past few years a number of his short stories have appeared in gay anthologies, including *Queer View Mirror 2*, *Quickies*, *Skin Flicks*, and *Boy Meets Boy*.

Brian Stein is a Toronto travel agent whose recent trip to China provided the inspiration for "The Occidental Tourist," his first published story. For more than twenty years, he wrote everything from speeches to annual reports, in government and the private sector. He's presently working on a collection of urban short stories.

horehound stillpoint's poetry and short stories can be found in many anthologies, including *Poetry Nation*, *Queer View Mirror 2*, *Sex Spoken Here*, *Quickies*, *Best Gay Erotica 1999*, and in the upcoming Rough Stuff. He is working on his new play, *14 Story Nightmare*.

Ron Suresha lives in Boston. His writing has appeared or is scheduled to appear in *Harvard Gay and Lesbian Review*, *Gay Community News*, *American Bear*, *White Crane*, *A&U*, *In Newsweekly*, and *Lambda Book Report*, and the anthologies *The Bear Book*, *Bear Book 2*, *My First Time 2*, and *Bar Tales*.

Royston Tester was born in England's industrial Black Country and has published in *Riprap* (Banff Centre Press), *Malahat Review*, *Prism*, *Quarry*, *Globe and Mail*, *B&A New Writing*, *Church-Wellesley Review* and *Queen Street Quarterly*. hands over the body is his first story-collection; *Enoch Jones*, a novel-in-progress. He lives in Toronto.

Robert Thomson is a Toronto-based writer with fiction and journalism having appeared in anthologies and magazines across North America. His short story collection *Secret Things* was published in 1994. Two new collections, *Need* and *Revenge*, are soon to be released. His first novel, *The Co-Dependent Cabaret* is slated for publication in early 2001. View Robert's website at: *www.globalserve.net/~impress*

Paul Vallance was born in 1958. He lives in East London and works for the National Health Service and is a regular contributor to the lesbian and gay photographic agency GAZE.

Jim Ventura is a playwright and composer by night, and a librarian by day. This is his first published work of fiction. He writes in a small 1910 bungalow that he shares with my partner of 13½ years and their little shih-tzu, Mai Ling, the best dog in the world.

Bob Vickery *(www.bobvickery.com)* is a regular contributor to *Men* magazine. His stories can be found in his two anthologies *Skin Deep* and *Cock Tales*, as well as in *Best American Erotica*, *1997*, *Best American Erotica 2000*, *Best Gay Erotica 1999*, *Friction*, and *Friction 2*.

Barry Webster is a classical pianist and writer of both fiction and non-fiction. His work has appeared in a wide variety of publications including *The NeWest Review*, *Pottersfield Portfolio*, *Dandelion*, *Quickies*, *The Washington Post*, and *The Globe and Mail*. He currently lives in Montreal.

Greg Wharton is employed by a non-profit arts education organization, husband of sixteen years to an extraordinary man, father to two cats, avid antique toy collector, designer of warped images, and writer. He lives in Chicago and travels, usually in his mind, throughout the U. S. and the world.

A. Vincent Williams is currently working on several projects, including an erotic-thriller screenplay, a science-fiction/fantasy novel, and a book of short horror fiction. This is his first submitted and published story.

Duane Williams lives in Hamilton, Ontario. His short stories have appeared in *Queeries, Queer View Mirror 1* and *2,* and *Contra/Diction.* He has published poetry in literary journals across Canada, including *The Malahat Review, Prism international, Arc, Dandelion,* and *The New Quarterly.*

Christopher Wittke has been writing *Bear* magazine's "The Wittke Wire: Men in Media" column for years and years. His work has also appeared in several anthologies including *Hometowns* and *Flesh and the Word 2.* "619 Words About Post-Coital Silence" is for Kelly, who was there at the time.

Nothing Kristofer Wölfe's poetry has appeared in many small print venues. His short story "Confessions of a Street Whore" was featured in *Queer View Mirror 2.* His life goals are to find love, learn reiki, make a film, and one day settle into a life which will bring something close to happiness.

Michael Wynne has contributed gay-themed fiction to *Quare Fellas, Queer View Mirror 2, Quickies,* and, most recently, *Chasing Danny Boy: Powerful New Irish Stories.* He lives and writes in Dublin, where he works with Poetry Ireland.

ABOUT THE EDITOR

James C. Johnstone's writing has been published in *Sister & Brother:
Lesbians and Gay Men Write About Their Lives Together* (Joan Nestle &
John Preston, eds., Harper SanFrancisco), *Flashpoints: Gay Male
Sexual Writing* (Michael Bronski, ed., Richard Kasak Books), *Prairie
Fire*, *Icon Magazine*, *The Buzz*, and the upcoming anthology *Heretical
Voices: Controversies Within The Queer Parenting Community* (Jess Wells,
ed., Alyson Publications).

He is co-editor, with Karen X. Tulchinsky, of *Queer View Mirror:
Lesbian and Gay Short Short Fiction*, and *Queer View Mirror 2*. He is also
editor of *Quickies: Short Short Fiction on Gay Male Desire*, the upcoming *Donors & Dads: True Stories of Gay Men & Fatherhood*, as well as a
collection of humorous erotic fiction called *Boners* which he is co-edit-
ing with Robert Thomson.